Arsenic and Adobo

Arsenic

and Adobo

Mia P. Manansala

BERKLEY PRIME CRIME
NEW YORK

BERKLEY PRIME CRIME
Published by Berkley
An imprint of Penguin Random House LLC
penguinrandomhouse.com

Copyright © 2021 by Mia P. Manansala
Excerpt from *Homicide and Halo-Halo* copyright © 2021 by Mia P. Manansala
Penguin Random House supports copyright. Copyright fuels creativity, encourages diverse
voices, promotes free speech, and creates a vibrant culture. Thank you for buying an authorized
edition of this book and for complying with copyright laws by not reproducing, scanning,
or distributing any part of it in any form without permission. You are supporting writers
and allowing Penguin Random House to continue to publish books for every reader.

BERKLEY and the BERKLEY & B colophon are registered trademarks and
BERKLEY PRIME CRIME is a trademark of Penguin Random House LLC.

Library of Congress Cataloging-in-Publication Data

Names: Manansala, Mia P., author.
Title: Arsenic and adobo / Mia P. Manansala.
Description: First edition. | New York: Berkley Prime Crime, 2021. |
Series: Tita Rosie's kitchen mysteries
Identifiers: LCCN 2020050117 (print) | LCCN 2020050118 (ebook)
ISBN 9780593201671 (trade paperback) | ISBN 9780593201688 (ebook)
Subjects: GSAFD: Mystery fiction.
Classification: LCC PS3613.A5268 A88 2021 (print) |
LCC PS3613.A5268 (ebook) | DDC 813/.6—dc23
LC record available at https://lccn.loc.gov/2020050117
LC ebook record available at https://lccn.loc.gov/2020050118

First Edition: May 2021

Printed in the United States of America

1st Printing

Book design by Kristin del Rosario

To Daddy,

Thanks for giving me my height, a great head of hair,
and most of all, a passion for food.

Your love was apparent in every bite.

Wish you could've seen this. Miss you.

Mahal kita

Author's Note

As a Filipino American born and raised in Chicago, I've written about experiences that are true to me. While Lila is a fictional character and very different from me, her perspective is still filtered through me and my worldview. There are scenes in this story that I considered to be harmless mystery genre tropes, especially tame since this is a cozy, but I was viewing this through the lens of an American. A homeland Filipino sensitivity reader pointed out that those scenes had a triggering effect on her because they hit so close to home regarding the way the PNP (Philippine National Police) enforces President Rodrigo Duterte's drug war.

For the sake of my readers, I'd like to provide content warnings for indications of evidence planting and police intimidation, as well as drug use, fatphobia, racism, and domestic violence.

Arsenic and Adobo has a deliberately light and humorous tone, but it is still a work of crime fiction. It would be a disservice to my readers and any survivors of these listed issues for me to gloss over these problems or treat their concerns in a flippant manner.

To learn more about Duterte's drug war, please check out these resources recommended by my sensitivity reader:

DrugArchive.ph: the repository of a drug war research consortium composed of Ateneo, La Salle, and UP researchers

On the President's Orders: Award-winning documentary on the drug war

Paalam.org: a remembrance site for the victims of the drug war

"Summary & Extrajudicial Killings in the Philippines": Report submitted to the UNHRC on the drug war

Glossary and Pronunciation Guide

HONORIFICS/FAMILY (THE "O" USUALLY HAS A SHORT, SOFT SOUND)

Anak (ah-nahk)—Offspring/son/daughter

Ate (ah-teh)—Older sister/female cousin/girl of the same generation as you

Bunso (boon-soh)—Youngest in the family

Kuya (koo-yah)—Older brother/male cousin/boy of the same generation as you

Lola (loh-lah)/Lolo (loh-loh)—Grandmother/Grandfather

Ninang (nee-nahng)/Ninong (nee-nohng)—Godmother/Godfather

Tita (tee-tah)/Tito (tee-toh)—Aunt/Uncle

FOOD

Adobo (uh-doh-boh)—Considered the Philippines's national dish, it's any food cooked with soy sauce, vinegar, garlic, and black peppercorns (though there are many regional and personal variations)

Almondigas (ahl-mohn-dee-gahs)—Filipino soup with meatballs and thin rice noodles

Baon (bah-ohn)—Food, snacks or other provisions brought on to work, school, or on a trip; food brought from home; money or allowance brought to school or work; lunch money (definition from Tagalog.com)

Embutido (ehm-puh-tee-doh)—Filipino meatloaf

Ginataang (gih-nih-tahng)—Any dish cooked with coconut milk, sweet or savory

Kakanin (kah-kah-nin)—Sweet sticky cakes made from glutinous rice or root crops like cassava (There's a huge variety, many of them regional)

Kesong puti (keh-sohng poo-tih)—A kind of salty white cheese

Lengua de gato (lehng-gwah deh gah-toh)—Filipino butter cookies

Lumpia (loom-pyah)—Filipino spring rolls (many variations)

Lumpiang sariwa (loom-pyahng sah-ree-wah)—Fresh Filipino spring rolls (not fried)

Mamón (mah-MOHN)—Filipino sponge/chiffon cake

Matamis na bao (mah-tah-mees nah bah-oh)—Coconut jam

Meryenda (mehr-yehn-dah)—Snack/snack time

Pandesal (pahn deh sahl)—Lightly sweetened Filipino rolls topped with breadcrumbs (also written pan de sal)

Patis (pah-tees)—Fish sauce

Salabat (sah-lah-baht)—Filipino ginger tea

Suman (soo-mahn)—Glutinous rice cooked in coconut milk, wrapped in banana leaves, and steamed (though there are regional variations)

Ube (oo-beh)—Purple yam

OTHER

Diba (dih-bah)—Isn't it?; Right?; short for "hindi ba" (also written as "di ba")

Macapagal (Mah-cah-pah-gahl)—A Filipino surname

Mga ninang—In Tagalog, you don't pluralize words by adding -s at the end. You add "mga" (mahng-ah) in front of the word

Oh my gulay—This is Taglish (Tagalog-English) slang, used when people don't want to say the "God" part of OMG. "Gulay" (goo-lie) literally means vegetable, so this phrase shouldn't be translated.

Tama na (tah-mah nah)—That's enough; Stop; Right/Correct (depends on context)

Tsinelas (chi-neh-lahs)—Slippers/sandals

Utang na loob (oo-tahng nah loh-ohb)—Debt of gratitude (though it goes much deeper than that)

Arsenic and Adobo

Chapter One

My name is Lila Macapagal and my life has become a rom-com cliché.

Not many romantic comedies feature an Asian-American lead (or dead bodies, but more on that later), but all the hallmarks are there.

Girl from an improbably named small town in the Midwest moves to the big city to make a name for herself and find love? Check.

Girl achieves these things only for the world to come crashing down when she walks in on her fiancé getting down and dirty with their next-door neighbors (yes, plural)? Double check.

Girl then moves back home in disgrace and finds work reinvigorating her aunt's failing business? Well now we're up to a hat trick of clichés.

And to put the cherry on top, in the trope of all tropes, I even reconnected with my high school sweetheart after moving back to town and discovered the true meaning of Christmas.

OK, that last part is a joke, but I really did run into my high school sweetheart. Derek Winter, my first love.

Too bad he'd aged into a ridiculous jerk with a puffed-up sense of importance and weird vendetta against my family. Pretty much tried to shut down my aunt's restaurant on a weekly basis. Odd behavior from the guy who'd wanted to marry me right after graduating from high school, but what can I say? I had exceptionally bad taste when I was younger. You're dumb when you're fifteen and hopped up on hormones.

Heck, I'm twenty-five and still make bad decisions based on those same dumb hormones.

Hence I was working at my Tita Rosie's restaurant rather than running my own cafe, which is what I'd been going to school for before I found out Sam was a cheating scumbag. That was right around the time my aunt sent me a distress signal, and here we are. So instead of grinding my own coffee beans or brewing the delightful loose-leaf teas I'd sourced for my dream cafe in Chicago, I now spent every morning preparing mugs of Kopiko 3 in 1 in my hometown of Shady Palms, Illinois, over two hours outside the city.

And yes, the town really was named Shady Palms. Rumor has it some rich dude from the Caribbean got homesick after moving to the area and tried transplanting a bunch of palm trees along the main street. Surprise, surprise, they didn't take, so he replaced them with tacky plastic replicas. Both the fake palms and the name stuck.

Anyway, the morning clientele at my tita's restaurant always included a bevy of gossiping aunties, none as loud or nosy as the group of fiftysomething-year-old women I privately referred to as "the Calendar Crew." Their names were April, Mae, and June—they weren't related, but all three of them were completely interchangeable, down to their bad perms, love of floral patterns, and need to provide running commentary on my life.

It was their due—after all, they were my godmothers (yes, plural). They bore the important title of "Ninang" and were my late mother's best friends. They loved and cared about me.

In their own infuriating way.

I brought over their morning plate of pandesal and they descended like a pack of locusts upon the dish of lightly sweetened Filipino bread, spreading the warm rolls with butter and dipping them in their coffee or drizzling them with condensed milk. And like locusts, once they were done devouring one thing, they moved as a pack on to their next victim: me.

"Lila, why's everything you wear always dark? You look like a bruha."

"And your hair's always in that ponytail and hat. Not sexy."

"Ay nako, what is this? You get bigger every time I see you!"

This last statement, accompanied by a firm pinch of my arm fat, was from Ninang April, who always had to have the final say. April always was the cruelest month.

I was used to these digs against my appearance—it was how older Asians showed affection. While I was no beauty queen (well, except for that one time, but that's a story for another day), my brown skin glowed and my long, black hair was thick and shiny from straightening it every morning. My pride and joy. Too bad I had to keep it under a baseball cap for work.

I could ignore my godmothers' first two comments—while being told you looked like a witch would bother most people, I considered it a compliment. I loved natural remedies, dark color palettes, and made bewitchingly delicious baked goods, so I'd learned to lean into the bruha image. Everyone needed a personal brand.

As for the baseball cap, it's not like I wore it as a fashion accessory. I worked in food service, and my family were sticklers for hygiene. It was either a cap or a hairnet, which, thanks but no thanks.

My weight gain, however, was a sore topic. Bad enough that I'd been eating my feelings and couldn't fit into my old clothes anymore; I didn't need them and their fatphobic comments rubbing it in. Then again, I hadn't been home in almost three years. The recovering Catholic in me recognized that these barbs were just the beginning of the penance they would make me pay for being away so long.

I waved my hand dismissively. "Ay Ninang April, I'm just adjusting to being back home. You know everybody eats well when Tita Rosie is around."

The Calendar Crew all nodded as they helped themselves to the coconut jam and kesong puti, or salty white cheese, that I'd added to the table.

"Why do you think we come here all the time? The decor?" Ninang Mae asked, gesturing around at the scuffed tables, mismatched silverware, and appliances from the 80s. "Nobody cooks better than your Tita Rosie."

A loud "Ha!" was the response to Ninang Mae's comment. We all turned toward the source of this rudeness, and my stomach clenched as I locked eyes with the only man I hated as much as my ex-fiancé: Derek Winter.

Derek sipped at a travel cup of coffee and tapped his foot in a cartoonish show of impatience. "Hey, could I get a table already?"

My godmothers all clicked their tongues in unison and began whispering furiously in Tagalog as I approached him. "I thought I made it very clear you weren't welcome here."

His eyes crinkled in amusement—something I used to find so attractive. His charms were wasted on me now.

"Now, Lila, is that any way to treat a customer?" the man behind him asked.

My eyes snapped to the newcomer—I hadn't realized Derek was dining with a guest. He'd always eaten alone before. Supposedly, dining solo made it easier for him to focus on the food so he could write his "reviews." I figured he just didn't have any friends.

And even more surprising than the idea of someone willingly spending time with Derek was his companion. What was Derek doing with our landlord?

"Mr. Long? What are you doing here?"

"What, a man can't have brunch with his son?" He clapped Derek on the shoulder, who flinched. "I've owned this plaza for a while now, but I've never tried your aunt's cooking. You missed another payment, so after seeing some of Derek's reviews, I figured I'd come see what the problem was. See if I could offer any assistance."

I narrowed my eyes at Derek. "The problem," huh? And since when were these two related? You'd think he would've told me his mom had remarried when we first saw each other again, but I guess this was just another of his little omissions.

I knew Mr. Long was just his stepfather, but still, looking back and forth between the two, I couldn't picture someone less likely to have sired him. Mr. Long was thin, wiry, and balding, with pale gray eyes and the red flush of the constant drinker. Derek, unfortunately, was still absolutely gorgeous, with wavy, sandy brown hair that matched his eyes perfectly, as well as the stocky build of a football player gone slightly to seed. The only thing they had in common, appearance-wise, was they were both White. Derek's hair had thinned quite a bit over the last few months though, so maybe the baldness would unite them.

Derek met my glare with a smirk and gestured toward his favorite table near the window. Honestly, how was it even possible to have a favorite table at a restaurant you allegedly despised?

"Of course, make yourselves comfortable." I smiled sweetly and added, "But no outside food or drinks allowed."

Derek rolled his eyes and started toward the door, but Mr. Long intercepted him. "Here, son, why don't you finish your drink and I'll put the thermos in the car? I gotta call your mom real quick, so go ahead and order for me. I don't know what any of this food is anyway."

I waited till Derek gulped down his drink and handed over the travel cup before hurrying to the kitchen to talk to my aunt and grandmother. Those two coming here together—especially after our latest warning about being behind on rent again—could only mean one thing for us.

Trouble.

Chapter Two

I banged into the kitchen, startling my aunt, who was adding longganisa, the short, fat sausages I'd named my dog after, to a breakfast platter.

My grandmother, Lola Flor, was grating coconut on the special
bench she'd brought over from the Philippines. Remaining her usual
aloof self, she said, "Is that how a lady enters a room? A little less
noise, ha?"

"I'm sorry, Lola. It's just . . . Derek Winter is here. With Mr. Long."

Tita Rosie blew a puff of air that made the old-fashioned bangs
curled over her forehead fly up. "Those two. OK, anak, I'll take care of
this. Just add some fried garlic and bring these plates to table six,
yeah?"

She washed her hands, quickly dried them on a nearby dish towel,
then grabbed a plate of pandesal to bring to the men.

I did as she asked, and when I reentered the dining area, Derek
was snapping his fingers to get my attention. The rude gesture, cou-

pled with his hideous uniform of year-round khaki cargo shorts (it was March in Illinois and there was like, half a foot of snow on the ground, yet he still wore shorts) and baggy sports jerseys, were what I had to put up with every time he dropped by for a meal. Which was surprisingly often, considering the negative reviews he wrote about us.

He was a notorious food blogger and critic for our local paper, which was pretty ridiculous since our town boasted a population of less than twenty thousand and consisted of chain restaurants with the occasional mom-and-pop shop sprinkled around the area. Shady Palms wasn't exactly a hotbed of fine dining options—when Starbucks came to our town, it was literally front-page news.

Though according to my best friend, Adeena, a bunch of fun, new places had opened up within the last couple of years. Not that I'd had the chance to check any of them out since I'd been so busy with the family restaurant. You'd think Derek would focus on these new places since that was literally his job as a food critic, but nope. He seemed fixated on us.

Sadly, Derek was the kind of guy who prided himself on "telling it like it is." In his mind, that meant calling people out over every imagined slight. He tried a new dish whenever he came to our place and managed to find fault with every single one, despite clearing his plate each time. Tita Rosie went out of her way to be gracious and make him feel welcome, and I hated it.

"Why are you killing yourself trying to impress this jerk?" I'd asked her several times. "We could be feeding him manna provided by the heavens and he'd still write a scathing review of the Lord's kitchen."

She pursed her lips the way she always did when she felt I was being blasphemous, then said, "Ay, it's not about impressing him. He can write what he wants. But you know his mother has issues, so he could use a little kindness. Besides, I hate seeing someone unsatisfied with their food. It means they're going unnurtured. Unfed."

An expression of pain crossed her face as she said that, causing a pang in my heart. In typical Filipino fashion, my aunt expressed her love not through words of encouragement or affectionate embraces, but through food. Food was how she communicated. Food was how she found her place in the world. When someone rejected her food, they were really rejecting her heart. It crushed her.

And I did not take kindly to those who made her feel that way.

Luckily, Tita Rosie was taking care of Derek's party, so I went over to table six to drop off the breakfast platters my aunt had prepared. I chatted with the family of four as I refilled their glasses of honey calamansi iced tea and delighted in their compliments. This refreshment was one of my concoctions—traditional, but with a bit of a twist. Just like all my creations.

I wandered around the restaurant with a pitcher of water in one hand and the tea in the other, topping up glasses as needed. I joked around with my godmothers and made them a couple more cups of instant coffee. I avoided Derek's table as long as I could, but as I gazed around the space to check on the customers, he looked up from his plate and we locked eyes.

Fudge. Not like I could avoid him now.

Pasting my customer-service smile on again, I approached the table. "Would either of you care for a refill?"

Mr. Long was too busy shoving pork and chicken adobo into his mouth to respond, but Derek pushed his empty glass toward me. As soon as I filled it with tea, he knocked it back and gestured for another refill.

"Thirsty, huh?" I said as I filled the glass yet again.

"Got a sore throat. It's been bugging me for a while and the tea helps."

Just when I thought he was finally going to compliment the restaurant, he wiped his mouth and asked, "Where are my chopsticks?"

I took a deep breath. "Derek, you've been here tons of times. You know we don't have chopsticks."

"Well, how am I supposed to eat my noodles?"

"With a fork, like everyone else."

"But noodles are supposed to be eaten with chopsticks," the would-be gourmet whined. "What kind of Asian restaurant doesn't have any?"

"The kind serving food from a country that doesn't use them."

At his blank look, I added, "We don't really use chopsticks in the Philippines. We mostly use a spoon and fork or our hands."

"Why?"

I shrugged. I served food, not history lessons. If he really wanted to know, he could google it.

Lola Flor came up at that moment and set a plate of suman and a bowl of ginataang bilo-bilo on the table. Mr. Long stopped gorging on the soy-sauce-vinegar-and-garlic marinated meats long enough to lean forward and say, "Ooh, that looks tasty. What is it, Mrs. M?"

He always called my grandmother "Mrs. M," which Tita Rosie thought was him being friendly. She said it reminded her of the Fonz referring to Mr. Cunningham as "Mr. C" on *Happy Days*. My lola and I were pretty sure he just didn't know how to pronounce our last name.

Lola Flor pointed to the suman, saying, "Sweet sticky rice cooked in coconut milk and steamed in banana leaves. The banana leaves give the rice its distinctive flavor. They're garnished with latik. Caramelized coconut curds," she added at Derek's confused look. "In the bowl is ginataang bilo-bilo. Chewy rice balls, tapioca pearls, jackfruit, purple yam, and saba banana cooked in sweet coconut milk. The best thing to eat on a cold day like this."

"That's a lot of coconut," Derek said, glancing at Mr. Long, who was looking oddly forlorn.

"I'm allergic to coconut," he explained. "Do you have any desserts without it?"

My grandmother just raised her eyebrow and said, "Not today," before walking away.

Remembering the amount of effort she put into hand-grating the coconut—the bench she used had a special coconut scraper attached to it—I could understand her impatience. However, it wasn't Mr. Long's fault he was allergic, and it was our duty to accommodate our customers' dietary needs. She needed to start taking these things seriously, but she was so inflexible when it came to her recipes.

Seeing the ube, or purple yams, in Derek's dish, I realized this was the perfect chance to test my creations on a customer.

"This is your lucky day, Mr. Long. I've been working on a fusion dessert for the restaurant, and you could be the first customer to try it. Would you be interested? There's no coconut in it, I promise."

He agreed, and I hurried back to the kitchen to grab the batch of ube crinkles I'd baked earlier that morning. I piled the cookies, their lovely violet color peeping through a light coating of powdered sugar, on a plate. I studied the offering, then added a small bowl of vanilla ice cream as well as a serving of my ube halaya, the purple-yam jam I'd used to create the cookies, to the dish. Perfect.

When I made it back to the table, Derek had already consumed the plate of suman and was preparing to tuck into the ginataang bilo-bilo. His eyes widened as I set the plate of cookies on the table.

"What's that?" He'd broken into a sweat and was tapping an offbeat rhythm on the table with his fingers as he eyed the plate greedily.

"I call them ube crinkles. I used condensed milk instead of coconut to make the jam, so they should be safe for you, Mr. Long. I like to think of them as a Filipino-American hybrid." I watched as Mr. Long and Derek each helped themselves to a cookie. I chewed on my lower lip as I waited for their reaction.

And waited.

And waited.

"So . . . how are they?" I finally ventured.

"Not sure what to think, actually. I've never tasted anything like it. Very delicate," Mr. Long said, helping himself to another cookie.

Derek added, "I think it's cute that you still dabble with baking, but it's way too sweet. You'd think all those years practicing at that fancy school would've taught you better."

And just like that, bitter memories of my ex-fiancé, Sam, critiquing my baked goods flashed through my mind. I remembered all the little jabs I had suffered at the hands of my ex, Mr. Big Shot Chef, as he condescendingly patted my hand, saying he was glad I had a hobby, but maybe I should stick with the business side of the restaurant and leave the food to him. Only to find him later stuffing down another of my date and walnut bars, or deconstructing one of my fusion biscotti flavors.

He knew I was good. But in his kitchen, there was no room for me to be great.

Shaking the flashback away, I looked at Derek, who was smearing ube halaya across the bottom of a cookie. He then added a scoop of ice cream and sandwiched it with another cookie before chowing down.

Was this dude seriously shoveling down the entire dessert platter despite insulting my food—to my face—a mere five seconds ago?

I snatched the plate away from him. "If the cookies are so disgusting, maybe you should stop eating them."

Derek rolled his eyes and grabbed another cookie. "I never said they were disgusting. God, you're so sensitive. If you can't take the criticism, you don't belong in the kitchen."

Mr. Long frowned, eyes darting back and forth between us. His gaze lingered on Derek's sweaty, pallid appearance as he handed Derek a handkerchief and then gestured for me to hand him the cookie plate. "Lila brought these cookies for me, son. I think you've had enough to write a proper review of them. You're supposed to be watching your sugar levels anyway, remember? Did you take your insulin?"

Derek glared at him, but accepted the handkerchief and wiped the sweat and crumbs from his face. "Of course I took my insulin. I'm not a little kid, Ed. I can take care of myself."

The stare-down between the two of them was making me uncomfortable, so I started to clear the plates from the table. When I grabbed the untouched bowl of ginataang bilo-bilo, Derek stopped me.

"I haven't tried this yet. I can't write a full review if I don't taste everything on offer."

I shrugged and slid it in front of him. "Knock yourself out. It's one of my favorite cold-weather treats, so I hope you enjoy it."

Usually consumed for breakfast or at snack time for meryenda, it had all the comfort of a warm bowl of oatmeal but enough sweetness to qualify as dessert. While it wasn't the most Instagram-worthy dish, the various textures of soft and chewy with a bit of bite, combined with the sweet creaminess of the thickened coconut milk and my lola's deft touch made it the Filipino culinary equivalent of hygge. Pure coziness and warmth in a bowl.

Derek spooned up a large portion, his eyes widening as he experienced the delicious interplay of all the different ingredients. For once, he was speechless.

I grinned as he seemed to squirm with delight. "Good, huh?"

He let out a long, drawn-out sigh but didn't answer.

I put my hands on my hips. "Oh, come on. Would it kill you to say something nice for a change?"

He responded by convulsing violently, then face-planting right into the dish.

Chapter Three

"D ude, that's not funny. Quit it."

My first instinct said Derek was playing around. He'd been an infamous prankster when we were in high school, and this looked like another one of his unfunny jokes. I was too annoyed about the mess he'd made, with gobs of coconut milk splattered all over the table, not to mention my apron, to take him seriously.

But when Derek didn't immediately pop up and grin like I thought he would, I looked over at Mr. Long. He stared at Derek, facedown in our chipped ceramic bowl, with an odd mix of horror and some other emotion I couldn't quite place.

The hair on the back of my neck rose as I leaned over Derek and started shaking him. First gently, then harder and harder as he refused to respond. Did he pass out? Have an allergic reaction or something?

With effort, I pulled him up and leaned him against the back of the chair so he could breathe easier. Not that I could actually see him breathing. Oh, dear Lord, was he dead?

I hadn't even noticed Ninang June making her way over till she shoved me aside. "Call an ambulance!" she yelled as she felt for his pulse. I shook myself. She was right. He could still be saved and my standing around gaping at him wasn't helping anyone. I whipped out my phone and called 911, giving them the restaurant address and explaining what happened. As I talked to the operator, Ninang June wiped off Derek's face to clear his airways, had Mr. Long help her lay Derek on the ground, and began administering CPR.

As I gave the 911 operator the play-by-play of what was going on, Derek's chest moved up and down ever so slightly on its own, and Ninang June was able to lean back and observe his condition.

The immediate danger now over, I tried to hang up, but the operator insisted on staying on the line until the ambulance showed up. I put her on speakerphone and laid my phone on the table, then looked around, taking in the shocked faces and heavy atmosphere filling the room. Luckily, it was an odd time of day and we were mostly empty, just the aunties and two other tables of our regulars.

I rushed over to the door and flipped the sign over to CLOSED and locked the door. I took two steps before remembering the EMTs would need to get in, so I propped the door open and ran back to the kitchen to get my aunt and grandmother.

Tita Rosie shot out and headed straight toward Ninang June, who was still kneeling by Derek's side. Before she could say anything, the wail of an ambulance siren filled the room and two EMTs burst in with a stretcher. Lola Flor stayed over by the other members of the Calendar Crew, who were no doubt filling her in on everything that had happened.

I was so focused on calming down the other customers that I wouldn't have noticed the emergency workers hefting Derek onto the stretcher if I hadn't heard him vomit as they rolled him out, Mr. Long following in their wake.

As the door swung shut, a heavy silence descended on the restaurant. My aunt stood stock-still, staring out the door long after the ambulance pulled away. Remembering the operator still on the line, I thanked her and hung up, pocketing my phone.

I looked around, not sure what to do. Comfort my aunt? Clean the table? Start ringing up the customers? My thoughts were broken when a child at table four started wailing, and my grandmother met my gaze across the room. With an imperceptible nod toward the table, she instructed me on what to do. I hustled back to the kitchen to prepare some salabat. The hot ginger tea would cure anything that ailed you, and I'd made a few modifications to boost the flavor and health profile.

I set the electric kettle and pulled out the jar of ginger, turmeric, honey, cayenne, and calamansi, the last ingredient adding a refreshing hit of citrus tang. While waiting for the water to boil, I filled mugs with a few spoonfuls of the ginger concoction and then topped them all off with the boiling water. I hefted the tray up to my shoulder and entered the dining room, where no one was speaking above a whisper.

My lola had set out plates of her homemade lengua de gato, the thin, crispy butter cookies matching well with my spicy-sweet brew. Everyone sat around sipping and munching, and I watched as the color returned to their cheeks and the tension left their bodies. Once the cups and plates were emptied, the customers all wiped the crumbs from their mouths and left money on the table, ignoring my aunt's insistence that they didn't have to pay. When she tried to hand the money back, everyone fled, leaving her standing with a fistful of cash and a bewildered expression on her face.

Finally, everyone was gone.

Well, everyone but the Calendar Crew.

"Lila, don't you have anything stronger?" Ninang Mae pointed toward the counter with her lips, gesturing to the bottle of Tanduay Gold Rum we kept for "emergencies." These emergencies were usually nothing more than an impromptu karaoke night, but for once I agreed with her and broke out the bottle.

I poured a generous shot in each mug except for my aunt's. She'd seen enough of the problems that alcohol could cause to avoid drinking it herself, but she let us imbibe in her restaurant as long as we were never foolish enough to try to drive home drunk.

I gulped down my drink, welcoming the fire as it coursed down my throat and burned my stomach, bringing tears to my eyes. As I dabbed away at the moisture, the phone rang. I started toward it, but my aunt waved me away, picking it up herself.

"Hello? Mr. Long! How is . . ." She paused, listening to the man on the other end. "I see. Sir, I'm so sorry, I . . . What?" More silence as she listened. "Mr. Long, we had nothing to do with it! We—"

He must've hung up on her because she suddenly stopped talking and put the phone down. Lola Flor stood up, and so did I.

I reached out to her. "Tita Rosie? Are you OK?"

She hadn't moved, hand still on the cradled phone. "Derek's dead. He's dead and . . . and the police are heading this way."

"W-what? Why?"

She turned scared eyes toward me. "Mr. Long thinks we killed Derek."

Chapter Four

My brain refused to process that comment into coherent speech, leaving me spluttering for a good minute. My grandmother was not so easily rocked.

"Diyos ko, that fool. He's going to use this as an excuse to kick us out. He's been trying to for months now." Lola Flor shook her head, pursing her lips the way she did whenever she saw me tinkering around with her recipes. Such a simple gesture, but it managed to convey just how big of a disappointment she found you.

My godmothers were already gossiping about what they knew of Derek and his family.

"Did you know Derek was still living with his mother when she married Edwin Long two years ago?" Ninang Mae said.

"Of course! Nancy's health has always been a problem. What was he going to do, leave her all alone in that big house? He may have been an entitled jacka . . . um, jerk, but he was always a good son," Ninang June said, with a quick glance toward my aunt.

Ninang April straightened up, adopting her "high and mighty pose" as the other aunties liked to call it. "Well, *we* know that good children stay and take care of their parents, but Edwin Long didn't agree. Told him he was there to take care of Nancy now, and Derek was an adult and needed to find his own place. Or start paying a larger portion of the mortgage."

The Calendar Crew all made a *tch* noise with their lips, indicating their displeasure. Even Tita Rosie was frowning at this information. "That wasn't even his house to make a decision like that. Poor Derek."

I fought the urge to roll my eyes. "Poor Derek" was almost thirty years old. I didn't find it all that unreasonable to have a grown adult start pulling their weight around the house or living on their own and said so.

That was a mistake.

All five wheeled around as one. I don't know if you've ever been stared down by an elderly Asian woman, but It. Is. Terrifying. Don't be fooled by the cute florals and jaunty visors—these women will end you, wielding nothing but their sharp tongues, bony elbows, and collapsible shopping carts.

"Lila, this is what's wrong with your generation. All you care about is yourself—your dreams, your needs, your independence. What about your family?"

This was the talk I'd been avoiding for the past few months. Filipinos were all about family. My whole life I'd had the concept of "family first" drilled into my head, and it's how I'd lived until I went away to college. It's not that I disagreed with it, exactly. Even someone like me felt utang na loob, that impossible to quantify sense of indebtedness and gratitude, to the people who'd raised me. But where was that magical line between selfishness and independence? Between my family and myself?

"Ninang April, now isn't the time for that." I glanced over at Tita

Rosie, whose usually lovely golden complexion looked pale and mottled. "Tita, you know Mr. Long better than I do. Was he just grieving and looking for someone to blame? Or do we need to talk to a lawyer?"

She didn't answer at first, just fidgeted with the glasses that were almost always perched on top of her head and rarely on her face.

I walked over and put my hand on her arm. "Tita Rosie? Are you OK?"

She plonked her glasses on her nose and shook herself. "I'm fine, Lila, stop fussing. And I'm not sure. He sounded serious, but he's wrong. Derek didn't have any allergies, so it couldn't have been my food. It couldn't have been my food," she repeated to herself.

Lola Flor cut in. "He was diabetic, though. And he died after eating our desserts. Maybe he wasn't careful enough about his sugar. He looked a bit ill when we were talking to him."

Remembering Derek's pallor and the sweat dotting his forehead, I had to agree with her. "If it was because of his blood sugar, our desserts are not to blame. He knew what he was doing. Mr. Long can't pin that on us."

The Calendar Crew exchanged glances. "You obviously don't know him very well. Isn't Adeena's brother a lawyer? Maybe you should call him, just in case."

My eyes narrowed at this statement. Adeena Awan was my best friend and her older brother Amir was indeed a lawyer. While it seemed like a harmless suggestion from well-meaning family friends, I knew my godmothers well enough to see what they were trying to do. It was a setup. They've been trying to get me together with Amir since he first got accepted at some fancy law school in Chicago.

I found this super annoying, since A) it was a legitimately good idea to talk to a lawyer and cover our bases, B) he was a family friend, so he likely wouldn't charge us for his help, and C) I've been crushing on him since high school. Not that anything would've happened.

Adeena would've killed me, and I'd started dating Derek pretty early into my freshman year.

But still, all of these things pointed toward the Calendar Crew being right about something involving my personal life, and I didn't know if I could bear that shame. Their "I Told You So" dance alone was enough to make me want to embrace the single life.

Though it would be nice to talk to Adeena about what just happened. The fact that I literally watched my ex-boyfriend—my first love—die in front of me, right after I made such a flippant remark, was finally starting to sink in. Where was she anyway? She worked at the cafe next door and had to have seen the ambulance pull up. I couldn't believe she hadn't barged in here yet, demanding to know what was going on.

"You know what, maybe I should talk to Adeena. I'm going to run next door to the coffee shop and see if she can take a short break." I pulled off my apron, then paused, asking, "Is that OK, Tita? Lola?"

My grandmother grunted her agreement and my aunt smiled and said, "Of course. Just give me a minute and I'll pack you some of my special adobo and rice."

After she handed me the package, I scooted out the door and walked all the way to the neighboring coffee shop. One of the few good things about coming home was getting to see my best friend every day and work right next door to her.

Java Jo's was a relatively new cafe that, despite its generic, lowbrow name, fulfilled my admittedly snobby coffee needs. Their pastry selection was boring and the quality subpar, but their drinks were first-class, thanks in large part to Adeena, barista extraordinaire. She worked there part-time to help pay for pharmacy school—which she'd put on hold temporarily—but was already threatening to drop out and follow her dream of opening her own cafe.

I advised against it since, although I had long ago joined the Disappointment to the Asian Community Club (DACC for short), pharmacy was the one thing keeping Adeena respectable in the eyes of her family.

It was bad enough that I had left our small town instead of staying to help Tita Rosie with the family restaurant. Bad enough that I had moved in with a boy without being married. But to return home without at least a degree (or a man) to show for it? Ultimate disgrace. I didn't want Adeena to have to deal with that.

I banged into the cafe and without preamble, yelled, "Kevin! I really, really need to talk to Adeena right now."

Adeena, working at the espresso machine, turned startled eyes to Kevin Conoway, owner of Java Jo's. He took in my appearance and the wild look in my eyes and said, "As long as you leave some food for me, sure. Go on to the backroom."

I followed my friend to the back and thrust my aunt's offering at her. "There's the chicken one your brother loves, but she came up with a new vegetarian recipe for you. Let me know what you think."

Quite a few Filipino recipes involve pork, and pork adobo was one of the most popular dishes. Adeena was a vegetarian and her family were Pakistani Muslims, so my aunt loved coming up with new variations to share with the Awans. Adeena watched with concern as I started rambling about how young jackfruit was the best meat substitute ever instead of telling her what was going on.

"Enough with the food. I can tell when you're dodging the subject." The familiar tinkle of her golden bangles comforted me as she took my hand and tried to sit me down on a rickety folding chair.

When I refused to sit, she asked, "Is this about the ambulance we saw earlier? I tried to go check on you, but Kevin dragged me back and said I was still on the clock. Told me to mind my own business and leave you in peace till you were ready to talk."

I drew in a shaky breath and decided to get it all out. "Derek's dead. He passed out while eating one of our desserts. Mr. Long went with him to the hospital, but I guess he . . . I guess he didn't make it."

Her eyes widened in horror and she pulled me into a hug. "Oh, honey, I'm so sorry. That must've been terrible."

"That's not even the worst of it." I paused, realizing how that sounded. "OK, I mean technically that *is* the worst since someone dying is bigger than my problems, but Mr. Long is blaming us for his death. Lola Flor thinks he's going to try and shut down the restaurant."

The shock finally started to wear off and reality seeped in. I had watched a man die in front of me. A man I knew and had once cared about. Had even loved. And loathed. Both of which were facts that everyone knew. And now his stepfather was accusing us of causing his death.

Collapsing into the chair next to her, I began to cry. What if he was right? What if Derek had an allergy we didn't know about, or his medication caused a weird reaction to one of our ingredients? We knew he was diabetic, but he was always eating sweets. What if our desserts pushed him over the limit? It's not like we did it on purpose, but we'd still be branded as killers.

We could lose the restaurant! Maybe even go to jail. And then where would we be? Tita Rosie had been running that place almost my entire life. And it's not like she and my grandma could start over again. The only thing the Macapagal family knew how to do, and do well, was cook.

While all these thoughts ran through my head, one of Adeena's hands clasped mine as the other rubbed my back in a soothing rhythm. Slowly, my sobs ebbed away. She got up to grab a box of tissues, which I used to mop up my face. Based on the smudges of black on the tissue, I was wearing more mascara on my cheeks than my lashes.

Adeena bit her lip and said, "Why don't you go to the bathroom and clean up? I need to make a call."

Grateful to be alone for a moment, I grabbed my purse and headed to the bathroom. Using the small jar of coconut oil I carried everywhere with me, I took off my makeup and splashed my face with warm water to get rid of some of the blotchiness. I dried my face as best I could with the rough paper towels, then headed back out.

Adeena quickly ended her call. "You, uh, you going for the no-makeup look?"

I shrugged. "Yeah, why not? I'm probably going straight home after this, so no point in reapplying."

She raised an eyebrow. "You put on a full face of makeup to go grocery shopping. I've seen you put on lipstick before heading to the gym."

"First of all, it's lip gloss, and I only put it on because my lips chap very easily," I said, crossing my arms. "Second, what are you trying to say? That I can't go out with a bare face? That I need makeup to look good?"

She rushed to reassure me. "No, honey, of course not. It's just, I know how you are and figured you'd want to look your best at a time like this."

Now it was my turn to raise an eyebrow. "Meaning?"

"There might be a news van waiting outside the restaurant."

"What?!"

A small, please-don't-hate-me smile spread across her face. "Also, I called Amir. He's on his way now to talk to you and your family in case you need legal counsel. He said not to talk to anyone till he gets there."

"I have to talk to other people? While I look like this?" I pointed to my red, swollen eyes and blotchy face.

"He'll be here in ten. Go make yourself camera-ready. Knowing my brother, he might have you make a public statement."

I hustled off to the bathroom again, calling over my shoulder, "You're lucky I need to put on my face, or there'd be two dead bodies to deal with!"

Chapter Five

Hair brushed until it shone, eyebrows and lashes mascaraed into place, and lips tinted their usual deep burgundy shade, I felt ready to face whatever awaited me outside.

Or so I thought.

A quick glance out the window showed our local news van and camera crew, plus a crowd of nosy onlookers lingering in the parking lot. Tita Rosie's Kitchen's position on the main strip of what constituted Shady Palms's downtown area must've drawn the attention of neighboring businesses and random bystanders. I briefly wondered if I could just hide out in Java Jo's for the rest of eternity. I had access to a bathroom, a kitchen where I could bake, and all of the caffeine. What more could I need?

Sadly, Adeena wouldn't let me take the coward's way out. After obtaining permission to leave from Kevin, she grabbed my hand and dragged me back to the restaurant, using her body to block me from the cameras.

Which would've been a sweet and gallant show of friendship . . . if the restaurant doors hadn't been locked. Instead, that night there would be news coverage of my best friend cracking up and being useless as our town's tiny news team swarmed me (do three people constitute a swarm?) while I fumbled for my keys.

I shouted, "No comment!" as I dug through my purse, which was larger than a diaper bag despite me not having (nor ever wanting) children. Just as I located my keys, which had somehow inserted themselves into my reusable boba tea cup, my aunt opened the door. I rushed inside, barely squeezing through the crack she'd opened, pulling Adeena in after me. The Shady Palms news team tried to follow us in, but I slammed and locked the door behind us.

"Have you heard anything new yet?" I asked Tita Rosie as we settled in and helped ourselves to the coffee and snacks on the table. Her response was to shake her head and pile a couple more pieces of suman on my plate.

While Adeena sat at a table gossiping with my godmothers, I alternated between checking my appearance in my phone and murmuring words of comfort to my aunt as she robotically sipped another cup of coffee. My grandmother, doing what she always did in times of distress, had yet to emerge from the kitchen. She'd disappeared into it shortly after my aunt received that fateful phone call, but her absence contributed to the aura of peace in the room.

The sharp *knock knock knock* at the door shattered that peace, and we all turned simultaneously at the sound, like a pack of meerkats.

There in the doorway stood a man I'd never seen before—trust me, I would've remembered. My first thought was "silver fox" as I took in his perfectly coiffed light brown hair that was tinged with gray in a way that said "dignified and sexy" rather than "old." My second thought, after taking in the contrast of his light hair and eyes with the rest of his features was that this dude was definitely mixed, probably

Asian and White. My third and final thought was that Tita Rosie looked exceptionally happy to see him, which hit me in a way I wasn't expecting.

"Jonathan," my aunt exclaimed, as she hurried to unlock the door. "What a surprise! Kumain ka na ba? Have you eaten?" She gestured toward me. "Lila, this is Detective Park. Get him something to drink, will you?"

I headed to the kitchen, but stopped when he held up a hand. "I'm sorry, Rosie, but I'm afraid this isn't a regular visit. Edwin Long stormed into the station yelling that his stepson is dead and that your restaurant killed him. Sheriff Lamb ordered me to check if his claims are substantiated."

Tita Rosie dropped the cup she'd been holding, and the only sound you could hear throughout the entire room was the mug shattering. The long-cold coffee she'd been drinking spilled out over the linoleum, staining the floor a muddy brown. I instinctively knelt down and began picking up the broken shards.

As I dropped the larger pieces in the nearby wastebasket, I asked, "So what exactly does that mean, Detective? Are we under investigation?"

My voice remained steady even if my hands didn't, and I ended up nicking my finger on one of the smaller pieces. The blood welled up at the same time as my tears, and I stuck my finger in my mouth to distract myself from the pain and fear.

Detective Park yanked some napkins from the holder on the table and handed them to me. "I'd give you my handkerchief, but this is probably more sanitary. You should wash that out properly, Miss...?"

I grabbed the napkins, wrapping them around my finger, and stood up. "Lila Macapagal." I nodded toward Tita Rosie. "I'm her niece."

My aunt cleared her throat, obviously urging me to be more polite, so I added, "I'd shake your hand, Detective, but as you said, I should go wash this out. Excuse me."

I stalked off toward the kitchen, where Lola Flor was wrapping up a tray of lumpia. As I rinsed out my cut and searched for our first aid kit, she piled a bunch of suman into a separate container and Saran-Wrapped it as well.

"What's with all the food?" I asked as I rubbed some ointment on my finger and put on a Band-Aid.

"We're closed for the rest of the day and there's no point in letting this food go to waste."

I waited for her to say more, but she continued boxing up the leftover food in silence. Typical.

I went back into the dining area in time to hear Detective Park say, "Where's the food Mr. Long and Mr. Winter were eating?"

I glanced over at the table where they'd sat, knowing what I'd find. Yup, it was spotless. My family ran a tight ship, so someone must've cleaned it up while I was at the coffee shop. Cleanliness was next to godliness, and there were few people who took godliness as seriously as my aunt and grandmother.

Try explaining that to a detective investigating a possibly mysterious death, though. To say that Detective Park was put out was putting it mildly.

"Rosie, I want to help you out here. But you do realize that destroying the evidence makes you look even more suspicious, right?" He rubbed at his right temple. "Please tell me you haven't washed the dishes yet. At least give me that."

My aunt began apologizing. "I-I'm sorry, I had no idea . . ."

"Tita, you have nothing to apologize for." I stepped between her and the detective. "Derek was alive when they took him away and we had no reason to believe there was a problem with our food."

He tried to interrupt me, but I kept going. "We run a restaurant, which means we have to follow certain hygiene standards. It's our protocol to bus a table as soon as the customer is gone so that it's ready for our next guest. My aunt's behavior wasn't suspicious, it was professional."

I was probably overreacting, but everything I'd said was true. Our family restaurant was a hole-in-the-wall in desperate need of remodeling, but my aunt and grandmother took pride in their work and I wouldn't have their work ethic construed as something criminal. Not to be cliché, but even the floors were clean enough to eat off. Besides, my family knew how the Shady Palms Police Department worked. I wasn't going to let them pull anything on us, not again.

Detective Park bit his lip, not in chagrin, but as if holding back a sharp response. After waiting a beat, he said, "Understood. Now, as I asked before, the table is clean, but have the dishes been washed yet?"

Tita Rosie spoke up. "Not unless my mother washed them already. I left them in the sink and brought out coffee and snacks since my guests and I were all a little rattled by the events of this morning."

She gestured to the Calendar Crew as she said this, and indeed, there were half-empty mugs in front of them, along with small bowls sticky with leftover ginataang bilo-bilo. The detective jotted all this down on his notepad, then said, "Could you come with me into the kitchen, Rosie? And, ladies, I have some questions for you once I'm done in there."

He had no business going into our kitchen. That was our space. I stepped forward, blocking his path. "I could bring them out to you if you want to start questioning them now."

He raised an eyebrow. "That's quite all right, Miss Macapagal. The fewer people in contact with the evidence, the better."

"You mean you don't want me tampering with it."

"That's not what I said." He jotted some notes down on his tablet. "Is there some reason you don't want me going into the kitchen?"

"No, I just . . ." I looked over at my aunt, who smiled at me with understanding. She also observed the sanctity of the kitchen.

"It's OK, anak. It'll only take a minute," she said.

After they disappeared through the swinging doors, the Calendar Crew gestured for me and Adeena to come close. As we huddled together, they whispered, "This doesn't look good, girls. Not at all."

I exchanged looks with Adeena. "What do you mean? We haven't done anything wrong. This is insulting, and a little scary, but the police have nothing on us."

Adeena joined my godmothers in shooting me looks of pity. "You have no idea who Detective Park is, do you?"

I fiddled with my necklace. "Of course not. I never made it a point to hang out with Shady Palms law enforcement, especially after the whole Ronnie thing. Besides, I haven't lived here . . ."

"In a long time," Adeena finished. "Well, he moved here a year or two after you left. He was supposedly some big shot back in the city, but moved here to be closer to his parents. Can't remember if he's semiretired or whatever they call it, but the department only calls on him when something big is happening."

"What was the last case they needed him for?"

"When that trucker was killed at the rest stop just outside of town last year."

My jaw dropped. Even I had heard about that back in Chicago. "He was the one who caught the killers and brought down that drug-smuggling ring?"

The four women at the table all nodded. Ninang Mae added, "And if they're bringing him in to investigate Derek's death? Well, doesn't it seem like they've already come to a conclusion about what happened to him?"

But why? Everyone knew Derek didn't take care of himself. It was ridiculous to think we'd do something to him. I dropped my face into my hands. "But we're innocent. So it'll be OK, right? We'll all be fine?"

Adeena grinned and tossed her hair. "Of course you will. Amir's on his way, isn't he? He'll take care of everything."

I wasn't one to play the damsel in distress, but at that moment, I clung to those supportive words like the lifeline they were. Amir "The Golden Boy" Awan was coming and everything was going to be OK. It had to be.

But behind Adeena's back, I could see my godmothers shaking their heads, like they knew what was to come.

Chapter Six

Someone will need to come over and collect the evidence. We have no pictures of the scene, but luckily the dishes haven't been washed yet. Send someone now before—" Detective Park was speaking on the phone as he swung back into the dining area from the kitchen, but stopped short when he saw our group listening in. "Just send someone."

I crossed my arms as he hung up. "Find what you were looking for? And what exactly are we being accused of?"

Detective Park held his hands out. "There are no accusations being thrown around. At least, not on the part of the Shady Palms Police Department. A complaint was made about the suspicious death of a young man in good health, so I was called in to make sure he died of natural causes."

"Derek wasn't in good health, though," Adeena said. "He was a diabetic with a sweet tooth and didn't always mind the doctor's orders. The fact that he was eating dessert before dying is proof of that."

Detective Park arched an eyebrow as he wrote this down. "I didn't realize the two of you were friends, Miss Awan."

"'Miz.'"

"Excuse me?"

"I prefer 'Ms.' not 'Miss' if you're going to use titles." She gestured to me. "We both do. And no, we weren't friends, but we've known each other since high school."

When that didn't seem to satisfy the detective I sighed and added, "We all went to high school together. He was a couple of years older than us, but he and I dated for a while. Adeena and I are both familiar with his history of diabetes and his general behavior."

The detective's eyebrow stayed arched as he asked, "You dated the deceased?"

I crossed my arms. "Yes, but we broke up years ago. Before I even left for college."

The Calendar Crew started whispering among themselves again at this, and I glared at them. Good thing the detective didn't understand Tagalog, because I did not appreciate the play-by-play they were giving of my old relationship.

Detective Park must've guessed the general content of their conversation, though, because he asked my aunt, "Rosie, is there somewhere I can conduct these interviews in private? And I'm sorry, ladies, but you'll have to stay in this room while I'm holding the interviews. No wandering around."

"Hold on, shouldn't we wait for Amir? I don't think he'd want us to talk without him around," I said.

"Ay, Lila, you worry too much. I just want to get this over with. You can use my office, Jonathan," Tita Rosie said, leading him toward a small room hidden near the back. "You sure I can't fix you something to eat? Or drink, at least? You look so tired."

I tried to hide a smile. A detective told her she's being blamed for someone's death and my aunt was more worried about his well-being than her own. That's my Tita Rosie for you.

Detective Park seemed to understand this as well, since he smiled and said, "Sorry, Rosie, I'm on duty. Maybe later though."

My aunt nodded, and Detective Park gestured at Ninang Mae to follow him to the office. We waited till the door closed before we all started speaking at once.

"Why do you think he wants to talk to us alone?"

"What do you think they're talking about in there? I hate not knowing what's going on."

"Do you think they'll actually find anything suspicious in the dishes they took away?"

"Don't worry about it, Lila. It's just like Derek to cause trouble, even in death."

My godmothers stopped clucking long enough to admonish Adeena. "Hoy! We do not speak ill of the dead. Diyos ko," they added, crossing themselves.

"So we're just going to pretend Derek was a saint, even though we all know what he was?" I asked.

Before my godmothers could respond, Lola Flor held up her hand. "Tama na."

"Enough," she said. We sat quietly at the table, nibbling our treats while waiting for the detective to call on us. Ninang Mae had just switched out with Tita Rosie when Amir arrived.

He rushed over to me. "I'm sorry it took so long, but I was in the middle of a meeting when Adeena called." He sat down and pulled out his iPad to take notes. "Walk me through exactly what happened. Start when Derek first arrived."

I took a deep breath. "Derek and Mr. Long came over to eat around ten. They finished their food and Lola Flor brought out dessert. But the dessert had coconut, which Mr. Long is allergic to, so I brought him a dish I'd been working on instead."

Amir nodded, taking notes on his tablet. "And then what?"

I tried to think back. "I think Derek had already eaten the suman when I came back, but the bowl of ginataang bilo-bilo was untouched. I gave Mr. Long the cookies, jam, and ice cream platter I'd made and both of them started eating."

I almost repeated the hurtful comment Derek made about my baking, but refrained. "Derek was eating too much of Mr. Long's dessert, so Mr. Long suggested Derek stick to his own food. I pushed the bowl toward him and he started eating. He seemed to be enjoying it, but then he suddenly . . . he just . . ."

"He passed out, facedown into the bowl," Ninang April cut in. "And you forgot to mention how terrible he looked. All sweaty and pale, diba? Edwin even gave Derek his handkerchief to clean himself up." She shook her head. "That boy was sick before he ever touched the desserts."

Amir stopped typing and looked back and forth between me and Ninang April. "Is this true? Because that's a very important detail."

I thought back, chewing my lower lip in concentration. "She's right. He also seemed to have trouble breathing. I didn't think much of it at the time. He was being so . . . himself, and it distracted me."

Amir continued typing. "What happened after he fainted?"

I flushed. "I, uh, thought he was joking at first. Just being a jerk, you know? So I yelled at him a bit. But when it became clear he wasn't playing, I pulled him upright and Ninang June performed CPR while I called 911. He was breathing, but barely. I didn't know what else to do, but the ambulance got here quickly and took him away. He was still alive when they left." I bit my lip. "I think? No, definitely. I remember hearing him throw up as they rolled him away."

Amir stopped typing and put a hand on my shoulder. "Lila, you did what you could. There wasn't anything else you could've done that would've saved him."

The warmth from his hand radiated through my body, and I luxuriated in it for a moment before pulling away. I didn't want to get used to his touch—not at a moment like this, and certainly not in front of Adeena.

"You don't know that. What if he was suffocating while I yelled at him? All because I thought it was a joke? What if there was food blocking his airway and I could've done something to clear it before Ninang June took over? What if my actions were the only things between Derek living and dying?"

Adeena wrapped her arms around me. "Why are you putting all this on yourself? It's not like you were the only two in the room. Auntie June is a trained professional nurse and even she couldn't do much before the ambulance got here. And for all Mr. Long's complaints, why wasn't he the first at Derek's side to try and help him?" She paused, as if something just came to her. "What was he doing when all this was going on?"

I looked over at my godmothers. "I'm not sure, actually. I was so focused on Derek. Did either of you see?"

Ninang June shook her head, but Ninang April said, "Not sure what he was doing immediately after Derek passed out. My attention was on all the action. But when June was giving Derek CPR, I saw Mr. Long playing with his food. I remember thinking it was a strange thing to be doing right then."

Ninang June frowned. "Maybe Derek has food allergies and Mr. Long was checking to see what was in the bowl? Poor man. What's he going to tell Nancy?"

Now it was Ninang April's turn to shake her head. "I don't envy him that. How do you tell a mother her child is dead?"

We all sat silently with that thought. I couldn't help but glance at my Lola Flor, who got up and walked to the kitchen (blatantly disregarding Detective Park's instructions to not move around the restaurant, but good luck telling her that). She'd gone through this before, the loss of a son. I was young when I lost my parents—they were a pleasant but hazy memory my aunt tried to keep alive for me.

But for my grandmother? Unforgettable.

An oppressive silence settled over the group, and no one seemed to be able to break it. Even my godmothers stayed quiet, though Ninang June seemed engrossed in texting, her arthritic fingers flying with surprising dexterity, only coming to attention when Tita Rosie came out to tell her it was her turn.

Amir stood up to greet my aunt. "Were you speaking with Detective Park?" he asked. She nodded and he groaned. "Without me around? Why would you do that?"

"I know, I know, I said the same thing. But Tita Rosie insisted on getting it all over with. She really seems to trust this Detective Park," I said, a sharp edge to my voice.

The corner of Ninang Mae's mouth tugged down at my tone as she came to Tita Rosie's defense. "It's fine, we didn't talk about anything special. What time I got here, when did Derek arrive, if he came together with Mr. Long . . . like that. Why such a big secret?"

She sniffed. "He also wanted to know if things happened the way Lila described. 'Did anything strike you as different?' or if she forgot to mention anything. Practically called her a liar!" She patted me on the arm. "Don't you worry, I set him straight."

That was not as reassuring as she thought it would be. "What do you mean 'set him straight'?"

"I told him, yes, Lila and Derek had a fight before he died, but everybody fought with Derek. Many people didn't like him, such a difficult young man. God rest his soul," she added, crossing herself.

I groaned and buried my face in my hands. Adeena put her arms around my shoulders. "Don't worry about it. You two having beef is public knowledge, and if the good detective does even the tiniest amount of investigating, he'll find out half the town had reason to hate him. Not like your restaurant was the only one he wrote about. It was just . . ."

"The one he attacked the most," I said, finishing her sentence. "Does that make it better or worse?"

I directed that question to Amir. He rubbed his jaw, square-set, recently shaven, and as perfect as the rest of him before saying, "Depends on how badly the negative press affected the other restaurants. Anyway, we're getting ahead of ourselves. You haven't been formally charged with anything and it's highly unlikely that your food was the cause of Derek's death."

He was right. Of course he was right. Ninang June switched out with Ninang April for the final interview, so I got up to help my aunt and grandmother, who'd gone to prepare a snack for everyone. Might as well get the opinion of people I trusted on whether or not my ube cookies were ready for public consumption.

I got to the kitchen just as my aunt and grandmother made their way out, hands filled with snacks.

"Lila, grab the tray with the coffee," Lola Flor commanded.

So much for sharing my treats with the group.

I followed her directions, almost bumping into Detective Park as he and Ninang April emerged from the office.

"Ope, sorry, Detective. Could I interest you in—"

"Ms. Macapagal, I'm sorry, but I'll have to stop you there." Detective Park held out a hand. "You weren't supposed to be walking around, remember? That kitchen is closed and you cannot serve food out of it until this investigation is over."

"I—What? What do you mean? I thought you said we weren't being charged with anything."

"You're not. But the fact is that a man died while eating here, and to be safe, we need to keep the kitchen closed until we analyze the dishes and get the health department over here."

"Wait a minute," Amir interjected. "You don't have a warrant. You can't take those dishes out of here."

Detective Park's head whipped around at Amir's voice. "Mr. Awan? What are you doing here?"

Amir stepped forward. "I'm their legal counsel. From now on, you can't question anyone in the Macapagal family without my presence. And those dishes stay here."

Detective Park smiled and shook his head. "Tough luck, Counselor. I already got the OK from the owner to take those dishes."

"Auntie Rosie, is that true?" Amir asked.

"I'm sorry, Amir, but I want to help out as much as possible. Nancy deserves to know how her son died, and if those dishes can help, so be it. Besides, Jonathan promised we'd be cleared in no time."

I set the tray down on the table. "And how long is 'no time'? One day? Maybe two?"

His brows knitted together. "We only have one health inspector and the lab is already backed up with other cases in the county."

"So?"

He let out a breath. "We're talking two or three weeks, minimum. Maybe more if the medical examiner finds something strange in Mr. Winter's system."

My aunt, grandmother, and I all reacted at once.

"Two or three weeks? That's ridiculous!"

"Jonathan, I have a business to run. How can I pay my bills if we're closed that long? I just got a shipment of fresh produce. What am I supposed to do with it?"

My grandmother just let loose the foulest string of Tagalog curse words I'd ever heard.

Detective Park shook his head. "I'm sorry, ladies. Until we figure out what killed Derek Winter, Tita Rosie's Kitchen is closed until further notice."

Chapter Seven

My aunt retired to her office after the detective and his crew left the restaurant. She said she wanted to get some paperwork done, but the rest of us out in the dining room could hear her sobs through the thin walls.

"We really need better insulation," was all my grandmother said before heading into the kitchen. She came out moments later with her jacket on and some foil-covered trays in hand. "We can't serve this food to customers, but he can't stop us from eating it ourselves."

"Um, Lola. He already stopped us earlier, remember? Shouldn't we be throwing this all away?"

She shoved one of the trays into Amir's hands. "I'd like to see him try. Do you think this food is going to kill you, too? No? Then eat up. No wasting food."

She marched out of the restaurant, hands still full with the other trays. My godmothers, all smart enough to be afraid of my grandmother, waited till she'd left before getting up themselves.

"We should go, too. Take care of your tita, ok?" Ninang April said.

Ninang Mae hugged me. "We'll come over to your house some-time tomorrow. I'll bring my ensaymada. I know it's your favorite."

I smiled my thanks, then turned to Ninang June, who also hugged me. I started to pull away, but she held tight, her lips close to my ear. "Come over to my place for dinner. I might have some information for you."

Before I could say anything, she'd released me and scurried off after the other two.

"That was weird," I said, facing Adeena and Amir, who were the only ones left.

"What'd she say?" Adeena asked as she peeled back the foil to check the tray's contents.

Her eyes lit up when she saw the lumpia, then wrinkled her nose when she broke one open and saw the ground beef inside. She shoved the tray to Amir, who happily dished up a plate.

"She wants me to come over for dinner. Said she had information for me." I handed Amir a container filled with sweet chili sauce.

He dribbled the sauce over his fried spring rolls before digging in. Between bites, he asked, "Auntie June was the one texting the whole time, right? I wonder who she was talking to."

I snorted. "She was probably just telling everyone she knew about what happened here."

What I said slowly dawned on me. I peered through the blinds at the parking lot, which was blessedly empty. When Detective Park and his team had left with the evidence, he delivered a general statement, basically repeating what he'd told us: investigating suspicious death, no crimes alleged, etc. The news van seemed to have left when the police did. Still . . .

"With the Calendar Crew on the loose, the whole town will know

Derek died here, if they don't already. How're we going to recover from that? Who'll want to eat at a restaurant where someone died?"

Amir nodded. "Unfortunately, I think you're right. Even if you're innocent, until we know the real cause of death, people will likely avoid this restaurant."

Tita Rosie emerged from the office in time to hear Amir's statement. "I'm not sure that matters now. You heard Jonathan. Closed for weeks while we wait for the results? We'll be out of business by then. We can barely pay the bills as is."

I looked down and noticed the stack of papers she clutched in her hand. I'd already gone through my aunt's accounts to figure out the problem areas—it was one of the first things I did after returning home. Figured I should put my expensive education to work, even if I didn't have a degree to show for it.

We were a fairly popular restaurant with the locals, yet couldn't seem to make ends meet and I didn't understand it. Till I looked through our records. My aunt and grandmother were wonderful cooks, but not very business savvy. Or at least my aunt wasn't. My lola was a killer at mahjong and pusoy, a kind of Filipino poker. She was also really slick when it came to day-to-day transactions. She was not a record-keeper, however, which made it difficult to track what needed to be done. And she sure did love the casinos, eating up what little profit we made.

Tita Rosie's problem was that she was too soft. Too soft to charge her customers the true value of her food. Too soft to go after her estranged, alcoholic husband who'd run off with most of her savings. Too soft to ask her son Ronnie, my good-for-nothing cousin, for help—he was a boy, therefore free to live his own life. Not to say that the rest of the family never lobbed guilt his way—he just managed to dodge it while I took nothing but direct hits.

"Tita Rosie, that's not going to happen. I'm not going to let them just take away your life's work. Trust me, OK?"

She smoothed my hair and kissed my forehead, something she hadn't done since I was a child. "Thank you, anak. I'm going home now. Think I need to lie down for a little bit. Do you all need anything?"

We shook our heads and she took her leave.

Adeena looked at her brother. "So what are the next steps?"

He frowned. "I don't think there's anything we can do until the police are done with their investigation. Or at least till the test results come back."

Looking at my crestfallen expression, Adeena said, "Hey, remember when West Haven stole Petey Pablo sophomore year and we worked together to find him and exact revenge?"

No, not Petey Pablo the rapper. Petey Pablo the parrot was the Shady Palms High mascot. I didn't care much for sports, but Derek had been on the football team and was devastated that their good luck charm had disappeared right before the big game. Plus I really loved that ridiculous bird. So Adeena and I teamed up to investigate our rival school and saved the day.

We'd actually earned a decent chunk of change that year finding lost items and spying on cheating boyfriends (I know, the irony) but I gave it up junior year to focus on college prep.

Reminded of those days, I tilted my head, formulating a plan. "You said our restaurant's closed until they learn how Derek died, right?"

Amir stared at me, having had to bail us out of trouble enough times to not like my line of thinking. "Yes . . ."

Adeena grinned. "So, we back in the game?"

I slung an arm around her. "Yep. Put on your sleuthing cap, girl. We're on the case!"

Chapter Eight

"You can't be serious," Amir said, his expression clearly showing he knew how deadly serious I was. "Let the police do their jobs. If you really want to know specifics, I can find out for you. Under no circumstances are you to investigate on your own, got it? It could be dangerous."

Adeena scoffed. "You're not our dad, Amir Bhai. You can't tell us what to do." As his expression darkened, she added, "Plus, how dangerous could it really be? That idiot probably went into diabetic shock and passed out. Or at worst, had an allergic reaction. It's not like we're trying to track down a serial killer."

She turned to me. "Oh, do you remember Robin? My friend from pharmacy school? They work in the lab for the county police department. I'll ask them to let us know if they hear anything."

"Awesome. I'll check in with Ninang June and see what she wants." Inspiration struck. "Oh, her daughter works at the hospital as an ER nurse. Maybe she was there when he was brought in. I'll stop by there first to see if she knows anything."

Adeena said, "Sounds like a plan. I'll text my friend and let them know what's up. I need to head back to the cafe though. Kevin's probably lost without me." She tossed her undercut, magenta-streaked wavy hair over her shoulder before waving goodbye.

Then it was just me and Amir standing there.

He'd finished eating, so I covered the tray, bussed his dishes, and began wiping off the table. He watched me in silence, seemingly content to just let things stand as they were. Which was fine with me. Conversations with Amir never went where you wanted them to.

As I shrugged on my coat and switched my no-slip work shoes for winter boots, Amir finally spoke up. "If you're going to go snoop around, I'm coming with you."

I rolled my eyes. "Amir, I appreciate your concern, but I'm just going to the hospital. Half the staff knows me and is related to me in some way. I'll be fine."

He put on his coat and wound his scarf around his neck, the ends draping just so down the front. "Not everything's about you, Lila. If I'm going to help your family, I need all the information I can get. Something tells me," he eyed me warily, "you might not be as cooperative as I'd like you to be."

The weight of our history sat in those words, an accusation of all the times he'd wanted me to be more forthcoming, more helpful, more "cooperative," as he put it.

But I couldn't. He knew why. And he claimed to understand. Didn't stop him from trying though. From wanting.

I didn't know how to respond, so I said, "We should take separate cars. I have errands to run and I'm sure you have other things to do."

I grabbed one of the foil trays and hurried out before he could naysay that statement. He wasn't the only one who could hold an unsatisfactory conversation. If there were an Olympic event for avoidance, I probably wouldn't bring home the gold, but I'd sure as heck place.

Amir and I managed to catch my cousin Bernadette while she was on break in the cafeteria. I say "cousin," but we weren't related by blood. Like most Filipino families, we extended that relationship to any close family friend. So even though I was an only child, I had enough godmothers, cousins, aunties, and uncles to populate a small village. Or at least a relatively small town that began to feel smaller and more suffocating the older I got.

Bernadette stood from the table where she was snacking on shrimp chips and wiped crumbs off her magenta-pink scrubs before giving me her usual friendly greeting. "Hey bruha, about time you came to visit me. You been with Tita Rosie for what, two or three months now? And you're only coming around now that you need me for something?" She made a noise with her lips and gestured to Amir. "Even Mr. Big-Time Lawyer here knows how to make time for his family. What's your excuse?"

I pasted a smile on my face as I screamed on the inside. "Missed you too, Ate Bernie. And in case no one told you, I've been busy helping Tita Rosie and Lola Flor run the restaurant. Maybe if your exboyfriend stopped being trash and came to help his mom, I'd have more free time." My smile grew bigger. "You talk to Ronnie lately?"

She stiffened, but managed to redirect that barb. "Speaking of exboyfriends, seems like yours is dead and the police blame you. What do you think you'll achieve by coming here? You know I can't give away confidential patient information."

It had always been like this between us, ever since we were little. She was only a year older than me, and the aunties were constantly putting us in competition against each other. Not Tita Rosie—she was above all that. But Ninang June was Bernadette's mother, and you better believe she pitted us against each other. My other godmothers say she and my mom were always trying to show each other up. Guess the rivalry continued beyond the grave.

Amir stepped in to smooth things over. "We know you're busy, Bernadette, so thanks for taking the time to talk to us. We would never want you to violate HIPAA, but if there's anything you could tell us, anything at all that would help?"

The stormy expression left her face as she beamed up at him— Amir always had that effect on women. "All I can say, unofficially, is that I was in the ER when he was brought in and it looked like diabetic ketoacidosis."

"Is that the same as a diabetic coma? What are the symptoms? How could you tell?" I bombarded her with questions.

She looked at me with scorn. "Since I can't tell you anything that I might've seen on his chart, I suggest you google it."

I sighed, and Bernadette shrugged. "Hey, I take my job seriously and I'm not losing it for you. You want more info, I hope you got an in with the medical examiner's office."

Sensing she was out of time (and patience), I played my final card. Handing her the foil tray, I said, "I know, and you're right. Sorry to bother you like this at work. Here's some leftover adobo and rice. Figured you'd be hungry and could share it with your shift members. There should've been lumpia too, but Amir ate them all."

She raised her eyebrows, but accepted the obvious peace offering as well as my apology. I think she knew it was supposed to be a bargaining chip and was surprised at the sincerity of the apology. Heck, I was too. Pretty sure we'd never apologized to each other our entire lives. But maybe it was time to bury the hatchet—despite the aunties egging us on, we had no reason to be in competition anymore. We were adults now and didn't have to keep playing these games. My mom was gone, our pageant and athletics days were behind us, and I could really use an ally.

Friend might be going a little too far though. Baby steps.

"Why don't you come over for lunch tomorrow? Before your shift? I'm sure Tita Rosie would be happy to see you, and you know she always makes too much food. I think she'd appreciate the distraction."

At her confused look, I explained, "Until the medical examiner figures out what killed Derek, the restaurant is shut down. We also have to wait on the health department to check the place out. Knowing Lola Flor, she'll use this as an opportunity to waste money at the casino, but Tita Rosie will be stuck at home."

Bernadette's expression softened. "So that's why you're here. You're trying to help out Tita Rosie."

I looked her in the eye. "Just because I left doesn't mean I was never there for my family. We all help in whatever way we can. Not all the Macapagal kids are deadbeats."

Now it was her turn to flush and apologize. "You're right. And lunch sounds great, thanks. I'll do what I can from here, and figure out a legal way to pass along the information."

Amir handed her his card. "If it helps, you can say that I asked for it in an official capacity. Edwin Long has made accusations against the family, so I'm representing them. Anything you say to me will be confidential."

I glared at him. How dare he railroad me? I was hoping that having her over in an attempt to bond would also shake out some new info, but there was no way she'd tell me anything if she could just report to Amir with no repercussions. And he knew that. This was his attempt to get me to stop investigating on my own. I'd planned on having him come with me to Ninang June's, but forget that. If he wanted to know what she had to say, he could charm her on his own time.

"You got my number, Ate. Feel free to text me whenever. You want Tita Rosie to make anything in particular?"

"It's freezing lately, so maybe some kind of soup? And something easy to pack for my baon to take with me to eat at work."

I laughed. "I'll let her know. See you tomorrow."

She waved us off, and I left without waiting for Amir. He caught up with me near the elevators.

"Hey, what's wrong?"

I wouldn't even look at him. "Don't play innocent with me. You know what you did."

"You mean help you out? She clearly wasn't comfortable talking to you, so I made it easier to pass on information."

We entered the blessedly empty elevator and he continued, "I told you to leave it alone, you wouldn't, so I'm assisting you the only way I know how. What's your problem?"

I knew he was right and I needed his help and that upset me even more. "If you really wanted to assist, you would've asked me how you could help. Did you ask me? No, you just did what you wanted since you always know best."

He looked away, running his hands over his perfectly coiffed hair. "You sound like Adeena."

I shrugged. "Adeena's right."

We lapsed into silence yet again as the doors opened and we stepped out. This uncomfortable quiet between us was fast becoming the norm.

His phone rang, the generic *Ring! Ring!* from landlines past. Ugh, even his ringtone was old-fashioned.

He checked the screen. "I've got to go. I'll call you later though, OK?"

"Just text me."

He smiled. "Still hate talking on the phone?"

I smiled back. "Always."

I let him walk to his car ahead of me, claiming to need to use the bathroom. We waved goodbye to each other, and I stood watching until he got in his car and drove away. I headed back the way I came, but turned down a different hall and stopped in front of an office door. The nameplate read:

ASSISTANT ADMINISTRATOR
JANET SPINELLI

Amir may have gotten his hooks into one of my sources, but he'd never figure this one out.

A girl's got to have some secrets now, doesn't she?

Chapter Nine

I stood in front of Janet's office, trying to hype myself up enough to knock on the door. *You're not in high school anymore, Lila. I'm sure it'll be fine. There's no way she still hates you. You're both adults. Sort of.*

Who was I kidding? This was a terrible idea. I was about to wander back the way I came when I heard someone step into the hall and a voice call, "Turning tail and running away again, Lila? That does seem to be your MO, doesn't it?"

I closed my eyes and counted to ten before responding. "Hey, Janet. I see not much has changed, has it?"

I turned to face my high school bully. Wow, she really hadn't changed. There were some laugh lines around her eyes (though I sincerely doubt they were caused by laughter), but the rest of her porcelain complexion remained as flawless as ever. I had to fight the urge to pick at the tiny pimples near my hairline.

She was still strawberry blonde and willowy, her breasts and bangs pushed up to impressive heights. Her left hand sported a ring with a rock so big it practically screamed "FAKE!"

She must've noticed me looking at it because she held it up and smirked. "You heard, right? Terrence and I are getting married. He's mine," she added unnecessarily.

"Yup. Congrats."

She waited for more, but that's all I had to say on that matter.

"That's it? After you tried to steal him from me senior year, I figured you'd have more to say."

Don't take the bait, Lila, don't take the bait. This woman is in charge of pretty much all patient information and she could easily get Bernadette fired. Don't push her.

When I didn't respond, she said, "You always had such a smart mouth. Why are you so quiet now?"

I fought the urge to roll my eyes. "Because that all happened, what, seven years ago? Maybe even eight? How are you not over it yet?"

She scoffed, so I added, "And if you recall, *he* came to *me* when he saw you for the bully you were. Besides, I remember you getting pretty cozy with Derek as well."

Her hand flew to her chest and literally clutched at her pearls. "How dare you! Just because you got dumped by your fiancé doesn't mean you have to lie about mine."

As usual, good news traveled fast around Shady Palms.

"Forget it. I was a fool to think you'd help me." I started to walk away, but knew I couldn't leave it like that and turned back around. "Congratulations to you and Terrence. He's a good guy and there aren't many of them left. I hope you make each other happy. Truly."

She stood there with her mouth hanging open as I walked away, trembling but proud.

I'd witnessed a tragedy, been interrogated by the police, recon-

ciled with Bernadette, told off Amir, and confronted Janet all in one
day. And it wasn't even dinnertime yet.

I checked my watch and saw I had another couple of hours to kill
before calling on Ninang June. There was only one thing I knew would
get me out of this funk, so I hopped in the car and headed home.

It was time to bake.

Chapter Ten

A pound of butter and Lord knows how much sugar later, my head was clear, my spirit was calm, and I had a delicious calamansi-ginger pie cooling on the counter. I twisted shut the lid of the jar I'd filled with the excess calamansi-ginger curd and sighed in satisfaction. Now this was bliss.

The sweetness of the coconut shortbread crust scented the air, interspersed with the zest of citrus and zing of ginger. If I could bottle this scent, I'd wear it forever.

My chubby dachshund, Longganisa, pranced around my feet, waiting for her share of my experiment. I tossed her a bit of the crust I'd trimmed off and waited for her reaction. Nisa was always my first critic. If it didn't pass muster with her, it was a no go.

She snapped up the shortbread in record time and got up on her hind legs, begging for more. A good sign for me, but disappointment for her.

"Sorry, baby, you know you can't have more than that. It's not good for you."

I poured out some of her diet kibble and set it in front of her. She looked down at her bowl, then up at me, and I swear, if a dog could raise an eyebrow in disgust, she would've. Go figure I'd pass my food snobbery on to my dog.

I poured a tiny bit of broth over the kibble to make it more enticing and went to check on my aunt. She was still napping in her room, so I left her a note saying I'd be at Ninang June's if she wanted to join us when she got up.

I poked my head into Lola Flor's room and noticed her lucky visor wasn't hanging from its usual peg. Yep, she'd gone to the casino.

I carefully put the pie into a carrier and headed over to Ninang June's, praying she actually had something important to tell me and that this wasn't her attempt to set me up with one of the Calendar Crew's roster of sons, nephews, and godsons. It wouldn't be the first time my godmothers sprung a surprise date on me.

Thankfully, no eligible bachelors were waiting for me. Instead, the Calendar Crew stood around the table setting down dishes and gabbing in Tagalog. Suddenly, I didn't know what was worse: having to small talk my way through what was essentially a chaperoned date or enduring the full onslaught of my godmothers' attention.

"Lila! What took you so long? Go wash your hands and help us."

"How's your aunt doing? We've been praying for her."

"What's that?" One of them poked at the carrier I'd set on the table.

"Calamansi-ginger pie with a coconut shortbread crust. I'm trying out a new recipe."

Luckily, my godmothers didn't share my grandmother's aversion to anything not "authentically" Filipino. The fact that food was one of Lola Flor's few tangible connections to her homeland, and that it meant more to her than just sustenance, was not lost on me. But her refusal to try anything new and insistence on me being a "real" Filipino grated on me. As a second-generation member of a colonized country, born and raised in the Midwestern United States, what did that even mean? But good luck having that conversation with her.

I washed my hands and helped Ninang June set the table. The leftover pork and chicken adobo my grandmother had pushed on them— green beans, chopped tomatoes, and white rice—already sat in the middle, so once we brought out the plates, glasses, and silverware, everybody dug in.

I reached for the bottle of patis, and as I added a few dashes of the fish sauce to my tomatoes, Ninang June said, "Bernadette told me you visited her at work. Was she able to tell you anything good? Last time we talked, she hadn't been able to get at his chart."

Of course Ninang June would've pumped her daughter for information already. "Sort of? She thinks Derek went into a diabetic coma and didn't wake up. She couldn't tell me any more without violating hospital regulations though. She did say that the medical examiner needs to run more tests before they can make an official announcement."

"What did that Janet woman tell you?" Ninang April asked.

I put my fork down. "How did you know I talked to Janet? Nobody was in the hall."

The aunties all gave me a pitying look. "Nobody was in the hall, but plenty of people were in their offices. You think people don't listen to a conversation happening right outside their door?"

Ninang June had been head nurse at the Shady Palms Hospital for years before quitting to run her late husband's business over a decade ago, and still kept in touch with much of the hospital staff. Maybe I could use her to get me some info on the DL.

I sighed and picked up my fork again. Food was the only thing that would get me through this conversation—my godmothers weren't in the habit of drinking wine with dinner, so this was going to be a long night.

"So if you've already received a report, why are you asking me about it?"

"We need to hear your end of the story. It's important to hear it from the original source."

Wow. I knew my godmothers loved tsismis, but who knew they took it this seriously? Guess I should be glad they didn't know about community listservs, because I could see them exploiting their powers for the dark side.

I'd lost my appetite but knew better than to leave food on my plate, so I stabbed another piece of chicken and stuck it in my mouth to delay answering.

Ninang April put down her spoon and fork. "Lila, stop stalling. You can't avoid us, you know that."

I really hated how well they knew me.

"I didn't learn anything."

They stared at me, waiting for more.

I sipped some water. "We, uh, got into a fight and I left."

"Amir wasn't there to help you talk to her?"

I slammed my glass down, water slopping all over the table. "No, he wasn't there when I talked to her. I don't need his help."

Ninang April snorted. "If you want Bernadette or Janet to talk to you, you definitely need his help." She smiled at my outraged look. "What? You girls have been competing since you were children. You think they're going to play nice now that you need them?"

"OK, first of all, I never wanted to compete with either of them. With Ate Bernie, well . . . you know." I glanced over at Ninang June. "As for Janet, she would always join in my activities just to taunt me! That girl made my childhood a living hell. I don't see where she gets off being mad at me."

My godmothers all *tsked*. "Ay, Lila, as self-absorbed as ever," Ninang April admonished.

"Ay, April, stop it," Ninang Mae said.

Thank you, finally someone on my side.

"She's so young, of course she's self-absorbed. You can't expect her to see what we see, diba?" Ninang Mae continued.

OK, I didn't need this. "Excuse me, I have to clean up this water spill. And I think it's time for dessert."

I got up to wipe down the table and get my pie. Ninang June joined me in the kitchen to make decaf coffee for all of us.

"Lila, don't take it too hard. We're just trying to help out."

That was the problem. Their idea of helping caused me nothing but stress.

Ninang June served everyone coffee and pie, and we all settled into a haze of sugar and happiness. My pie got a thumbs-up from everyone, but Ninang April (of course) offered me a useful bit of feedback.

"The balance of sweet and sour is well done, but you need to cut the richness. Either a thinner layer of filling or maybe some whipped cream would be good. Also, the ginger is interesting, but I think it'd be better to just let the calamansi shine on its own."

After we finished the pie, I wondered how long I'd have to sit there sipping subpar coffee before I could politely say my goodbyes.

As if sensing my listlessness, Ninang June said, "Lila, before you leave, you should know we invited you over for a reason."

She pulled a sheet of paper out of her blouse pocket and slid it across the table toward me. "Don't tell Rosie we gave you this, but we made a list of anyone who could be a suspect in Derek's death. You know, in case the medical examiner says he didn't die naturally."

I stared at the paper but didn't pick it up. "Um, I appreciate the effort, but it's not like he was murdered. What we need is someone who can speed up the lab results, or at least get the health department to clear us ASAP. Do you know anyone like that?"

"Don't worry, we've made a few calls. Things will start moving quickly. But just in case . . ." Ninang June gestured at the paper.

"Good. Now that that's settled, I should head home and check on Tita Rosie. Thanks for dinner." I shrugged on my coat and went to the front room to put my shoes back on, leaving the list where it lay.

Ninang June came over to say good night and give me a quick hug and kiss goodbye.

It wasn't until I was searching for my keys outside that I realized she'd also managed to slip the suspect list in my pocket.

Chapter Eleven

I t was weird to wake up the next morning and not have to rush to the restaurant. None of us knew what to do with ourselves. I'd told Tita Rosie that Bernadette was coming over for lunch, so as soon as we finished breakfast, she headed to the restaurant to pick up supplies to prepare a feast for our one guest. Lola Flor said she was going out and wouldn't tell us where, but my aunt and I both knew her destination.

I took Longganisa out for a run, which I hadn't been able to do since I started working at the restaurant. We both had stubby legs and were out of shape, so she made the perfect running buddy. I guess I underestimated how out of shape we both were because a mile out, just as we were about to reach the riverwalk, she splayed out on the pavement and refused to take another step. The lazy little sausage made me pick her up and walk back.

I had deliberately avoided the Main Street Plaza, which housed our restaurant, because I didn't want to be reminded of the other day. However, I figured that short run had earned me a little treat, so I swung by Java Jo's to grab a coconut milk latte for myself and a stale pastry for Nisa.

Even though it was right next door to our restaurant, the spaces were a world apart. My aunt hadn't updated the decor since she bought the place in the late 90s (and the original owners hadn't updated the decor since at least the 70s). Tita Rosie's Kitchen was meant to be warm and comforting, the feeling of having a meal at your home away from home. However, what was once "cozy" and "rustic" was now just small and outdated.

In contrast, Java Jo's was all black and white and stainless steel. Very clean and modern-looking with the only splashes of color coming from Kevin's framed artwork. You'd think an interior like that would seem cold, even sterile, but the ever-present steam from the cappuccino station, the burble of the espresso machine, and the smell of quality ground coffee beans made it heavenly.

Kevin was cool with me bringing Nisa inside as long as no other customers complained, so I sat at a table near the door and waited for Adeena to join us. After handling the short line, she made her way over with a tray bearing Nisa's pastry plate, a giant mug with my latte, and several small paper cups filled with her latest creations.

She had a magical touch, experimenting with beverages the way I did with my bakes, and we were each other's guinea pigs and suppliers. It was thanks to her that my calamansi iced tea was a hit (my original ratios of honey to citrus were off), and my Sunday contribution to the coffee shop was the one day the pastry case sold out. Adeena was always on Kevin to expand the menu and be more adventurous, but he continued slinging the same boring (yet quality) beverages and the same dry pastries from a commercial supplier.

The one thing she was able to talk him into was the Sunday specials, which she and I lived for. She'd spend days thinking up what to offer, and then test my strong sense of smell and trained palate. Over time, we developed a little tasting ritual that we'd go through every week, which I used to indulge my weekly dairy allowance.

I popped a Lactaid pill, and Adeena handed me the first paper cup. I closed my eyes and took a long sniff. The scent of cinnamon and cloves tickled my nose. I sipped the brew slowly, letting the liquid flow over my tongue, holding it there a moment to let all the flavors permeate.

I swallowed. "Did you just take your chai spice mix and add it to coffee?"

She grimaced. "That obvious?"

I shrugged. "It's been done."

She bit her lip and handed me the next cup. I repeated the ritual, only this time a floral bouquet flooded my nose and mouth. I choked it down, but barely.

"Too heavy-handed with the rose?"

I gulped down water, too intent on washing the taste of potpourri out of my mouth to bother answering.

She sighed and handed me the final cup, which turned out to be liquid gold. I'd never had hot chocolate that was so rich, yet drinkable—I drained the tiny cup and immediately wanted more.

"That's the winner. Hands down, the best hot chocolate I've ever had. What's in it?"

She grinned. "You know I can't give away my secrets."

I pouted a bit, so she added, "Unless you've finally decided to settle down here in Shady Palms and open a cafe with me?"

"Uh . . ." was my very articulate reply.

Nisa came to the rescue by whimpering loudly and pawing at the door. "Oops, I better let her out before she goes all over the floor."

Remembering the list Ninang June gave me, I pulled it out of my belt bag and handed it to her. "Oh, before I forget, Ninang June slipped that in my pocket last night. I think she's being ridiculous, but you know more about these places than I do. Let me know what you think, OK?"

Adeena frowned, obviously sensing I was trying to change the subject, but took the list and waved me off. She couldn't exactly accuse me of training my dog to get me out of awkward situations, so I escaped this time. Unfortunately, this conversation had been coming up more and more frequently and I didn't know how to answer.

When I was in Chicago, the two of us would spend hours fantasizing about how Adeena would move to the city after finishing school, and we'd open our own place together, taking the Chicago cafe scene by storm. But over the past year, and especially now that I was back in town, she seemed more and more content to stay in Shady Palms and open a business here.

Which I just couldn't understand. I didn't exactly like Shady Palms, but Adeena loathed it here. If I felt stifled by family expectations, she was drowning in them. One of the reasons Amir and I never explored our feelings for each other was because of Adeena. It was no secret that Amir was the golden child of the family. The one who did everything right, the oldest, the boy, the one who not only met expectations but smashed through them at every opportunity.

Adeena was the afterthought. Sure they loved her, but not a day went by that she wasn't reminded of what a disappointment she was. They hated her clothes and hair. She had yet to graduate from pharmacy school, not because it was too hard for her, but because she'd rather sling beverages than get a proper degree. And worst of all, she refused to meet with any of the nice young men her parents hoped she'd someday marry.

Because she was a lesbian. Something her parents knew—she'd come out to them her first year of college—but conveniently ignored.

Hence her big-city dreams: diverse populations meant diverse palates and lifestyles, things that were sorely lacking in our little town.

So what happened? Why the big push to get me to settle down in Shady Palms?

I made it home in time for a quick shower before Bernadette arrived. When I entered the kitchen, the warming aroma of almondigas, meatball soup with vermicelli noodles, enveloped me. I hadn't had this soup in years, and had forgotten how much I loved the rich, garlicky broth and slippery noodles, atop which floated delicately spiced pork meatballs. This was going to be a real treat.

I set the table, then helped Tita Rosie bring out the soup as well as the leftover adobo and rice from yesterday. A few slices from last night's calamansi pie were waiting in the fridge. We just needed Bernadette to show up.

So where was she?

After another fifteen minutes passed, Tita Rosie moved the soup back to the stove to keep it warm and I hunted for my cell phone to see if Bernadette had texted me saying she'd be late. I finally found it when I heard my ringtone out in the area where I'd left my boots.

I rushed over to answer it and was surprised to see Adeena's name flashing across the screen instead of Bernadette's.

"Hey girl, what's up?"

Adeena's voice was shaky. "Lila, I'm so sorry. I don't know how to tell you this, but . . ."

My hand tightened around the phone. "But what?"

"My friend from the lab said they found traces of poison in the dishes from your restaurant. They can't say if it matches anything found in Derek's system, but they know this much: He was murdered."

Chapter Twelve

Before I could fully process what Adeena said, the doorbell rang. I scurried away without answering it. "Oh my gulay, there's someone at the door. Do you think it's the police? Do they think my family killed Derek?"

Adeena's voice flowed, warm and reassuring, through the phone. "You're innocent, so there's nothing they can do to you, right?"

We both paused, knowing that wasn't quite true. The law tended to work differently for people like us.

She continued, "Go answer the door. The longer you take, the more suspicious you look. I'm calling Amir to let him know what's going on."

I thanked her and hung up, but stayed in the hallway staring at the front door. Whoever was on the other side got tired of ringing the bell and started pounding on the door. Tita Rosie bustled by to answer.

"Lila, what's wrong with you? That's probably Bernie out there and it's freezing!"

She was right.

Bernadette stomped inside, both to knock the snow off her boots and also because she was pissed at me. "What the hell, Lila? Have you been standing here this whole time?"

"Bernadette, language!"

She flushed. "Sorry, Tita Rosie."

My aunt gestured for Bernadette's coat and led her into the dining room. "Come in and warm yourself up. I made almondigas for lunch."

Bernadette's eyes lit up. "My favorite! You remembered?"

Tita Rosie smiled. "Of course I did. I even added extra fried garlic, just the way you like it."

Bernadette swooped in and hugged my aunt, who patted her a few times on the back, the awkward gesture contrasting with her beaming face. Unfortunately, the doorbell rang yet again, interrupting this love fest.

We all looked at each other, Bernadette and I in alarm and Tita Rosie in confusion.

"Who could that be?" Tita Rosie asked, moving to open the door.

Bernadette and I huddled together. "Did you hear about the poison?" she asked.

I nodded. "That's why I didn't answer the door right away. I thought you were the cops. How did you hear about it?"

"The usual office gossip. Guess I'll forgive you for letting me freeze on the front porch, but don't think you can avoid the cops this time . . ." she trailed off as Tita Rosie and Detective Park stepped into the room.

I forced a smile. "Hello, Detective. We were expecting you."

"You were?" He raised an eyebrow, glancing back and forth between Bernadette and me.

"Oh don't worry, she didn't tell me anything. Not that I didn't ask her, of course." I hurried to clear Bernadette from suspicion. "I got the info from . . . another source."

"I see. And you're not going to tell me who this source is?"

Tita Rosie cut in. "Excuse me, Jonathan, but what are you talking about? Source for what?"

He sighed. "I'm sorry Rosie, but this isn't a social visit. We received an anonymous tip that had the chief speed up the results on the dishes we took from you. They tested positive for arsenic. I've got a warrant to search your home and restaurant."

I stiffened and stopped my aunt from responding. "This all seems pretty quick. I think we need to get our lawyer here."

"Anak!" My aunt grabbed my arm. "We have nothing to hide and Jonathan's right. The sooner they solve this case, the sooner I get my restaurant back. Right?" she asked, looking at the detective.

He smiled, as if he'd already anticipated my aunt's answer. "Of course, Rosie. I'm just trying to do my job here, you know."

"Tita, we really should wait for Amir to look this over—"

"Ay, Lila, stop fussing." She lowered her glasses onto her face to look over the document. "This seems to be in order. Do we need to do anything?"

"A team is going to search your house while I head over to your restaurant to lead the search there. You should all stay here, OK?"

He made the call and waited until another officer knocked at the door. He let him in, showed him the signed document, and instructed the team on what to search for. They went to work and Detective Park took his leave.

I watched him for a moment before coming to a decision. I grabbed Bernadette and pulled her aside. "Ate, do you think you can stay with Tita Rosie while this is going on? Amir should be here soon, but I don't want her to be alone for this."

She nodded. "You going over to the restaurant?"

"Of course. I can't let them do this to us. Besides, I don't exactly trust them. Not after what happened with Ronnie . . ."

Bernadette's lips pulled into a thin line at the mention of her ex-boyfriend and his troubles. "Go. I'll take care of Tita Rosie. You handle your business."

I hurried out to my car, trying to push down the sense of panic that'd been rising since I first got Adeena's call.

We'll be fine, I told myself. We didn't do anything, so they couldn't possibly find anything on us. Right? Right.

I sure hate it when I'm wrong.

Chapter Thirteen

I pulled into Main Street Plaza parking lot, a lump rising in my throat as I saw the stream of police officers entering our restaurant. I cut off the engine and hopped out, interrupting Detective Park's conversation with one of his officers.

"Ms. Macapagal? What are you doing here?"

"I wanted to be on the premises while it's being searched. Just in case."

Detective Park's nostrils flared, a sight I would've found amusing if it wasn't also terrifying. "Just in case of what?"

"I have a right to be here," I said, though I wasn't sure that was true. Still, act like you know what you're talking about, Lila!

He was about to give in to me, I knew he was, when a shout from inside interrupted us. We looked at each other and both ran inside toward a group of officers in the kitchen. One was holding an open bag of jasmine rice in his gloved hands.

He nodded at Detective Park. "Just like the note said, sir."

Before I could puzzle out what he meant by that, another officer came up to us holding a duffel bag I'd never seen before. He held it out to Detective Park, the bag's contents rattling as he gestured toward me.

Detective Park pulled on gloves and took the bag from the officer. "Ms. Macapagal, does this look familiar to you?"

I shook my head, eyes still locked on the bag.

"That's funny, because it was in your locker." He sighed. "I think we need to have another talk. Down at the station."

I felt light-headed and gripped a table to steady myself. "I . . . But I've never seen that bag before! Someone must've put it in my locker. It's not mine!"

Detective Park flipped out. "Are you accusing my officers of planting evidence? Is that what you're doing, Ms. Macapagal? Trying to pin this on the Shady Palms Police Department?"

I backed away, my hands in the air to show I was being cooperative. "Sir, I didn't say it was one of your officers. I just said someone else must've put it there because it's not mine."

"Save it for the station," he said, gesturing toward the door.

"Am I being arrested?"

"No. I just want to ask you some questions." He grabbed my arm to keep me upright as my knees started to wobble from his very unreassuring answer.

As he walked me out to his car, Adeena popped out of the coffee shop next door to see what was going on. Before getting in the backseat, I yelled, "Tell Amir to meet me at the station!"

She nodded, whipping her phone out of her apron, ready to go to battle for me.

As the car backed up and pulled out of the lot, dread settled into my stomach. Looks like I needed his help after all.

Chapter Fourteen

Detective Park drove to the station in silence, then bustled me into an empty room with a table and a few chairs that obviously valued function over style—and their function was to keep me as uncomfortable as possible while I waited for Amir to arrive. All very familiar emotions as I sat there wondering what could possibly happen next.

"Do I need a lawyer? I think I should wait for Amir," I told Detective Park, as I fiddled with the bottle of water he gave me, feeling the need to fill the silence as he sat there watching me.

"You can if you want, but you're not under arrest. There's no reason to wait for him."

He must've read the skepticism in my face, because he shrugged and said, "Hey, the sooner you answer my questions, the sooner you get out."

Remembering there was also a search at my house, I figured now would be a good time for me to get some information as well. "How's my aunt doing? Did they find anything at our house?"

The friendly expression he'd adopted as he tried to get me to talk was quickly replaced by a somber one. The change was so quick and unsettling, my body physically reacted. The spasms in my stomach brought to mind the day I was foolish enough to think I could run a half marathon. As I'd stood there at the starting line, at an ungodly hour on Lake Shore Drive, surrounded by people who'd been training for this year-round, my stomach twisted in anxiety, fear, and nausea, wondering what the heck I'd gotten myself into. That same feeling crept over me as I watched Detective Park debate just how much information to disclose.

"We didn't find anything in your house. Your aunt and grandmother seem to be cleared from suspicion, unless we find something in that bag of rice."

I blinked at him. "Oh, that's a good thing, right? Why did your expression change?"

He ran his hand up the short-shorn hair on the back of his head, the nervous gesture oddly boyish and charming on someone like him. "I just feel bad for Rosie, is all. But I've got a job to do."

He got up and walked out for a minute, returning with a large cardboard box. He pulled out the half-full bag of rice they found in our restaurant kitchen, this time in a labeled evidence bag. "Could you tell me about this, Ms. Macapagal?"

My eyebrows scrunched up as I studied the bag. What was so special about it? "I don't really know what to tell you, Detective. It's the same brand of jasmine rice we've been ordering in bulk since I was a kid. We use it for most of our dishes."

"And did you use this bag the day Derek Winter came to your restaurant?"

I laughed, then sobered up when he glared at me. "Sorry, it's just impossible to tell, you know? All the bags look the same. Besides, we pour the rice into storage containers to keep them fresh once we open them. If that bag is still half full, we must've opened it recently."

"Why do you say that?"

"My aunt is nitpicky about cleanliness and food hygiene. As soon as we open a bag, we pour the whole thing into a storage container. We don't usually leave open bags laying around."

"'Usually'?"

"Well, I mean nobody's perfect. Could be one of us started filling the container and got called away to do something and never finished the job."

He noted this all down without further comment, which made me even more nervous. What could I possibly be saying that was important enough to write down in an official capacity?

"Sir, why all these questions about the rice? Considering it's sitting there in an evidence bag, do you think there's something significant about it?"

"Did you know that rice has higher levels of arsenic than other foods?"

Whoa, really? I ate rice every day for just about every meal. "I had no idea."

"Not enough to kill, usually, but enough to make people sick. Your friend Derek had unusually high levels of arsenic in his bloodstream." Sensing my protest, he held up his hand. "Now that could easily be explained by the fact that he seemed to frequent your restaurant quite often and maybe it built up over time. However, the police chief received an anonymous tip leading us to believe that the rice was purposely contaminated with arsenic."

I slammed my hands on the tabletop, pushing myself out of my seat. "That's ridiculous! Why would we purposely poison our custom-ers? That restaurant is all we have! Plus my family eats the food there every day and we're just fine." Realizing my actions and tone could be misconstrued as aggressive, I quickly sat back down and folded my hands together. "Sorry. It's just, you know. Upsetting."

A thought occurred to me. "Are you saying that you narrowed down the substance in Derek's system to that exact bag, Detective? I mean, you just found it, right?"

Detective Park frowned at me. "It would be impossible to narrow it down to this specific bag, and we haven't had time to run tests on it yet."

Oh, thank goodness.

"But we did have time to test the dishes we removed, and the ones Derek ate from had large traces of arsenic in them while Mr. Long's did not. So how many people had access to the food and the opportu-nity to poison the dish?" Detective Park asked.

He had us there. But how?

"Are you positive that arsenic is what killed him? And that it was added before Derek ate our food?"

The detective raised his eyebrows. "Are you suggesting that not only was the poison added after Derek ate the food, but that it's not what killed him? Then how did such a large amount of arsenic get in his system, and how did he die, Ms. Macapagal?"

Well of course it sounds ridiculous when you say it out loud like that, Mr. Detective.

I crossed my arms and scowled to cover up my embarrassment. "I don't know! Mr. Long was there too, maybe he did it. Besides, it's not my job to prove how or why, Detective. That's your job."

Detective Park's nostrils flared. "I don't need you to tell me what my job is, Ms. Macapagal. I know exactly what I need to do."

He followed this statement with an intense glare and an even more intense silence. I squirmed in my seat as the quiet grew oppressive. I'd nearly reached the breaking point when—

Knock, knock.

Amir entered the room, breaking the tension so completely I sighed audibly with relief. He stood behind me, hands on the back of my chair. "You have no right to be questioning my client without me present, Detective."

Detective Park grinned at him, the jig finally up. "Ah, Mr. Awan. I was wondering when you'd get here. And just so you know, your client spoke freely and of her own volition."

My jaw dropped. "But I asked for him! I know how this works."

"Sorry Ms. Macapagal, but you asked if you needed a lawyer. I said no, and you started talking."

"I . . . that's . . . Amir, can he do that? Does that count?"

Amir rubbed the space between his eyebrows. "If you never actually said, 'I want my lawyer,' or 'I won't speak without my lawyer present,' then yeah. You chose to speak to him without me around."

I started to protest, but he held up his hand. "Anyway, I'm here now and unless there's something you can hold her on, we're leaving."

Amir motioned toward me and I started to get up, but the detective waved us to sit down. "You're being rather hasty, Counselor. Perhaps we need to run a few more tests to connect Ms. Macapagal to Derek Winter's murder, but I'd like to see you talk your way out of this."

He reached into the cardboard box and pulled out the duffel bag they'd found at the restaurant, this time with an evidence tag on it. He unzipped it, exposing mounds of cash and baggies full of pills, some of them still in prescription pill bottles.

Amir glanced at me, but I shook my head, eyes locked on the kaleidoscope of drugs and money spilling out of the bag. "My client claims to have no knowledge of this bit of evidence."

Detective Park leaned forward, elbows on the table and fingers steepled together. "Really, Ms. Macapagal? Then why was it in your locker in the restaurant office? And before you ask, yes, it was locked. Your aunt gave us the keys."

"But that doesn't make sense! I don't even know what those pills are! Why would I have them?"

The detective smiled. "Oh come now, Ms. Macapagal. A young woman as worldly as you surely knows about recreational drug use. We're in the midst of an opioid crisis, haven't you heard?"

Amir nodded slowly, apparently catching his drift, which was nice because I had no idea where he was going with this. "That's right, Detective. You were the one who broke up that drug ring and handled the trucker's murder."

"Exactly," he said, eyes glittering like a hawk. "And it all stopped for a while and our little county found peace. But now it seems like it's starting up again, and I absolutely will not stand for that."

It took me a minute, but I finally caught on to what he was insinuating. "Wait a minute! I am not involved with whatever—"

"It starts with just one death, doesn't it?" Detective Park interrupted me. "But then it spirals. One person parties a little too hard, and emergency services doesn't get there in time. Or we're out of Narcan, because it's happening all too frequently and our resources are spread thin." He shook his head. "Why'd you do it, Lila? Did Derek find out about your little side hustle and threaten to turn you in? Or were you in it together and things turned sour? A lover's spat gone wrong?"

My mouth opened and closed soundlessly, like a goldfish. His accusations were so wild, I didn't even know how to begin to combat them.

"Detective, this is outrageous. You're grasping at straws trying to paint my client as some drug kingpin, but you have no proof." Amir put his hand on my shoulder. "If you're done insulting Ms. Macapagal and wasting our time, we'd like to leave now."

Detective Park held up a hand. "Do I have proof that she's one of the higher ups? No, you're right. But I do have evidence that she's involved and that's more than enough to move forward."

I stared at him, the seriousness of his last remark sinking in. "Amir? He's not . . . I mean, he can't, right?"

Amir's grip on my shoulder tightened. "Are you charging my client, Detective?"

"Absolutely. Possession with intent to sell, for beginners. We need to run checks on that extremely suspicious lot of cash as well. And when the medical examiner gives us a more thorough report, we might even throw in murder. Though I'm sure we could work something out if you choose to confess now, Ms. Macapagal."

I shook my head wildly. "I have nothing to confess. I'm innocent."

He grunted. "Save it for court. Mr. Awan, we need to process your client now. You'll have to come back during visitation hours tomorrow."

I panicked, grabbing Amir's arm as he stood up. "Wait! Are you just going to leave me here?"

Amir gently loosened my grip, trying to keep a smile on his face, though a pained expression slipped through. "Don't worry Lila, it's just one night. I need to talk to your family and let them know what's going on. I'll be back tomorrow, and we'll figure this out."

He squeezed my hand and leaned forward, eyes burning with conviction. "I swear to you, I will fix this. Just trust me, OK? Everything will be fine."

And then he left. Just left me there as Detective Park had another officer take my fingerprints and photo, as well as all of my belongings. Dear Lord, I had a mug shot now. What would Tita Rosie and Lola Flor think? I hoped Amir would break it to them gently. I also hoped Lola Flor wouldn't shoot the messenger.

Chapter Fifteen

After being processed, I was led to a (thankfully) empty cell. I wasn't sure I could deal with a rando up in my space after all that had just happened.

I sat on the wooden bench attached to the wall, which was every bit as functional as the chairs in the interrogation room. I drew my legs up onto the bench, hand clutching the area of my shirt where my necklace should be. It was taken away during processing and I felt scared and naked without it. My mind refused to focus on the fact that I had just been booked on bogus drug charges and, based on the evidence, was going to be locked away for some time.

Instead, I did the breathing practices Adeena taught me. Well, I tried to, but having a well-honed sense of smell could be more of a curse than a gift in certain settings. Rather than inner peace, each deep inhalation brought whiffs of a sour, unwashed odor emanating from the empty but not-quite-clean latrine.

So now what? I guess I could put my trust in Amir and the legal process (ha!), but this seemed like a good time to go over all the details of the case that I knew so far. How much info did I actually have? Well, someone put arsenic in Derek's dish. That same poison matched one found in his system. How did it get there? The only people close enough to his food were me, Tita Rosie, Lola Flor, and Mr. Long. My family clearly didn't do it, but that just left . . . Mr. Long?

But that didn't make sense. Derek was his stepson. He didn't seem to like Derek much, based on my godmother's gossip, but he must've cared about him somewhat. Why else would he be coming after us so hard? Unless it was all an act.

I shook my head. But what was the motive? And why at our restaurant? There was an anonymous tip called in about us, so my family was tied to it somehow. Why us?

I thought back over the suspect list my godmothers gave me. Luckily Adeena still had it, so it hadn't been taken away with my other possessions. The list was short and populated with restaurant owners that Derek had attacked in his column, so even though the details were fuzzy, I could recall the general info:

> *Stan and Martha Kosta—Stan's Diner*
> *Diana Torres—El Gato Negro*
> *Akio and Yuki Sato—Sushi-ya*
> *George and Nettie Bishop—Big Bishop's BBQ*
> *Mike Krasinski—Pierogi Palace*

Stan's Diner and Big Bishop's BBQ were Shady Palms institutions. In fact, Derek and I had spent a good portion of high school hanging out in the sticky booths at Big Bishop's BBQ, often with Adeena and Derek's best friend, Terrence, in tow. George and Nettie Bishop were like family. I couldn't believe he'd dare desecrate such a special place, but there's no way the Bishops had anything to do with his death. I mentally crossed them off the list. I knew I'd eventually have to go there in person to talk to them, but I couldn't handle that right now. Too many memories tied to that place.

Stan's Diner, however, was on the other side of town, an area I wasn't particularly familiar with. I wouldn't say Shady Palms was segregated, at least not as noticeably as Chicago was, but let's just say Stan's Diner and Pierogi Palace were in the older part of town, where a particular set of clientele preferred to stay. Big Bishop's BBQ, El Gato Negro, and Sushi-ya were on the other side, where people whose families hadn't been in Shady Palms (or the U.S.) for generations upon generations settled. Tita Rosie's Kitchen, which was lucky enough to be located on the Main Street strip of downtown, was directly in the middle.

As I tried to recall the information the aunties had scribbled next to each name, the sound of footsteps and clinking keys interrupted my thought process. Looked like I was getting a cellmate. I put my feet back on the floor and braced myself for what was coming. I didn't expect to see a familiar face.

"Marcus?" I said, recognizing one of Ninang Mae's younger sons. "I didn't know you were a cop. Heck, I didn't know you were old enough to—"

"I'm not a cop," Marcus Marcelo replied, as he opened the cell door and gestured for the woman he was escorting to enter. She scowled at him, but followed his instructions, moving to the opposite side of the cell to sit and sulk.

After locking the door behind her, he clarified, "I'm a corrections officer. And I'm sorry, Li—Miss Macapagal, but while I'm on duty, you'll have to refer to me as Officer Marcelo or C.O. Marcelo. I don't need anyone thinking I'm giving you preferential treatment."

He nodded toward the woman, then addressed her. "Mrs. Sato, your husband is being questioned right now. I'll come get you when it's your turn, but until then, play nice, OK?"

He turned to leave, but I stopped him. "Marcus, I mean Officer Marcelo, wait! Do you know how long I'll be here? Have you heard what's going on? Is my aunt OK?"

Marcus sighed, but moved closer so we wouldn't be overheard. "I can't tell you much, but it's serious. Detective Park has enough evidence to put you away on those drugs he found." He searched my face for a moment, probably remembering my cousin Ronnie and wondering how alike we were. I stared defiantly back. Satisfied, he moved on. "As for the murder, it's shaky at best. But he's used to getting his way around here, Lila. I hope you have a good lawyer. You're going to need one."

I took a deep, shaky breath, willing away the tears and nausea. "You'll let me know if anything else comes up, right?"

He shook his head, but in a voice only I could hear, said, "I'll do what I can."

He stepped away and spoke again, this time at a regular volume. "I'm sorry, but my hands are tied." He glanced at the woman he brought in, who was studying us.

He nodded at her before leaving and I returned to my seat, noting that I had the full attention of my cellmate. She looked me up and down, assessing every part of me, so I did the same. She was East Asian, probably Japanese, and her straight black hair was cut to her shoulders in an asymmetrical bob. She might've been pretty, but her red, swollen eyes and the rivers of eye makeup staining her cheeks made it difficult to tell.

She was older than me, but her skincare routine (or fantastic genes) made it impossible for me to tell how much older. She could've been anywhere between late twenties and early forties, but was probably somewhere in between. I was in the middle of comparing our general size if it came down to a fight when she finally spoke up.

"You knew Derek."

It wasn't a question.

I straightened up, planting my feet on the floor to steady myself. "I don't know what you're talking about."

She stood and moved toward me, fists balled up. "I heard that cop or whatever he is talking to you. He mentioned drugs and something about a murder. Is that why you're in here? Did you kill Derek Winter?"

I stood up and moved aside, trying to put distance between us, which wasn't easy in a six-by-eight jail cell. "I don't care what you overheard. I had absolutely nothing to do with Derek's death."

She moved closer and I circled to the side. "Then why are you here?" she asked.

"Why are you here?" I countered. "You seem to know Derek. How are you involved?"

"I . . . just found out Derek died. He was supposed to meet—" She cut herself off, tears gathering in her already reddened eyes as a wave of grief washed over her features. "I thought my husband—never mind, it doesn't matter now."

She was babbling, but I managed to put the pieces together. "You're Yuki Sato, aren't you? You and your husband own that new sushi place that Derek reviewed last summer."

Her eyes widened. "How did you know?"

"Marc—Officer Marcelo—called you 'Mrs. Sato' and I knew that Sushi-ya was owned by a couple named the Satos. Wasn't hard to put two and two together." I stared at her. "I don't understand. From what I know, Derek left terrible reviews about your restaurant. You should hate him, but you seem to really be grieving his death. Almost as if—"

"We were friends," she interrupted. "That's all. The reviews were a misunderstanding."

If my godmothers' notes were correct, that was one heck of a misunderstanding.

"OK, but how did you become friends?" I made sure not to put an emphasis on the word 'friends,' though I wanted to. "He still wrote those reviews. How could he possibly make it up to you?"

She sighed and made her way over to one of the benches. "After those reviews, the health inspector started coming around and came up with a laundry list of infractions, even though my husband and I were sure we were up to code. We had no way to challenge him though, and he's the only health inspector in town. What he says goes, and he wanted us to pay an outrageous fee to keep operating."

"Wait, were these actual health code violations he was busting you on? Because this sounds a lot like extortion."

She shrugged, but more to signal helplessness than nonchalance. "Like I said, I was so sure they had nothing on us. But when the inspector came to visit, he pointed out all these problems that I'd never noticed, like the lights being too dim in certain areas and the bathroom door being open during operating hours. And of course, he came the one day our ventilation system was broken."

Questionable, but still no connection to the case. "And what does this have to do with Derek?"

"I tracked Derek down at the news office and made a big scene, saying it was his fault that jerk was on our backs. He took me aside and said he'd talk to the health inspector since he was a family friend. After they talked, the inspector said he'd cut our fees in half if we hired a particular contractor to fix the problems."

Hmm, that setup smelled fishier than a barrel of patis left out on a summer day. I wonder if Derek was purposely writing bad reviews to sic the health inspector on these restaurants and then taking a cut of the fees the inspector charged them. Depending on how damaging those reviews and fees were, that could be a motive for murder. I'd need to check if he did the same thing to the other restaurants on the list, but I was pretty sure I knew why Derek went easy on the Satos.

Yuki had been so open and vulnerable during her confession, I figured it was time to go for the jugular. Take advantage of her grief and strike while her guard was down. "And how long were you and Derek having an affair?"

SLAP!

Yuki wasn't the only one who'd let her guard down, because I was completely unprepared for the vicious backhand that cracked across my face. Jesus, Mary, and Joseph, that tiny woman could pack a wallop.

I cried out from the force of the strike, bringing Marcus running over to our cell. "Hey! What's going on in there?"

He took in the expression on my face and the mark blooming around the area covered by my hand. "Mrs. Sato, I can't have you attacking prisoners in my care. Looks like you're going to be charged after all."

"Prisoner?!" I exclaimed.

"Oh please, I barely touched her," Yuki said.

We eyed each other.

Marcus sighed. "Yes, Miss Macapagal. Until bail is posted, you're under arrest and in our care. And Mrs. Sato, you haven't been released yet. Guess you're spending the night here as well."

"But, Officer—"

"I won't be pressing charges, Marcus. And if there are no charges against her, she can go, right?" I asked.

Marcus looked back and forth between Yuki and me, trying to figure out what had gone down before he arrived. "You sure, Lila? I mean, Miss Macapagal?"

"Of course. I wouldn't want any bad blood between us restaurateurs. I'm sure we'll run into each other, and I don't want it to be too awkward when we do." I smiled at her. "We have lots to discuss. Right, Yuki?"

She studied my face, like she did when she first arrived. "Of course. I think talking to you again would be . . . most enlightening."

Marcus grunted. "In that case, you're free to go, Mrs. Sato. Nobody's pressing charges, so you and your husband are being let off with a warning. Just keep it down next time, OK?"

Yuki got up and exited the cell. Before walking off with Marcus, she said, "Come by Sushi-ya once you get out, Lila. It'll be on me."

With one last inscrutable look, she was gone. Leaving me blissfully alone again, trying to figure out where this new puzzle piece fit.

Chapter Sixteen

After a sleepless, starving night (I wouldn't eat and barely drank anything they gave me because I refused to use the toilet in that cell), Marcus finally came and released me into Amir's custody.

I barely had time to grab all my possessions and settle my necklace into its rightful place before Amir hustled me over to court for my arraignment. My head was spinning from lack of food and sleep, so I struggled to follow the proceedings, but I guess the gist was that I could be released on bail and wouldn't have to go back to that jail cell, praise be.

He led me out to the courthouse lobby, where Detective Park waited with my aunt.

I managed an awkward hi and a wave before Tita Rosie swept me up in her arms, giving me the first hug I'd received from a Macapagal since I was in elementary school. She was soft and warm and smelled of Pond's Cold Cream, and if she held me any longer, I was going to burst into tears. Luckily, this hug was a bit too much PDA for her and she soon pulled away.

"Oh, anak, are you OK? I tried to get you out immediately, but they said they had to follow all the procedures. Still, Amir and Joseph worked very hard to get you bail."

Joseph was our accountant, Ninang Mae's son, and Marcus's older brother. Our families had had high hopes of us getting together, but both of us could see that was a nightmare waiting to happen. I was the one who introduced him to his wife, so we remained friendly.

Before I could thank Amir for his part in getting me released, Detective Park stepped forward. "I'm sure C.O. Marcelo already told you this, but you're technically not free. You're just being released on bail into the care of your aunt. You still need to appear in court. If you don't make your court date, you forfeit the bail your aunt put up. Do you understand?"

I swallowed, or attempted to, but my throat felt like sandpaper. "Yes, sir. Any idea when I have to go to court?"

"You're lucky. A judge has agreed to see you rather quickly. Your court date is in two months."

OK, that didn't sound so bad. Gave Amir plenty of time to prepare my defense. "What about our restaurant? When can we open?"

He glanced at my aunt. "We finished processing the scene, but you still need to be approved by the health inspector. He's out of town right now and I think he won't be back for a couple of weeks."

Tita Rosie paled. "A couple of weeks? What are we supposed to do until then?"

"I'm sorry, Rosie, but those are the rules. Until you get approval from the inspector or we solve this case, Tita Rosie's Kitchen is closed." Detective Park tried to put his hand on my aunt's shoulder, but she brushed it off. He hesitated, then nodded curtly at us and left.

Amir ushered our group out of the station and into his car. The immensity of the situation pressed down on me, grinding me down into Amir's luxury leather car seats. I was so tired. None of this would've happened if I'd just stayed in Chicago. Sure, that cheating rat of an ex-fiancé, Sam, was there, but so were my friends and my dreams.

I pictured jogging along Lake Michigan or on the 606 above the city with Nisa, dodging cyclists and couples and befriending new dogs. Popping into Jennivee's Bakery for a slice from one of their sky-high cakes. The thrilling push and pull of a city filled with so many different people, from so many different places, who minded their own business and didn't know a thing about my history.

Suddenly I couldn't stand being in Shady Palms for another minute.

"Tita, you said you needed some supplies from Seafood City, right? Want me to drive up to Chicago and get whatever you need?"

Before she could respond, Amir said, "Lila, have you been listening to anything we just told you?"

I sighed, rolling my eyes. "Yes, Amir. I just need some time to think, OK? Besides, I'd be gone for less than a day. What's the big deal?"

Tita Rosie leaned forward, putting her hand on Amir's shoulder. "It's OK. And he's right, anak. Besides, with the restaurant closed, we won't be needing those supplies for a while. Not sure what we're going to do about the restaurant . . ."

I didn't know why it hadn't occurred to me earlier. I guess I was just happy to be out of jail. But if there was one thing I knew, it was that we were dead broke. Like, our savings account was literally empty and their cards were close to maxed out. So how could she possibly have posted bail for me?

I twisted in my seat to look at my aunt. "Tita? How were you able to bail me out? I know what our finances are like. Did you take out a loan? Is that why you talked to Joseph?"

"Don't worry about it, anak. As long as you show up on your court date, they said we get our property back." Tita Rosie got out of the car and rushed into the house before I could respond.

I whipped around to face Amir. "What did she do? Did she put up the restaurant?"

He grimaced, obviously not pleased to be the one to break it to me. "The restaurant was already under threat of closure, so the value wasn't high enough to cover your bail. They wanted your house too."

"Oh my—but she said she gets everything back as long as I don't skip my court date, right?"

"Except for the initial ten percent she put down, yes."

Ten percent may not sound like much, but considering how far behind we were in our payments, even that small amount was enough to induce panic. "So you're saying that we have two months to gather enough evidence to prove I'm not guilty of drug trafficking and murder or I go to jail. Even if you do manage to prove that, we still have to cover that down payment and pay you too."

Amir started to protest, but I shushed him. "We'll argue about that some other time. With the health inspector out of town and the restaurant already in so much trouble, the longer this all drags on, the higher the chance that my family . . ."

He looked away. "Loses everything. I'm sorry, but that's how it is."

I gazed at the house my family had lived in since my grandparents first immigrated to the States in the 80s. This house and our restaurant were more than places to sleep, eat, work. They represented everything my family had sacrificed so that I could have a better life. I owed my aunt and grandmother everything. Guess it was finally time to put my dreams aside to make sure their sacrifices meant something.

Well, at least until I paid them back that ten percent.

Chapter Seventeen

I needed to figure out who killed Derek Winter.

Which meant I should've started investigating immediately, but I figured a night in prison meant I was due for a hot shower and a good meal. The burning, pin-sharp spray from the new showerhead I'd installed as a Christmas present, followed by a huge bowl of the almondigas I'd missed out on from the day before were just what I needed. A tray of mamón, my grandmother's special little chiffon cakes, fresh from the oven, was the cherry on top. Their restorative powers worked wonders on my mood, but one thing was missing to bring me back to 100 percent: a good dose of caffeine.

A trip to Java Jo's and a chance to hash out a possible plan with Adeena was the perfect way to kill two birds with one stone. Or some other less murder-y, more animal-friendly proverb.

Lucky for me, the crowd at Java Jo's was fairly light for late Saturday morning and Adeena was able to join me at my favorite corner table by the window. "Your usual coconut milk latte, but I added a bit of honey and cayenne to it. You look like you could do with a pick-me-up."

I sipped at the sweet, creamy brew, the cayenne hitting me in the back of the throat and giving me life. "You, my friend, are an angel incarnate. This is exactly what I needed."

She grinned. "Maybe you should get arrested more often. You're way nicer than usual. Or maybe it's the shot of honey that's sweetening you up."

I drew myself up straighter, putting on a haughty expression. "Hmph, I was going to share this bag of mamón that Lola Flor left for me, but I guess I'll have to eat them all myself. I mean, I'm pretty hungry from being in jail overnight. It was a very traumatic experience, after all."

OK, so maybe I was laying it on a little thick, but still. I may not have been in a maximum-security prison, but I had just been through one heck of an ordeal. Would it hurt her to fawn over me just a little bit longer?

Not sure if it was the realization of what I went through, or the temptation of her favorite snack, but she plopped down next to me and took my hand. "I'm sorry, honey. You want to talk about it?"

I handed her one of the little chiffon cakes, the top slathered in butter and sugar, and helped myself to one of the cheese-topped mamón. I tore it in half and a faint curl of steam rose up, as well as the smell of sweet butter and the sharp tinge of cheddar.

"Not really, but I don't have much of a choice. Did your brother tell you anything?"

She broke off a bit of cake and dipped it in her chai latte. "Not much. Just that they found something pretty incriminating in the restaurant and that's why you got locked up." She rolled her eyes. "He takes client confidentiality very seriously, so wouldn't tell me much more than that."

I laughed. "Well, I'm glad that my lawyer isn't blabbing the story all over town, but he should know I tell you everything anyway." Well, almost everything.

I sipped at my drink and sighed. "They found drugs in the restaurant, Adeena. A big duffel bag full of filled prescription pill bottles and money and Lord knows what else was in my locker. I have no idea how it got there. You know I don't mess with that stuff."

The color drained from her face, an impressive feat considering she boasted quite a bit more melanin than I did. "Drugs? What kind of drugs?"

"I have no idea. Detective Park didn't specify, and it's not like they let me near enough to read each individual label."

"Do . . . do you have any idea how they got into your locker?"

I frowned. "No clue. They were obviously planted there, but when? They weren't there when I started my shift. I went in there to grab my apron."

"What about after?"

"Not sure." I took a sip of my latte and thought back to that day. "After everything that happened, I just wanted to go home, so I didn't bother putting my apron back. It needed to be washed anyway."

"I see." She took another bite of her mamón, but chewed it without her usual gusto. "Do you think the person who killed Derek was the same one who planted the drugs?"

"It'd have to be. Why else would it be in my locker? What I can't figure out is how they got them in there. We keep everything locked up because of Ronnie."

Ronnie was my screw-up cousin and Tita Rosie's only child. He didn't live in Shady Palms anymore, but when he did, he'd had a habit of rifling through our belongings, stealing and/or selling off our stuff to support his other, equally illegal habit. Which was another reason it was so ridiculous to be accused of being a drug runner.

"Anyway, you know I don't mess with that stuff. Not after Ronnie. I'd never do that to my aunt." I shook my head. "Besides, I got dreams. I'm not stupid enough to waste my time and money on that sh—"

Adeena put her mamón down, not even pretending to eat anymore. "Being stupid has nothing to do with it. Drug abuse is a serious problem, and I don't appreciate you acting like you're too smart to be affected by it."

My mug was already at my lips, but I lowered it without drinking after Adeena's impassioned statement. "What's gotten into you? You know how I feel about drugs. What they've done to my family. Why are you defending those fools?"

Adeena got up. "You know what, I have to get back to work. I'll talk to you later."

She cleared off the table, grabbing both our mugs and placing them on a tray to bring back to the kitchen. I wasn't finished with mine yet, but I wasn't about to argue with her.

"Yeah, sure." I stood up too, slipping on my jacket. She started to walk away, but I placed a hand on her arm. "Adeena, are we OK? I didn't mean to upset you."

She sighed, pushing back a tendril of hair that'd escaped from its clip. "Yeah, we're fine. I'll explain some other time."

Something that Amir said at the station came back to me. "Wait, Amir told me that the county had been cracking down on drug-related offenses lately. Did I miss anything big while I was gone?"

She gave me a strange look. "You haven't been home in almost three years. You missed a lot of things. You're so—" She shook her head. "Never mind. I'm not ready to talk about it right now. Maybe later, OK?"

I nodded, not really sure what there was to talk about. "Um, you want to grab a late lunch? We can't open the restaurant till the health inspector gets back or the case is solved, so I thought we could start tackling that suspect list the aunties gave me."

Adeena smiled. "I'd like that. I get off at two, so swing by then, OK?"

I hadn't realized how tense I was till my shoulders sagged in relief. She really wasn't mad at me. "Sounds good. I think I'll take a nap till then. Something tells me this is going to be another long day."

As if on cue, Kevin popped up with a tray of biscotti. "Oh, Lila, are you leaving? Wanna take some of this biscotti with you? Nobody's touched them and I'd hate to throw them all away."

Adeena widened her eyes and shook her head in warning, but I grabbed a few anyway. I loved checking out other people's biscotti to benchmark my own.

"It's not worth it," Adeena said. "Trust me."

I shrugged. "Even mediocre biscotti is still biscotti. I could use the sugar rush."

I reached out toward the tray in Adeena's hands, dipped the cookie in the last of my latte and took a big bite.

Crunch, crunch.

Barely two bites in, I felt a sharp pain and spit out part of my tooth. Oh heck no. Sure it had been some time since I'd seen a dentist because it was way too expensive on my crappy insurance, but there's no way my teeth were so bad they'd crack on a cookie.

I held out my hand, chunk of tooth on full display. "Are you serious? These biscotti are so bad I chipped a tooth?"

Kevin panicked. "I'm so sorry! I knew they were a little old, but I didn't think they'd be that hard."

I stared at him. "You fed me expired biscotti?"

"Um, there's a good dentist two doors down. Give him my name and tell him to bill me. I'll take care of everything." He put his hands together in a pleading gesture. "Please don't tell my customers about this."

I stood there glaring at him, but Adeena nudged me. Might as well use this to my advantage. "All right, but you have to cover my dental bill in full and give Adeena her own section on the menu. Oh, and I might need her to sneak out a little early for the next couple of weeks without you docking her pay. Deal?"

"Whoa, that's . . . you're kind of asking for a lot."

Adeena balanced the tray in one hand and put her other hand on her hip. "Kevin, that's nothing compared to what my brother would make you pay if he found out about all this. He is Lila's lawyer, after all."

He paled. "You drive a hard bargain, ladies. OK, Lila, you've got a deal. Now you better head over to the dentist if you want it taken care of today. He's usually busy in the afternoon."

D r. Jae's Dental Clinic was fairly new—I didn't remember it being here the last time I was in town. The inside lacked the musty carpet smell most clinics had, and all of the magazines were less than a year old—a sure sign of quality.

I explained what had happened to the receptionist and she nodded grimly. "You're the third one this year."

It wasn't even spring yet. I really needed to sit down with Kevin and talk to him about his baked goods. Adeena was bluffing, but he was a lawsuit just waiting to happen.

The receptionist checked the appointment book and said Dr. Jae would be ready in about twenty minutes. I sat down on a couch that couldn't decide if it wanted to be comfortable or chic and managed to fail at both. I looked through the magazine offerings, finally settling on the November issue of some foodie publication.

I became so engrossed in the glossy photos and autumnal recipes that I didn't hear the receptionist call my name. She had to come around the desk to tap me on the shoulder, curtly informing me that Dr. Jae would see me now.

Muttering an apology, made even more embarrassing by the fact that my chipped front tooth gave a whistly quality to my words, I entered the room she indicated.

A bespectacled Asian Adonis in scrubs awaited me.

He held out his hand. "Lila, right? I'm Dr. Jae. It's a pleasure to meet you, though I doubt you feel the same about the situation."

I tried not to stare as I gave him a respectably firm handshake and closed-lip smile. "Nice to meet you, Doctor. The receptionist said you've already dealt with several pastry catastrophes?"

He laughed, which was what I'd hoped for. Figured if I led with a joke, he'd ignore the gaping hole where my tooth should've been.

"Don't worry, I'll have that lovely smile restored in no time." He smiled and gestured to the chair. "Please have a seat."

Needless to say, it was the best dental experience of my life. Not only did he fix the tooth, he threw in a cleaning for free. The fact that Kevin was covering the expenses made it almost pleasurable.

After he finished, Dr. Jae walked me to the receptionist, who handed me the bill. She explained that it was charged to Kevin, but I needed him to sign the paperwork and bring it back. I thanked her and promised to be back the next day with the completed forms.

"We're closed on Sundays," she informed me. "Just bring it back when you have a chance."

Dr. Jae gave me his card and said to call immediately if there was any pain or discomfort.

"It was great meeting you, Lila." He escorted me to the door, then hesitated. "Are you new in town? I feel like I've seen you around a few times, but only recently."

I hit him with a full-wattage smile, made extra dazzling, thanks to my newly reconstructed front tooth. "I was born here but went away for college. I moved back at the end of last year. My family owns the Filipino restaurant a few doors down."

His face lit up. "You're related to Rosie? Such a wonderful cook, and the kindest, warmest person I've ever met. Showed up my first day with a tray of noodles for my staff and me, welcoming us to the area."

His smile slipped away. "I heard what happened. How are you all holding up?"

Ha, where to start? I watched my ex-boyfriend die in front of me, got accused of his murder and also of being a drug kingpin, was arrested, got slapped by a murder suspect, and my family's livelihood depended on me finding the real killer ASAP. Oh, and I'd almost lost a tooth due to some shoddy biscotti, the final betrayal.

Before I could figure out a way to convey all that without scaring him off, the *bing-bong* sound from the door opening alerted me to Detective Park's presence. He stood frozen in the doorway, eyes darting back and forth between me and Dr. Jae.

"What are you doing here?" he asked.

I put my hands on my hips. "This is a dentist's office, what do you think I'm doing here? Why are you here, anyway? Ready to lob more wild accusations my way?"

"For the last time, Ms. Macapagal, I am just trying to do my j—"

"Hey, quit blocking the door!" Adeena's forceful voice rang out behind Detective Park. He moved into the lobby and Adeena pushed her way into the clinic. "Lila, you've been gone forever. You OK?" She looked the detective up and down, obviously not excited to see him, and then turned toward the dentist. "Jae! How you been?"

She reached up for a high five, which he gamely returned. "Hey, Adeena. You here to meet up with another of Kevin's victims?"

She put an arm around my shoulder, boxing Detective Park out of the conversation. "Yup, Lila's my best friend. We've known each other since high school."

She must've felt the vibes in the room, because she added, "We're hitting up that Mexican restaurant for dinner tonight. Want to join us?"

This was news to me.

Detective Park said, "Sorry, he already has plans."

We all turned to look at him. "What?" he said. "He does. We're supposed to get dinner tonight."

Dr. Jae, however, waved his hand at the detective. "We get dinner together all the time, Hyung. You'll be fine without me for one night." He smiled at us, his entire face beaming with pleasure. Wow, he was adorable. "I'd love to join you for dinner! El Gato Negro, right? Does eight o'clock sound OK to you?"

Adeena grinned, winking at me. "It's a date!"

Chapter Eighteen

After I managed not to die of embarrassment, I dragged Adeena out of the dental clinic and shoved the paperwork at her. "You deal with this. I'd kill you now, but I'm already under investigation for murder. I'm going to go sleep for a few years. See you in time for lunch."

I woke up an hour later even groggier than before my nap, which wasn't ideal, but I couldn't afford to waste any more time. A quick walk with Nisa to shake the cobwebs from my brain, another hot shower to make me feel human again, and then off to grab Adeena for some very late lunchtime reconnaissance.

We decided to hit up Stan's Diner since it was the first on the list. Plus, we figured it was time we finally visited this supposed Shady Palms institution ourselves. See what all the fuss was about.

As I drove across town, Adeena pulled the suspect list out of her bag and looked it over. "OK, according to Auntie June, the owner is Stan Kosta. A bad review from Derek led to a surprise visit from the health inspector, who gave Stan a failing grade and made him hire a contractor to fix the problems so he could open up again. Got hit with a hefty fine as well."

Hmm, just like Yuki Sato's story. I was going to have to pay her a visit soon.

I pulled into the packed lot at Stan's Diner—not the most creative name, though as someone whose family restaurant was called Tita Rosie's Kitchen, I couldn't really judge. At least that failing grade and fine hadn't seemed to hurt his business all that much. Adeena and I exited the car and hurried through the last of the gray winter slush to yank open the door. A blast of hot air seared our faces, the warmth almost oppressive after the briskness of the wind outside.

"Hey, close that door, you're letting all the heat out!" the big burly man working the grill bellowed at us.

We rushed to comply and studied the man in front of us. He looked like a diner cook from the 50s in his old-school paper cook's hat and dirty white apron. The woman working the register, likely his wife, told us there was a twenty-minute wait for a table or we could seat ourselves at the counter.

I wanted to wait since I hate eating at the counter (honestly, who eats sitting next to each other?) but Adeena yanked me to a spot right in front of the grill. I was going to protest, but she nodded toward the cook. If I were to believe the dingy name tag hanging on the grill-man's apron, that put us directly in front of Stan Kosta, the owner of this establishment and first suspect on our list.

We looked over the menu. I appreciated a good greasy spoon, but most didn't pay a lot of attention to their vegetarian offerings. Stan's provided plenty of tasty comfort food, but not a ton of vegetal variety.

I leaned close to Adeena, so as not to offend Stan. "Will you be OK ordering here?"

"I think it'll be alright. They offer an all-day breakfast menu, and the pecan waffles are just what I need right now. How about you?"

I looked over the menu, paralyzed by indecision. Since I'd moved back home, I'd mostly been eating my aunt and grandmother's cooking. Don't get me wrong, I loved it and I'd bet good money my family could cook circles around anyone in town, but once in a while you crave something different. And good ol' greasy American diner food was something I missed from my late-night drunken college jaunts.

"You want a recommendation, go for the meatloaf. With a side of mashed potatoes and gravy, and maybe some green beans if you're one of those girls who needs something green with each meal," Stan said as he slid the bacon double cheeseburger he'd been grilling onto a toasted bun and topped it with a perfectly fried egg. "Order up!"

I smiled at him, figuring this was the perfect opportunity to get on his good side. "Usually the greens aren't a prerequisite, but I'm definitely ordering dessert, so I have to pretend to be at least somewhat virtuous."

He laughed. "I like that. In that case, go for the peach cobbler or apple pie. If you don't like fruit, there's plenty of other options and they're all great. My wife makes all the desserts."

He jerked his thumb toward the woman at the cash register. Ha, I knew she was his wife. Next to her sat a dessert case to rival some of Chicago's best bakeries. If I weren't trying to get my life back on track and prove to my family that I was an adult, I would've just skipped straight to dessert. There was a lemon icebox pie with my name on it sitting in that dimly lit case.

"So should I put in that order for meatloaf or what?" Stan asked.

I hesitated. I never really understood meat loaf—just dense, dry lumps of ground meat and bread topped with . . . ketchup? Even embutido, the Filipino version, never appealed to me.

It wouldn't hurt to butter the guy up though—might make him

more talkative. Plus, I hate when people ask me for recommendations and then don't take them. If you already know what you want, why even ask me?

OK, so technically I hadn't asked Stan, but as the owner, he should know what he's talking about, right?

"Yes sir!" I saw they had Filbert's root beer and ordered one as well. Adeena asked for her waffles and some coffee.

"Comin' right up." Stan got to work prepping our order: mixing the batter and ladling it onto the waffle iron, slicing the meat loaf and hitting it with a nice sear, then plating everything up. Extra gravy on the side for me, with a mini carafe of real maple syrup and cup of whipped butter for Adeena. Oh my gulay . . .

The steam rising up from the platter enveloped my face in an oddly comforting, lightly herb-scented aroma. I took a deep breath, detecting a hint of rosemary and tarragon.

While I was participating in my olfactory delight, Adeena wasted no time in tucking into her plate of tasty breakfast treats. Waffles were her desert island food—as long as you switched up the flavor or toppings once in a while, she could easily eat nothing but waffles for the rest of her life.

My desert island food was just as versatile: crepes. Both savory and sweet, from the classic Filipino lumpiang sariwa to the simplicity of a sprinkle of sugar and squeeze of lemon, I couldn't get enough of them. Maybe I could convince my family to do a Filipino-themed crepe bar on Sundays. Might be a good way to pick up new business.

"You just gonna sit there smelling your food or you gonna eat it?" Stan stood over me, hands on hips, still gripping his spatula.

"I'd think as the chef you'd want people to appreciate and savor your food," I said, finally forking up a chunk of meat loaf.

"As the cook, I just want people to clear their darn plates. How fast or slow they eat the food is none of my business."

"So why are you heckling me if it doesn't matter how long it takes to eat?"

"'Cause you weren't eating. Different story."

"You're a difficult man, Stan."

He shrugged. "Tell me something I don't know. Now go on, eat your food."

I rolled my eyes, but obediently popped the piece of meatloaf into my mouth. My eyes instantly widened and then closed in pleasure as I chewed. "Wow. I was expecting something dense and heavy, even a little dry, but this . . . I didn't know it was possible to make meatloaf that was so tender and fresh-tasting."

He nodded. "It's the herb mélange, plus my secret ingredient. And don't even ask, you're just wasting your time."

That was rather presumptuous, as my mouth was full and I hadn't planned on asking anyway (I hated handling raw meat), so his secret was safe from me. Well, about his ingredients, anyway. But about his involvement with Derek and the health inspector . . .

I turned to Adeena. "Can you believe Derek gave this place a bad review? The food here is amazing!"

She'd been too busy shoveling waffles into her face to get my cue, but she quickly caught on. "What? Oh, right! Yeah, this has got to be the best waffle I've ever had. And I've had a lot of waffles. They're so packed with flavor, you don't even need the butter and syrup."

Stan grunted. "Doesn't hurt though, right?"

"Real maple syrup and proper butter? Too much of a good thing is still a good thing."

He refilled our water glasses, then raised the pitcher in salute. "Cheers to that."

Darn it, he didn't take the bait. I elbowed Adeena to continue.

She cast around for something else to comment on and her eyes fell on her mug. She picked it up and took a sip of coffee. "Hmm, he was right about the coffee, though. Your food is prime, but your coffee-brewing skills could use some work."

He frowned. "Oh, and you're some coffee expert?"

"Well, I'm the barista at Java Jo's, so yes."

"Ah, so you work at that hoity-toity coffee shop across town? No wonder I've never seen you in here before. You girls too good to stop by my place?"

Adeena said, "Dude, chill. We literally just said that your food is fantastic. These waffles don't need your negativity stinking up the joint."

Stan laughed. "Yeah, you're right. And you're right about the coffee, too. I never got into that fancy stuff. It's hot and caffeinated, and that's all you need, in my mind."

He went to rub the back of his head and realized he was still holding the spatula. He put it down, saying, "It's just that hearing that guy's name still makes me so mad. What was his deal?"

"You mean, why the bad reviews?" I asked.

He nodded.

"I don't know. Maybe you had an off day? Got his order wrong? I can't remember what he said in his article, but he never seemed to review restaurants he actually liked, so . . ."

He stiffened. "I have off days like everyone else, but not in the kitchen. That kid called my food 'tired and generic, lacking flavor as well as class.' I can take criticism as well as anyone, but that was just for starters. It's one thing if he doesn't like my food. Everyone has their own tastes, right? But then he started outright lying about what happened here. Said I served him chicken that was still raw in the middle and hinted that he saw something running around in the kitchen, and how those had to be health-code violations. And the one day, *the one day* that my freezer is on the fritz is the day the health inspector decides to pay me a surprise visit. Because of what that liar wrote. Had to pay a huge fine and hire a contractor to fix my freezer ASAP. The inspector wasn't going to let us operate until it was done. Even tried to get me to hire a specific contractor, but I told him it was fine, I knew a guy. It didn't scare away my old customers, but it sure ain't bringing in any new ones."

I said, "Yeah, I know what you mean. When he set his sights on you, it was like he didn't care that he was trashing real people and harming their livelihood. The truth meant nothing to him. He just wanted a reaction out of people. What a sad way to live."

I'd decided to go the commiseration route to see if that'd endear him to me, but the more I spoke, the more the truth of my words hit me. That really was the person that Derek had become. And I didn't mourn that. But I did remember the person he was. The kid who'd cared for his mother through all of her troubles. Who'd had a wicked sense of humor and was always up for a good prank. Who'd been the first person to try all my baking experiments and make me feel like I really did have some talent in the kitchen, despite everything my grandmother said. And that filled me with immense sadness.

Stan leaned his elbows on the counter. "Sounds like you're familiar with his brand of reviews."

I shook off the curtain of gloom that was threatening to descend upon me. "Yeah, my family owns Tita Rosie's Kitchen, which has been his latest target. In fact . . ." I trailed off, not knowing how to finish that sentence. I needed him to open up to me, but I couldn't afford to be too honest.

Unfortunately, the rumor mill, as well as the daily paper, had already made its way to this side of town.

"Wait, why does that sound familiar? Oh sh—" Stan cut himself off and called his wife over. "Hey, Martha! Get on over here."

She bustled over, annoyed at being interrupted mid-conversation with a departing customer. "What do you want, Stan? Can't you see

I'm busy?" She turned around and waved to her customer. "Come back soon, you hear? Bye, sweetie!"

"Stop your gossiping, will you? Now you won't believe who this is—"

"The girl they think killed Derek Winter. Supposedly got arrested for dealing drugs as well." She rolled her eyes at her husband. "Of course I know who she is. What do you think people been talking about since she came in here?"

Martha looked me up and down. "You don't look like no killer. Though I can't say anyone around here would blame you if you were."

"Martha!"

"Oh come off it, Stan. Everyone around here hated that boy and knew he was full of it."

"So Derek was well-known around here?" I asked.

Her lip curled. "He started coming here early last year, almost every day for a month straight. Tried just about every item on the menu and found fault with all of them. Never had a kind word come out of his mouth. No compliments, not even a thanks."

The young waitress came around to refill Adeena's coffee mug. "He was also a terrible tipper. Surprise, surprise."

We hadn't had a chance to talk to her since Stan took our orders, but she was good about working the room and making sure everyone had what they needed. Knowing what I did about food service and how tips were basically what paid your bills, that made me even madder at Derek. He was a poor tipper at our restaurant too, but I thought he just had a grudge against me and my family. The fact that he was like that with everyone told me everything I needed to know about the person he'd become.

"Yeah? He always tipped poorly at my place, but I figured it was 'cause he hated me. Can't believe he was like that with everyone," I said.

Adeena had polished off her waffles and was nursing a cup of coffee she'd doctored with a bunch of cream and sugar to cover the actual taste. "Tells you a lot about what kind of person he is. Or was, I guess I should say. He ordered coffee from the cafe all the time and never left a tip." She shrugged. "Though he always insisted that Kevin be the one who made it for him, so it's not like I was missing out on anything. Still, not cool."

Martha put a hand on her chest, shaking her head. "I really don't know what was wrong with that boy. His mother is so sweet. A little troubled, but sweet. And she worked so hard to raise him all on her own after his dad abandoned them."

The waitress jumped in. "You'd think it would've gotten easier after she married that real estate guy, but I don't know. She seemed quieter. Went out less. And Derek became . . . Derek."

We were all silent for a moment before I asked, "So he was like this with all the restaurants he reviewed?"

The three of them nodded in unison. Stan said, "He chose a local place, frequented it for a month or so, wrote a bunch of vicious reviews about the place, then when he thought he'd caused enough damage, he moved on to the next one."

Martha added, "I guess we were lucky that he was foolish enough to choose us first. We've been here in Shady Palms for over thirty years. He was just starting out and didn't have a following yet. The only reason the health inspector came by was 'cause he's friends with Derek's stepfather."

"Wait, what? The health inspector is friends with Mr. Long?" Hmm, Yuki did say the health inspector was a family friend of Derek's. Mr. Long must've been their connection.

Stan nodded grimly. "Best friends. Which makes me wonder if that's how he knew to visit that day we were having problems. Who else would've tipped him off? Why else would he have hurried over here if we weren't scheduled to be inspected? Real fishy if you ask me.

But it's a small town. He's the only guy we got. Who am I gonna report him to, you know? And like I said, not like we lost a ton of business or nothing. So we let it go. The Torres family though, that was ugly."

I perked up and tried not to look at Adeena, but I knew we were both thinking that was the next name on the list, the owner of El Gato Negro.

"The Torres family? Who are they?" I asked, all wide-eyed innocence.

Stan and Martha exchanged glances. "They used to own a Mexican restaurant on the other side of town. But now it's, uh . . . under new ownership, I guess you could say."

"Let me guess: that was Derek's work?"

"Bingo."

"What's their story?"

"They were new to town. You know how it is. People didn't know them, so when they opened their restaurant, business wasn't exactly booming. But it wasn't bad. Till Derek started writing his reviews. That's when the whispers started."

"What were people saying?"

Martha fidgeted a bit. "You know, the usual. Food poisoning and unhygienic practices. Things like that."

I could tell there was more to the story. "And?"

Stan shook his head. "Like I said, it got ugly. There were claims that the owners had, uh, what's the right . . . undocumented? Yeah, undocumented immigrants working for them. Don't know if that's true or not, but they started getting threats soon after."

Now it was time for me and Adeena to exchange glances. "Someone started a rumor that they had undocumented workers and that's all it took to shut them down?"

Martha twisted a napkin between her fingers, not meeting our eyes. "The threats eventually escalated to vandalism. Someone shot out all their windows."

I gasped and Adeena looked sick.

Stan shook his head in disgust. "I know. Luckily no one was hurt. They got kids, too. Young kids. Didn't want them exposed to the hate that was spreading, so they packed up and left."

"Last I heard, they moved in with the woman's parents back in the city and are staying with them until they find work and a new place," Martha added, shaking her head. "Such a shame. We chatted with them at church a few times. They were a real nice family."

"How long were they in Shady Palms?" I asked.

"All said and done, maybe less than a year?" Martha hazarded, looking at Stan, who nodded agreement.

Yikes. To uproot your life, move to a small town to raise a family and start your own business, only to be run out by a pitchfork-wielding mob . . . they would've been my number-one suspects, but how could they kill Derek if they weren't even here anymore? Unless . . .

"The people who took over the restaurant. Were they friends with the Torres family?"

"I think they're related, actually. That's what I heard, anyway. They look nothing alike, so not sure how true that is," Martha said.

So maybe they had something to do with it after all. If the new owner was close to the family that had been driven out of town, it was possible they felt the need to retaliate. Seemed more likely than Stan and Martha, anyway. As they'd said, it had a slight impact on their reputation but not their business. The neighborhood locals clearly loved the place and the food was excellent. Speaking of which . . .

"I do believe it's dessert time. Martha, can I get a slice of your lemon icebox cake?"

Stan frowned. "You haven't finished your meal yet."

"Oh, and a box for my leftovers. After all this good food, I'm gonna need to go for a run later. Knowing I have this meatloaf waiting for me will provide a heck of a push."

He chuckled and handed over a Styrofoam box while Martha went to get our desserts. I've never known anyone with the capacity for sugar that Adeena has. She'd demolished her waffles, which she'd drowned in syrup, and then ordered a slice of triple chocolate tuxedo pie, another sugar bomb. If I ate the way she did, I'd have lost a foot to diabetes by now.

Martha slid our desserts in front of us, and Adeena and I hummed in appreciation after taking our first bites. The lemon icebox cake was cold and creamy, with a background sweetness and a whole lot of tang. As I often did when sampling delicious desserts, I tried to deconstruct what was in it.

Graham crackers, cream cheese, whipped cream, and a ton of lemon curd seemed to be the basis of the recipe. Similar to the ginger calamansi pie I'd made, but simpler and no-bake, if I decided to buy the graham crackers instead of making my own. Definitely worth experimenting with, as I had a jar of calamansi curd tucked away in the fridge just begging to be used. I made a note on my phone to try this later, maybe as a summer offering.

As per usual when eating out, Adeena and I swapped plates so we could taste each other's desserts.

"What do you think, girls?"

I grinned at Martha. "Delicious. I love how the lemon cake is sweet and tangy, but you don't go too far in either direction."

Adeena added, "It's the perfect counterpoint to my chocolate pie, which is divine, by the way. Rich, creamy, and so satisfying."

Martha beamed and left to go ring up a customer.

Stan nodded his satisfaction. "I like you girls. Feel free to come by anytime for some good food and gossip."

I glanced at Adeena. "What do you mean?"

He raised an eyebrow. "You telling me you didn't come here fishing for information about that Winter boy? You girls, who've lived here your whole lives and never once came to this part of town. You just happen to come to the diner the Winter boy wrote about, the Winter boy who happened to die earlier this week in your restaurant? That what you want me to believe?"

I rubbed the back of my neck. "Uh . . . yes?"

He shook his head. "Miss, I'm simple. I'm not stupid."

I started to apologize, but he held up his hand. "It's fine. I know why you're here. Word is both you and your aunt are in trouble. You're just looking out for your family, yeah?"

I bit my lip. "Yeah. We had nothing to do with his death. Tita Rosie's a good person and these rumors are destroying her. She's already worried they're going to take away our restaurant, now she's stressed that I'm going to be taken away, too. It's too much, you know? It's just too much . . ."

I choked up and couldn't finish the sentence. Adeena put her arm around me and pulled me close. "We're not gonna let that happen. You hear me? We're gonna figure this out."

Stan nodded. "I've met your aunt a few times, you know. Doing volunteer work at the church." He paused. "I'll keep my ears open. People 'round here like to talk. If I find out anything good, I'll let you know."

I didn't know what to say. "I . . . thanks, I . . ."

He held up his hand. "Miss Rosie is good people. I can tell you're cut from the same cloth. If you say your family didn't do it, I believe you."

Tears sprang to my eyes and I barely managed to choke out a "thank you" before running out to my car. I sat in the driver's seat, tears rolling down my face, embarrassed by my overly emotional reaction. I guess it was just so reassuring that this complete stranger believed in us. Believed in me. Nice to be reminded of all the kindness there still was in the world.

A whoosh of cold air announced Adeena's arrival as she opened the passenger door and slid in. She dropped my bag of leftovers in the backseat.

"You forgot that."

"Oh, thanks."

"And to pay your half of the check."

I winced. "Sorry. I'll get you next time."

"Oh don't worry, you're paying for dinner. You also ran out before leaving your contact information, so I gave him both our numbers. You need to get better at this detective stuff, or we'll never have any informants."

I let out a shaky breath. "Thanks, Adeena. What would I do without you?"

"I really don't know," she said without a trace of sarcasm. "Here's hoping you never have to find out."

Chapter Nineteen

When I got home, Marcus was in the living room with all the aunties, enjoying a meryenda of coffee, cheese, and the last of the mamón. I brewed a pot of tea and set out the ube crinkles I'd been experimenting with.

"I didn't expect to see you so soon, Marcus. Or is it C.O. Marcelo?" I grinned and held out the tin. "Try some of these cookies. I remember you having a particular fondness for ube."

"You remember right." Marcus popped a whole cookie in his mouth before stacking several more on his plate. "Whoa, these are so good. Thanks, Lila."

Ninang Mae smacked him upside his head. "What do you mean, 'Lila'? That's your ate, show some respect!"

I flushed. "Ninang Mae, it's fine. I don't really care about that stuff."

Tita Rosie smiled at me. "She's right, Mae. As long as they respect their elders, what's the harm in not using the titles among themselves?

I mean, Lila and Marcus aren't that far apart in age. Marcus, how old are you now?"

He swallowed a mouthful of cookie. "I'm twenty-one, Tita."

Ninang Mae huffed. "No member of my family will be so disrespectful, especially not in front of all my friends. Now, Marcus, tell us everything you know."

Poor Marcus. He probably wasn't supposed to tell us anything, but he seemed to not care about the bounds of professional privacy as much as Bernadette and Amir did. Or at least, he wasn't as scared of losing his job as he was of angering the aunties.

He picked up another cookie. "Well, I'm sorry to say it's not looking too good. Along with the arsenic in Derek's dessert dishes, they seem to have found narcotics in his system, similar to the ones found in Li—I mean, Ate Lila's locker."

I wrinkled my brow. "Wait, so he was drugged first? Maybe someone forced him to eat the poison?"

He shrugged, not so much in nonchalance as discomfort, his words coming out more like questions than statements. "Uh, well, it seems more likely that he purposely took the pain medication? You know, for uh, recreational use?"

"So maybe an overdose?"

Ninang June shook her head. "I doubt it. The EMTs would've recognized the symptoms of opioid overdose and used Narcan or something similar. Unfortunately, this kind of thing is becoming more common. Not in Shady Palms necessarily, but throughout the county."

I sighed and nibbled on an ube crinkle, so lost in thought I couldn't even enjoy how the light coating of powdered sugar gave just enough sweetness to the subtle, almost vanilla-like flavor of the purple yam. It all turned to sand in my mouth.

I put the half-eaten cookie down. "So what does this mean for me?"

Marcus rubbed the back of his head, the rasp of the short-shorn bristles grating on my already fragile nerves. "You need to prove that those drugs didn't belong to you. It's their main piece of evidence. Or that the arsenic got into Derek's food through some other means. If you can't prove those things, then I don't know."

Ninang Mae frowned. "Amir's good, but Detective Park is relentless. He doesn't care that Rosie is a friend. If he thinks he's right . . ."

Those ominous words hung in the air for a moment before Ninang June spoke up. "So, Lila, have you checked out anyone on the list yet?"

I glanced at Marcus and Tita Rosie, who didn't seem surprised. Guess that was to be expected—not like my godmothers to keep a secret for long.

"I've met two so far. Adeena and I went to Stan's Diner today to meet Stan Kosta and his wife. I don't think it's them. They had reason to be angry, but it hasn't hurt their business at all, so it'd be foolish for them to risk a murder. Plus, how would they even get the poison in our food?"

"You're all forgetting something," Ninang April said. "Yes, the fact that arsenic was in the dishes is very strange, but how quickly does it kill? Did anyone bother looking it up?"

Ninang June leaned back in her chair and tapped her chin. "Arsenic tends to be more slow-acting, taking anywhere from two hours to maybe four days, depending on the dosage. He vomited, which is definitely a sign of arsenic poisoning, but it's also a sign of most other poisons. And it was less than an hour from when he started his meal till he passed."

We waited for her to say more, but she had her thinking face on and wouldn't talk to us until she was good and ready. Ninang April picked up the thread of the conversation again.

"June, if I understand you correctly, that means while Derek may have had arsenic in his system, it was a low enough dosage that symptoms shouldn't have appeared yet. Which points to something else as the cause of death."

Ninang June nodded. "It doesn't make sense, but that's what I think. Also, the arsenic was only in Derek's dessert dishes? Nothing on any of the other plates?"

Marcus shook his head. "When Detective Park was out, I took a look at the report. The dishes were all mixed together from other tables, but arsenic was only found on two dishes, and one of them was the almost-full bowl of whatever Derek was eating when he passed out. The other still had banana leaf and bits of sticky rice on it, which we assumed was his other plate."

I nodded. "He ate suman, so chances are good the other plate was his. But it doesn't make sense. They seemed to think arsenic was in our rice, so it should've been in all the dishes, not just the dessert ones."

As I said that, another thing occurred to me. "Wait, that definitely doesn't make sense. The tainted bag held jasmine rice, but we don't use that for the desserts. We use glutinous rice. We're being set up!"

Ninang April nodded her approval at me. "That's a huge discrepancy. So what do you think happened?"

I tried to think outside the box. "Someone added arsenic to the dishes and bag of rice after Derek had already eaten. Is it possible for there to be another kind of poison in his system that didn't show up on the lab report?"

Marcus shrugged. "Dunno. My job is just supervising the people that get arrested. I don't have anything to do with like, on-the-street stuff. This is all stuff I heard 'cause people in that building love to talk."

Ninang June cut in. "From what I know, labs test for the most common toxins in a case like this. If there was something else in his system, then it was a substance they hadn't tested for."

"But why wouldn't they test for everything? This is a murder!" Ninang Mae exclaimed.

Ninang June shrugged. "We share the facilities with the entire county and there's limited resources. Plus they found drugs and arsenic in the initial screening, so why waste taxpayer time and money?"

"But do you think there's enough evidence to convince the lab to test for anything else?" I was desperate for anything to turn the case in my favor.

Ninang June nodded. "I think so. If Detective Park won't run it, I could pull some strings, but it's best not to go behind his back."

Marcus pulled out his phone. "You're right. Should I tell him what we talked about?"

I shook my head. "You're not supposed to be involved in this, remember? I don't want you getting in trouble. I'll tell Amir and he can pass it on. I don't think the detective will take it very seriously if I tell him."

I left to go make the call, then went to go check on Tita Rosie after I'd finished. She'd disappeared into the kitchen pretty early on and hadn't come back. "Tita? Are you OK?"

She was at the kitchen counter kneading dough. "Of course, anak. I just needed to get started on the ensaymada for church tomorrow. You know it takes a long time to let the dough rise, and then we have to rest it overnight."

The brioche-like bread covered with butter, sugar, and occasionally cheese was my favorite treat and one of the few things I looked forward to every Sunday. "Wait, I thought that was Lola Flor's job? Where is she anyway? I haven't seen her all day."

My aunt blew a puff of air up at her bangs. "You know how your lola is. Not like she tells me anything. Anyway, I have a lot to do right now, anak, so go keep mga ninang company."

I nodded and went back out to the living room at the same time Amir called me back with an update.

"Hey, what did the detective say?"

He laughed. "Told me to mind my own business and stick to defending criminals. However, he's a fair man. He really does care about doing the right thing, so he's going to ask the medical examiner to run tests for basically any poisonous substance in the database. It's going to take time, though."

"I'll take what I can get. Thanks, Amir."

We hung up and I grabbed the cookie I'd abandoned earlier. This time I savored it. I had a chance now. The medical examiner would prove that someone else killed Derek and this was one big frame job.

Ninang June coughed. "Lila, didn't you say you talked to two suspects on the list? You told us about Stan and his wife, who was the other one?"

"Yuki Sato. We actually shared a jail cell for a while last night. Marcus, anything you can tell us about why Mrs. Sato was brought in?"

He started to laugh again but cut himself off. "Sorry, that was messed up. It's just hard to picture that tiny woman getting into such a loud screaming match with her husband."

I held my hand up to my cheek, which was covered with an extra layer of concealer and powder to hide the souvenir from my run-in with Yuki. "Don't let her size fool you. That woman has a temper and packs a wallop. Felt like that time Ate Bernie 'accidentally' hit me in the face with a tennis racket."

"Oh, is that why you quit playing? She told me you were banned from the junior league for chucking your racket at a ref."

"He made a bad call! The ball was clearly in bounds, and I should've won—OK, you know what, not important." I took a sip of tea to calm myself down.

Ninang June tried to hide a smirk as she said, "Let's get back on track. So Mrs. Sato was brought in for a domestic dispute? Did her husband call the police?"

Marcus was working on what must've been his tenth cookie. He wiped some crumbs from his mouth before saying, "No, a neighbor called it in. Disturbing the peace, since they were having this fight on the sidewalk outside their restaurant. The neighbor tried to ignore it, but eventually they got tired of the Satos scaring away customers."

"Do you know what the cause of the fight was?"

"They were speaking in Japanese when they got to the station, but I managed to pick up the gist of the conversation," Marcus said. "She accused him of hurting someone, and he said it was her fault. Or something like that."

I raised an eyebrow, impressed. "Since when do you know Japanese?"

He ducked his head, not meeting my eyes. "I, uh, watch a lot of anime. Like, a lot. I can't speak it or anything, but I can understand a basic conversation."

Ninang Mae smacked him again. "Oh, so you can learn a new language from watching your stupid cartoons, but you can barely speak Tagalog? Your own language? Gago."

I ignored Ninang Mae's rant as I put two and two together. "Oh my gulay, did they get into a fight because she accused her husband of killing Derek? She didn't come out and say it while we were talking, but those two were definitely having an affair."

"Oh, that's what I wanted to tell you! Derek came into the station awhile ago to charge Mr. Sato with assault, but he never filed the paperwork. Said he changed his mind and that it was just a disagreement between men."

"Well then, I know where I need to go tomorrow. Yuki told me to stop by her restaurant sometime and I think I'm going to take her up on that. In the meantime, I'm getting dinner at that Mexican restaurant. What was it called again?"

"El Gato Negro!" Marcus said. "I love that place. And the waitress is really cute. Can I join you?"

"Well . . ."

I tried to ignore the laser-eyes Ninang Mae was shooting me, but it was tough. She'd been trying to set me up with her bevy of sons and nephews my entire adult life, and I just knew she was going to start pushing Marcus on me as well. He'd filled out nicely, was rather cute, and a sweet kid, but too young for me. Though if he knew the waitress, maybe that'd provide an in at the restaurant.

To clinch it, he added, "Actually, I should introduce you to the waitress. Her family pressed charges against Derek, so she might have some information for you."

"That would be great! Adeena will be there, too, but the more eyes and ears we have at the restaurant, the better."

I purposely didn't bring up that Dr. Jae would also be there since I didn't need the aunties grilling me about him and his potential dateability. Romance was the last thing on my mind, but the aunties' need to matchmake and meddle overthrew any of my particular wants or needs.

Marcus looked excited at the thought of a night out. "Great! Want me to pick you and Adeena up so we can ride together?"

"No, thanks, I need to run a quick errand later and can pick up Adeena on the way. How about we meet at the restaurant at eight o'clock?"

Marcus grinned. "Awesome! See you there."

Ninang Mae, who only ever heard what she wanted to hear, clapped her hands and literally squealed. "You're going on a date! I can't wait to hear all about it!"

Dear Lord, why did this keep happening?

Chapter Twenty

I repeated, "This isn't a date, this isn't a date, this isn't a date," over and over to myself like a mantra as I cleaned up the house. I took Nisa out for a quick jog and chanted it as we ran, matching the rhythm of each footfall. I even said it as I took my third shower of the day, singing it out like a show tune.

But as I blow-dried my hair, applied makeup, and stood in front of my closet to figure out what to wear, I couldn't bring myself to say it.

I knew this wasn't a date, though imagining a romantic night out with my dentist and Ninang Mae's son while Adeena chaperoned was both hilarious and horrifying.

Problem was, it was stirring up memories of the last time I actually had been on a date. It was with Derek, shortly after I'd broken up with my ex-fiancé and moved back to Shady Palms. We'd run into each other one day while I was brooding on the riverwalk, and I'd thought it was a sign.

I'd been leaning against the railing, looking out over the frozen river, two weeks after I'd walked in on Sam and known that my life in Chicago was over. It was the first time I'd been out since returning home, the first week of January being particularly frigid here, but I needed to get out. After years of being away from my family, I couldn't deal with the constant supervision and questions about where I was going and with who and what time I'd be back. So I'd slipped out without saying anything and went to my favorite place.

"Lila? Is that . . . is that you?"

A chill ran through me when I heard that voice, a chill that had absolutely nothing to do with the weather. How his voice could still have that effect on me, after all this time and after the way we'd ended things . . .

"Hello, Derek," I'd said, turning around. My first love stood there grinning at me, looking just as gorgeous as he had a decade ago.

"Wow. You're even more beautiful than I remembered." With a hesitance that I'd never seen in him, he asked, "Would you like to get something to eat? I'd love to catch up."

And that's how it all began. At first, I'd thought it was strange that we never dined in Shady Palms, instead driving out to nearby towns where we didn't know anyone. He'd claimed he wanted to avoid all the local gossips, which I'd appreciated.

Of course, this was before I knew anything. Before I knew who he'd become. Back when I thought we could pick up where we left off, when I thought the surest cure to my heartbreak was a new love. I mean, that's how it worked in just about every rom-com ever, and why would they steer me wrong? But then my aunt and grandmother found out about us. As Lola Flor screamed at me, Tita Rosie explained what he'd been doing to them. To us. Derek's betrayal, coming so soon after Sam's . . .

I shook my head, as if I could physically shake these dismal thoughts away. No need to dwell on that. No one knew I'd been seeing him when

I got back, not even Adeena. And no one needed to know. It was just a couple of dates, it hadn't meant anything.

Nothing at all.

I pulled on warm leggings and an off-the-shoulder black sweater, which managed to be sexy and cozy at the same time. Casual but cute, especially if paired with dangly earrings, booties, and a nice scarf.

"How do I look, Nisa?" I modeled my outfit to my tiny sausage dog. She tilted her head as if seriously considering it, and barked.

"You're right, how could I forget?"

I went over to my jewelry box to put on the necklace my parents left me. It was a simple disk of green jade on a golden chain, and the one physical reminder of them I was able to carry into adulthood. I wore it everywhere, even to bed, taking it off only to shower or swim.

I rubbed the smooth, cool surface of the pendant, remembering my first year of high school when I worried the chain was getting too small for me to wear. My grandmother had wanted to just replace the chain, but I wouldn't hear of it. My aunt came up with the idea of extending it by adding one of her gold bracelets to the back.

"That way," she said, settling the necklace over my head, "you still have the original, but you have a piece of me with you as well. To remind you we're always with you."

She smiled, but even at that age I could see the sadness in her eyes. I wasn't the only one who missed them.

My phone rang, pulling me out of my memories. I didn't recognize the number and went to reject the call, then remembered Stan had promised to call if he had any info.

"Hello?"

"Lila, we need to talk," a somewhat recognizable female voice said. The voice managed to be both hesitant and harsh at the same time— whoever it was clearly did not want to be having this conversation.

"May I ask who's speaking, please?"

"Oh God, are you seriously that polite, Miss Perfect? It's Janet."

The night in prison had put her out of my mind, but that argument in the hospital came back in full force. "Oh. Hey. What can I do for you?"

"More like what I can do for you." She paused, likely wanting me to beg her for more information. When I didn't, she said, "Look, I could get in a lot of trouble for this, but I didn't like the way our last conversation ended. I talked to Terrence about it and he wants me to try again. Will you let me do this for him?"

Stunned, I said, "I'm sorry too, Janet." I glanced at the clock, noting I was going to be late picking up Adeena. "Look, I have to be somewhere soon, but do you want to meet for lunch tomorrow? Sushi-ya is close to the hospital, right?"

"Oh that's fine, I mean I'm only sticking out my neck for you. Why not put it off another day?" She sighed in frustration. "Whatever. See you at one thirty tomorrow. Don't be late."

I agreed, but before I could say goodbye, she managed to get a final shot in. "Oh, and since I'm doing you such a big favor, lunch is on you tomorrow."

And then she hung up on me.

Hmm, guess I couldn't expect her to change that much.

I spritzed on my perfume, a special blend of citrus and ginger I created myself, and bundled up before heading out. I made it to Adeena's fifteen minutes late, which in Brown People Time (BPT) meant I was actually a little early.

I texted her to let her know I was there, then spent a few minutes going over the list Adeena had returned to me, adding notes and questions. I'd just crossed out Stan and Martha's names when the passenger door opened and Adeena slid inside, calling out to her family, "I'm going out with Lila, be back later!"

I waved at her parents and aunties who'd gathered at the door, watching us disapprovingly. "What's with the looks?" I asked as we drove off.

She rolled her eyes. "They heard you got arrested and think you're a bad influence on me."

I raised an eyebrow. "Did you tell them that you're the bad influence in this relationship?"

"Oh, that's another thing. One of my aunties got it into her head that we're dating since we spend so much time together."

I glanced over at her. "What's wrong with best friends spending time together? Plus, I haven't been home in forever. Did you stress that we were ju—that we were friends?"

I almost said "just friends," as if romantic partnership was superior to platonic friendship, but stopped myself. Adeena hated that term and idea. And I'd learned, time and again, she was right. There was no hierarchy to love.

Adeena rolled her eyes. "And that just because I like girls doesn't mean I like every girl in existence since that's not how sexuality works? Of course I did. You think it did any good?"

I snorted. Nothing else needed to be said. We both knew how our families were when it came to stuff like that. Still, this was the perfect opportunity to get her back for her earlier teasing.

"You should've told them that Dr. Jae was going to be at dinner, too. Their daughter on a date with a dentist? They'd love that."

Her eyes flashed. "Don't you dare mention it to them! I can just see them latching on to him, showing up at his job with samosas and welcoming him to the family." She shuddered.

We got to El Gato Negro around 8:15 or so. When we went inside, Dr. Jae was already sitting at a table, nervously downing a basket of tortilla chips and salsa all by himself. As we watched, he stopped a server to ask for a refill on chips.

"Hey Doc, you been here long?" Adeena plopped into the seat

across from him, setting her bag and coat next to her. "Sorry Lila, you know I take up a lot of space. We can use this as the bag and coat seat if you want to pass your stuff over."

This was a setup! I knew it.

I glared at her, saying, "Marcus is joining us for dinner, too, so you should hang your things on the back of your chair."

"Who's Marcus?" Dr. Jae asked as I slid into the seat next to Adeena.

"A family friend who's helping us with the c—with some stuff." Probably shouldn't go blabbing to everyone about our investigation.

Our waitress came by to introduce herself as Elena and ask for our drink orders. "Oh, are you waiting for someone else? Would you like to wait?"

"Nah, who knows when he'll show up. We can get started without him." I was driving, so I stuck with horchata, and Dr. Jae echoed my order. Adeena got one of their giant fishbowl margaritas.

We all helped ourselves to the chips and variety of salsas. Adeena preferred the fiery red chile sauce, while I loved the tangy green tomatillo. Dr. Jae, that coward, stuck with the mild tomato salsa.

Adeena was incredulous. "Aren't you Korean? How can you not like spicy food?"

He shrugged. "My dad's White. And I know what you're thinking, but Park is apparently an English surname, too. My mom's maiden name was Kim."

"So because of your dad, you don't like spicy food?" I asked.

"He can't handle it, so my mom never made it for us. The only spicy thing I eat is kimchi, and even that has to be served with bowls and bowls of rice. I love all the other stuff though, especially the seafood dishes. Unfortunately—"

"The majority of those dishes are cooked with red pepper paste and spicy as heck. I get it. Most Filipino food isn't spicy, or at least not where my family's from, so when I met Adeena, I couldn't handle it. But her family's food was so delicious, I slowly built up my spice tolerance every time I ate at her house. Give it time."

He laughed. "I'm almost thirty. How much time do I need? I've made peace with it. Jonathan's the chile fiend. He takes after our mother in that respect. Got our dad's personality though."

"Jonathan? Oh, you have a brother? Older or younger?" I asked.

Now it was Adeena's turn to laugh. "Are you serious? You don't know who his brother is?"

"Should I?"

"It's Detective Park," she said, watching my expression carefully.

I choked on my water, almost spewing it all over Dr. Jae, but managed to only dribble it down my front. Just the picture of class and grace. No wonder I never won those beauty pageants my mom made me enter. Well, except for that one time, and that was on a technicality.

Dr. Jae handed me some napkins, worry creasing his forehead. "Are you OK? I hope this isn't a problem. I know there's some, uh, stuff going on between you two."

"You mean because he thinks I'm a drug-dealing murderer? Yeah, no big." I tried to play it off. "I guess I just didn't make the connection since you two are so different. I mean, you seem so easygoing and friendly, and he's . . ."

"Intense?" he provided, likely sensing my struggle to not insult his brother.

I smiled. "That's one way to put it. Seriously though, you're two different people. What your brother thinks isn't a reflection on you. Unless you agree with him?"

He flushed. "Of course not! Do you think I'd accept a dinner invitation from someone I thought was a killer?"

"I don't know, maybe you're undercover as an unassuming dentist so that I lower my guard and give you precious information," I teased.

He scoffed. "Who would willingly do something like that? That's so dangerous."

Adeena swirled the water in her glass. "Yeah, Lila, who would do something super dangerous like spy on murder suspects to try and solve a case? Utterly ridiculous . . ."

I coughed. "So, have either of you eaten here before? What's good?"

Elena, our waitress, arrived with our drinks at that moment. "Everything's good, but our specialty is our duck mole. It takes two days to make and has over twenty ingredients in it, lending it a very special, savory flavor."

My mouth started to water the minute she said the word "duck," which was one of my favorite meats. "Oh my goodness, yes. Give me that, please."

She chuckled and added, "If you prefer seafood, our special of the day is pescado a la veracruzana. It's a much lighter dish, with fish smothered in tomatoes, olives, and capers."

Dr. Jae said, "Sounds perfect for me! I'll have that, please."

Adeena perused the menu. "I'll take the chile rellenos, with a side of corn tortillas and refried beans. Wait, are the beans cooked in lard?"

Elena nodded. "Yes, but we also make a vegetarian version and I swear it's even better than the original. I'd recommend the nopales, as well."

Adeena grinned. "Sold!"

I watched Adeena eye the waitress as she walked away, and I couldn't blame her. Elena was totally her type: black cat-eye glasses, dark lipstick, and a multitude of piercings. Pretty sure I saw a tattoo snaking out from the tight, long-sleeved black tee she was wearing as well. Which reminded me of Marcus. Wonder if she was the one he was talking about earlier. Where was he anyway?

I texted him: You still coming?

I put my phone back down on the table, where it buzzed almost immediately.

Sorry can't. Explain later. Tell the cute waitress I said hi!

I rolled my eyes. "Marcus can't make it. Told me to say hi to the cute waitress. Wonder if it's the same one Adeena's obviously—"

Adeena cut me off with a sharp elbow to the ribs. As I clutched my side, she said, "So, Jae, tell us about yourself! You've been in Shady Palms for what, a year?"

He dabbed his mouth with his napkin before answering. "Closer to three, actually. Came here shortly after I graduated from dental school to set up my own clinic."

I helped myself to another chip. "I had no idea you'd been here so long. You must've gotten here not long after I left for university."

His hand paused halfway to his mouth, the chip dripping salsa onto the tabletop. "Wait, are you still in school? How old are you?"

I smiled. "I'm twenty-five. I was working on a bachelor's in hotel and restaurant management since my aunt and grandmother don't have any business training. Took some time off near the end of the program to get proper restaurant experience, so I haven't finished my degree yet."

He sighed in relief. "That makes sense. For a minute, I worried I seemed like an old man to you two."

Adeena laughed. "Even if we were fresh out of college, that would make us what, twenty-two? Maybe twenty-three years old? I mean, fairly young in the grand scheme of things, but not exactly children."

I laughed, too. "Not that our families would ever acknowledge that, of course."

Dr. Jae nodded, commiserating. "I'm turning thirty soon, and my mom still insists on packing a lunchbox for me every day. I finally got my own apartment last year and you'd think I'd said I didn't love her anymore from the way she was carrying on."

"Let me guess, the fact that you moved out but aren't married yet absolutely baffles her?" I asked.

He nodded. "She's pretty old-school, but my dad stepped in before it became an issue. As a compromise, I moved to a building that's only five minutes away. I let them think I was making a big sacrifice, but I do like being closer to them in case of emergency. I just don't need to, you know, actually live in the same place."

"So, you said you're turning thirty soon. How soon?" I asked.

His ears turned red and he cleared his throat. "End of the month, actually."

Adeena and I glanced at each other and grinned. We both had the same idea.

"Let me guess," she said. "You plan on having a low-key celebration, maybe dinner with your family where your mom makes your favorite dish, but otherwise no fuss. Am I right?"

He choked on his horchata. "How did you know? That's exactly what I have planned."

"Not even a night out with friends?" I asked. "Have a few drinks, reminisce on where your twenties have gone?"

"I don't really have any friends out here. And I don't have time to drive out to the city on a weekday to meet up with my old ones."

I was just teasing him, but now I felt bad. "I'm sorry, Dr. Jae. I didn't mean . . ."

He waved me off. "First of all, call me Jae. 'Dr. Jae' outside the office is weird. It's not like I'm a pro basketball player."

At our blank looks, he added, "Julius Erving? From the 76ers? He was a legend!"

Adeena and I looked at each other and shrugged. I said, "I know the 76ers are a basketball team, but that's it. This is Filipino heresy, but I think basketball is so boring."

Jae's jaw dropped. "How could you say that? The Chicago Bulls—"

Elena appeared at that moment, bearing a giant tray laden with our meals. "Haven't won a championship since I was three years old. Anyway, here's the special for Dr. Basketball Fanatic."

Jae chuckled. "Yup, that's me."

She winked at him as she put down his plate. "Sorry, couldn't resist. The duck mole for the lady with the fantastic hair . . ."

I smiled at her. "The secret is coconut oil. And, spoiler alert, you're getting a great tip."

"That's what I like to hear! Since you use hair oil, remind me to tell you about the special beauty oils my mom and I make." She set down my platter and reached for Adeena's. "And for my lovely fellow vegetarian, I believe you ordered the chile rellenos, with a side of tortillas, refried beans, and nopales?"

Adeena clapped her hands in excitement. "If it's all as good as you made it out to be, we might have to bump that great tip up to 'excellent.'"

"And I think I've found my new favorite customers. Anything else I can get you right now?" We shook our heads. "Alright then, enjoy your meal! Buen provecho!"

We all dug in, and for the second time today, Adeena and I made completely inappropriate noises to display our satisfaction.

Jae raised an eyebrow. "I've never met people so enthusiastic about their food before."

I blushed, but Adeena was unfazed. "We're both in the food business, Doc. It'd be sad if we didn't have this kind of passion, don't you think?"

"Hmm, my receptionist does make fun of me for getting excited every time a shipment of the latest dental equipment arrives. I guess nerding out over our professions is a given, huh?"

"Speaking of which, was dentistry your choice or your parents'?" Typical Adeena bluntness.

He seemed to know where she was going with this. "Mostly mine. Jonathan was the cool, smart guy. Aced all his classes, track star, probably would've played football if my mom had let him. He got the dangerous job protecting people, which made my parents anxious but proud. I was the bookworm. I really loved studying and discovered that I liked helping people, but I wasn't cutthroat enough for academia and didn't want the high stakes of being a medical doctor. I did do my GPR at a hospital, which was fascinating but reaffirmed my decision. Dentistry was the perfect choice for me."

I snagged one of Adeena's tortillas to drag through the leftover mole sauce on my plate. "You seem pretty close to your family. Is that why you moved here?"

He nodded. "We both wanted to be closer to our parents since our dad's health isn't great. Jonathan made a lot of sacrifices to come out here. Hard to leave behind a fancy career and move away from your kids to settle down in the middle of nowhere, even if your marriage is long over and your kids are grown. Logistically, it was easier for me since I hadn't set up a practice yet."

He sighed and took a sip of his drink. "Still hard not really having anyone other than my family around, though."

"Family first, right?" I said with a shrug.

I thought I'd hidden the bitterness that came when I uttered that phrase, but Adeena picked up on it. "No offense, but you two sound really spoiled right now. Having families like ours might be kind of annoying, but it's also a privilege."

I crossed my arms, her comment stinging more than I thought.

She sounded like Bernadette. "Adeena, nobody complains about their family more than you do."

"And I also know that when things go down and life is against me, my family will always have my back. We all take care of each other in our own way. Yours is the same. How many people can say that and actually mean it?"

Jae looked at Adeena in admiration. "You, my friend, have more layers than I gave you credit for."

Adeena grinned. "I'm like an onion. Many layers, lots of flavor, and I provide incredible depth. Lucky for you all, I'm not as pungent."

As we all laughed at her silliness, Elena sauntered back with a water pitcher and refilled our glasses. "Can I interest you all in some dessert? We've got buñuelos, flan, and tres leches cake. All family recipes, all fantastic."

Jae said, "Um, I'm a dentist, so I don't think—"

"We'll take one of each, Elena, thanks," I said. She grinned and left, and I turned my attention to Jae. "You're allowed to enjoy sugar in moderation, you know. Live a little."

He smirked. "Lila, I appreciate the sentiment, but you realize that you create sugary treats for a living, right? You're not exactly the most objective observer here."

I returned his smirk. "I've never had a cavity in my life."

His jaw dropped.

Adeena added, "My people literally soak fried dough in sugar syrup on the reg and I've only had one cavity. She's right, fellow outsider. Live a little."

He leaned back in his chair, finally relaxing a bit. "Fellow outsider, huh? How so?"

I glanced at Adeena. "How much time you got?"

Elena came back with our desserts and we paid proper obeisance. The flan was out of this world. I've tasted plenty of flan in my life, as they were a staple at Filipino fiestas. But this was flan on a whole other level. The custard was silky smooth and the caramel on top had smoky overtones that played well with the creamy sweetness. Whenever I tried a dessert, my first instinct was to dissect it and put my own spin on it. This flan was too perfect to mess with.

I took a break from this taste of heaven to tell Elena, "Oh, almost forgot. My friend Marcus wanted me to tell you he said 'hi.' I guess he's a bit of a regular here?"

Elena's smile fell a bit before stretching back to its previous form. "Oh, you know Marcus?"

"Yeah, he's my godmother's son. He was supposed to join us tonight, but I guess something came up. How do you know him?"

Elena pushed back a curl that'd escaped from her bun. "We had some trouble with a previous customer. Got to the point where we almost pressed charges, but decided against it. I met Marcus at the police station. He started visiting pretty often after that. Said he wanted to make sure Der—uh, that customer didn't come back."

I tried to play it cool, but her slip-up was exactly what I needed. "I'm sorry, but were you about to say Derek? As in Derek Winter?"

Elena made a disgusted noise. "Don't even bring up that pendejo around me. He told nothing but lies about my uncle and his family."

"Your uncle? Was he the original owner of this restaurant?"

She frowned. "Yeah."

When she didn't elaborate, I asked, "So what happened?"

She crossed her arms. "Why you wanna know?"

"Unfortunately, I'm very familiar with Der—um, that guy. And he loves stirring up trouble. Just curious about what mess he got into this time."

She hesitated, struggling with whether she wanted to defend her family or tell me to mind my own business. The need to set the record straight won out.

"He told some pretty damning lies about my family that got them into a lot of trouble. Tío Hector and Tía Perla were new in town, and who was the town gonna believe? The White boy who'd lived here his entire life, of course."

Jae looked a little uncomfortable with that last statement, but Adeena and I just nodded grimly. We knew how it was around here.

"We tried pressing charges, but without any money for a lawyer, it wasn't gonna go anywhere. Anyway, my tío and his family couldn't hack it. The restaurant wasn't making any money and they were scared for the safety of their kids, so they left."

Elena shook her head. "This restaurant was their dream. So my mom took over the lease."

"That's pretty amazing. What were you and your mom doing before this?" I asked.

"I was in school for business administration. Helped my mom run an online store selling handmade soap, candles, beauty and wellness products, things like that. The restaurant doesn't leave a lot of free time, but we love doing it, so we've kept it up."

Adeena said, "That's so cool! Do you have a business card? I'm always looking for organic, cruelty-free beauty products."

Elena looked at her appraisingly. "You clearly take good care of your skin. You're practically glowing." She handed over a business card that matched her goth aesthetic, bearing the title WhichCraft Beauty Brews. "I'd love to be your craft hookup. We do big business with herbal remedies and teas, as you can guess from the name. Most of the plants we use in our products are grown in our greenhouse."

She scribbled her phone number on the back of the card and slid it to Adeena, who grinned. Her goal accomplished, I tried to steer the conversation back on topic so I could accomplish my own.

"So when's the last time your uncle and his family were in town?" She eyed me suspiciously. "Why?"

"Oh, just . . . making conversation, I guess. You all seem close, so it's a shame to think that you probably don't see them much anymore because of what happened."

A shadow passed over her pretty face. "They haven't been back since everything went down. Bad memories, I guess, and they weren't sure how safe it would be."

Elena got called away to take another order before I could think of a response.

Jae cleared his throat. "So what's with all these questions? Seems a bit personal for friendly chitchat with our waitress."

Adeena and I looked at each other, having a conversation with our eyes and the barest of body language.

Should I tell him? My eyes asked.

Eyebrow raise. *His brother is the detective on the case. Do you think that's wise?*

Eye roll. *What's he going to do? Tattle on me?*

Shrug. *He could.*

Shifty look at Jae. *Maybe he could get inside information.*

Smirk. *Maybe you just want to get inside his pants.*

Pointed look at Elena. *Like you're one to talk.*

We both burst out laughing, which probably made us look like a couple of weirdos, since we'd been staring at each other silently the whole time.

Jae leaned back in his chair, studying the two of us. "Do I even want to know what just happened?"

I grabbed the last buñuelo, dragging the crispy fritter through the piloncillo syrup pooled on the plate. "Just girl talk. You know how it is."

"But you weren't even speaking!"

Adeena smiled at me. "And yet everything that needed to be said was said."

He shook his head. "You two are . . ."

Adeena and I took turns finishing his sentence.

"Fascinating?"

"Gorgeous?"

"Mysterious?"

"Hilarious?"

"Super weird?"

He laughed. "All of the above. But I was going to say, 'lucky.'"

"Lucky? How so?" I asked.

"Watching you two play off each other is a lot of fun, and I can already tell your bond is special. You've found someone who gets you. Not everybody's so fortunate." He looked off into the distance, as if seeing his past relationships through a different lens.

I flushed, and Adeena's eyes dropped to her lap. Was she thinking what I was thinking? How we'd both almost let our friendship lapse more than once? How my years away had strained all my relationships, including this one? I was keeping a pretty big secret from her, but I was sure she'd been less than honest with me as well. Maybe it was time we had a talk.

Before either of us could respond, Elena stopped by with our check, which Jae gallantly covered. Normally Adeena and I would put up more of a fight (you did *not* want to get into a fight with an Asian person over who's going to foot the bill), but I was still paying off student loans and Lord knew what was going to happen to our restaurant. Adeena was too busy making heart eyes at Elena to realize Jae had paid the bill.

"Lovely meeting you, Elena," I said, getting up and holding out my hand.

"The formal type, huh? I like that," Elena said, shaking my hand.

Jae and Adeena did the same, though Adeena's handshake lingered for a little longer than necessary. "Hey, maybe you could stop by Java Jo's sometime tomorrow? Sunday is the day I'm in charge of the menu. I'll hook you up with something good."

Elena grinned at us. "Sounds great. I just might do that."

Then she left to go assist the latest batch of customers, her hips swinging to a rhythm only she could hear.

"Ooh, Adeena, things are looking up. And if it seems to be going well, maybe you could ask a few questions . . ."

She threw me a look but didn't respond. Ah well, it was worth a shot. Besides, I'd learned enough to see there was a strong connection and motive, and it'd be way too obvious if we pushed any harder. My next step was to figure out why the Torres family almost pressed charges, which meant I had to meet up with Marcus again. Sigh.

Adeena, Jae, and I headed out and Jae walked us to my car. "Thanks for inviting me out tonight. This was a lot of fun. I don't know many people here outside of my family and patients, so maybe we can do this again sometime soon?"

"You free tomorrow night? With the restaurant closed, I figured I should continue exploring the eateries in this town. Who knows how long I'll be stuck here?"

Adeena frowned at that last statement. "I've got a family thing going on, so I can't make it. Don't go anywhere good without me!"

I thought over the next few restaurants and suspects on my list. I was going to the sushi place with Janet, so that was out. Barbecue was delicious, but not my favorite thing to eat in public. Besides, I still wasn't ready to face the memories Nettie Bishop would bring up. Which left . . .

"Jae, you up for some pierogis?"

His eyes lit up. "Absolutely! My grandmother is from Poland and I'd kill for some potato-cheese pierogies as good as my babcia made every Sunday. I didn't know Shady Palms had a Polish restaurant."

I hesitated. "This isn't going to cause problems between you and your brother, is it? Us being friends? I wouldn't want him to think . . ."

I trailed off, unsure of how to finish that sentence.

"I'm a grown man. He doesn't get to tell me who I can and can't hang out with." Both the tone and the look that accompanied it were surprisingly fierce—seemed like Adeena wasn't the only one with big-brother issues.

He paused, then asked in a lighter tone, "Would you like me to pick you up so we don't both have to drive tomorrow?"

"Uh, sure. That'd be nice. I'll text you my address. Same time tomorrow night?"

"Absolutely. See you then!"

He waved at Adeena and headed to his own car, and I got into mine, pretending like it was no big deal that we were getting dinner two nights in a row.

For once, things were starting to go my way.

Chapter Twenty-one

Sunday morning. Time for church.

While this ritual was one I always regarded with dread, it was particularly unwelcome today. It had only been a few days since Derek died, and I'd been lucky enough to avoid the newspaper and town gossip. This wasn't something I could ignore while at church and the thought of having to deal with all the whispers and judgmental stares made me want to fake an illness to stay home, like I did when I was a kid. But I also knew, just like when I was a kid, Lola Flor would see right through me and I'd have to deal with her lecture all day, so I dragged myself out of bed and threw on my Sunday best.

When we arrived, the Calendar Crew were already in our pew, so we walked down to them. As luck would have it, our pew was near the front of the church, so we were subjected to all the stares and whispers as we made our way over. My grandmother marched forward, her head held high, and I imitated her. My aunt lagged behind, obviously shocked at our reception.

It only got worse near the end of the service, when the priest said, "And to our brothers and sisters who are ailing or no longer with us, including JoAnn Doblecki, Martin Johnson, and Derek Winter. Let us pray."

We all bowed our heads and prayed along with him, but I could feel the stares of the congregation like icy pinpricks in my back.

After the service, we gathered in the church basement as usual, waiting for our turn to chat with Father Santiago. He'd been with our parish since I was a kid, and was well-loved in the community. I used to have a standing appointment to go running with him every Tuesday, something I hadn't taken him up on since I'd been back. Maybe it was time to start again.

Mary Ann Randall, the head of the PTA, and her legion of soccer moms were hogging up his time as usual. What was unusual was when Father Santiago made eye contact with me and tried to make his way over, they blocked his path and refused to let him leave on the pretense of asking him more questions about "his lovely homily."

I rolled my eyes and made my way over to the table laid out with goodies the parishioners had brought. My aunt's tray was usually the first one emptied, but this morning it sat untouched before her as her "friends" avoided eye contact, filling up on nearby (read: less delicious) treats instead.

The Calendar Crew must've noticed because Ninang April strode toward her and made a big show of picking up a piece of ensaymada and taking a huge bite out of it.

"Can you believe I get this whole tray to myself? How blessed I must be!"

Ninang Mae and June soon joined her, and their exclamations of delight soon drove a few curious bystanders over to the table. Armed with mugs of tsokolate, the Filipino hot chocolate my grandmother blended herself, and plates of ensaymada, our area soon became the social hotspot it usually was.

Father Santiago managed to pull himself away from the PTA Squad and strolled over toward me. I handed him his usual cup of tsokolate made with sugar substitute and a half piece of ensaymada, which brought a smile to his face. He already looked younger than his fiftyish years, but that simple gesture erased even more years from his face. I felt better just being by him. He'd come over from the Philippines over thirty years ago, yet his rich, calming voice still carried the accent of his youth.

"So Lila, you've had an interesting couple of days, it seems."

I grimaced. "Not the word I'd use, but I guess you could say that. Who was the first to tell you? Was it one of the aunties," I gestured toward my godmothers, "or the PTA Squad?" I nodded toward the gaggle of moms scowling at me for daring to talk to the community priest.

He smiled. "Neither. It was your tita." He waved at my aunt, who lit up and waved back.

"Tita Rosie? Really?"

"After you got arrested. She was frantic and came to me for counsel."

I couldn't believe it. She loved Father Santiago as much as the rest of the community and held him in high esteem. But my aunt wasn't a talker. And, knowing her, she wouldn't want to bother him. Not that he'd consider her a burden, but that's how Tita Rosie was—game to listen to everyone else's problems without judgment, but keeping her cards close to her chest. The fact she'd confided in our priest drove home the seriousness of the allegations.

The crowd around my aunt was dispersing—her tray was finally empty. As she wiped her hands on a dish towel, I realized she'd be heading over soon, so I needed to talk fast.

"Father, what did she say to you?"

"Lila, you know I can't tell you that. My parishioners come to me in confidence. I would never betray them."

I sighed. "I know. I'm just so worried about her. All she's done since this thing with Derek happened is fret at home about the restaurant. And now me, I guess. I don't know what to do."

"What do you mean? I gave you that suspect list days ago," Ninang June's voice boomed behind me, making both me and the priest jump. "Sorry, Father. Honestly, Lila, haven't you started investigating yet? What happened to all those plans you made yesterday?"

Father Santiago looked alarmed. "June, what are you saying? Didn't the police say Derek was murdered? You can't have Lila investigate, it could be dangerous!"

My godmother waved her hand dismissively. "Ay, Father, you think I would send my own goddaughter into trouble? Her mother would never forgive me, God rest her soul. I just thought she could ask a few questions is all. You know, eat at the other restaurants Derek reviewed. That's not asking too much, diba?"

For once, I agreed with her. "She's right, Father. Someone planted drugs in my locker. And not like, a tiny baggie of weed. They're trying to get me put away on drug trafficking. You know my family. You know why this is so messed up. The police aren't even looking into other suspects since they think they have enough evidence against me."

Father Santiago didn't look convinced, so I added, "Besides, I never go to these places alone and all I'm doing is asking questions at these restaurants. What can they do to me?"

He shook his head. "I hope you're right, Lila. For your sake, and your family's." As he left, he made the sign of the cross, which I'm sure was meant to be reassuring.

It wasn't. And now I had to face lunch with Janet.

Chapter Twenty-two

After church, I'd planned on heading straight to Sushi-ya, hoping to get a chance to talk to Yuki before Janet got there. Unfortunately, my grandmother had other plans for me.

Any other Sunday, we'd be heading back to the restaurant for Sunday lunch. Much of the congregation would follow us for a good meal and a good time. Those Sunday lunches were what had sustained my aunt's business through the rough times. If nothing else, my family could count on Sunday to turn a profit.

But not today.

Tita Rosie's Kitchen was closed until the health inspector came to clear us. In the first bit of good news we'd had in a long time, Detective Park called my aunt after Mass to say he'd convinced the health inspector to interrupt his vacation for a quick evaluation of our restaurant. Monday he'd be over and we'd pass, like I knew we would, and everything would go back to normal. But until then, nothing was normal. Until then, we had to keep busy or go bananas.

Because of this, Lola Flor was in a worse mood than usual—which was really saying something—and had commandeered me to be her personal valet for the day. She made me drive her around to all her errands for the rest of the morning. I only managed to dump her on my godmothers by begging them to take her out to the casino so I could do some investigating.

I dashed into the sushi restaurant right on time (which was actually late in Janet's world), expecting to see her sitting there, looking at me with her disapproving scowl, but a quick sweep of the room showed me she wasn't there yet. I settled into a table near the door and played a phone game while I waited for Janet.

And waited. And waited. Ten minutes passed by, then fifteen. I texted her. No response. Called her cell phone. No response. I even looked up her office number and called her there. Nothing.

After thirty minutes, I knew I'd been stood up. Since that source of info turned out to be bupkis, I might as well treat myself to a nice lunch and work the Yuki and Akio Sato angle. I hadn't seen Yuki yet, but was pretty sure that was her husband behind the counter. I moved from my table over to an open spot in front of him.

"Konnichiwa! Welcome to Sushi-ya. What can I get for you?" the man I assumed to be Akio greeted me as he put together a plate of California rolls.

Did I start with the full court press right away? No, better to ease into it. Yuki wasn't around, so he was unsuspecting. Plus I didn't have Adeena with me to lighten the mood if it got too tense. Luckily, Ninang June's list included bits of Derek's reviews, so I knew which areas to poke.

I skimmed the menu. "Hmm, I usually go for the tempura bowl, but I remember reading a bad review about it." I glanced up and caught the man's stormy expression. "Oh, sorry! That was rude of me.

But a friend told me she loves this place and comes all the time for lunch, so I thought I'd check it out myself."

His expression softened, ever so slightly, so I added, "You're the owner, right?"

He grunted in acknowledgment.

"So then what would you recommend? You'd know what's best." I smiled, trying to butter him up.

"Ah, so then it's the omakase? Chef's choice?"

I nodded and he grinned, sharpening his knife so enthusiastically I leaned back, even though the counter and glass pane separated us. "No one ever picks the omakase! Miss, I'll prepare you a meal you'll never forget."

As he got to work, a sullen-faced pre-teen girl handed me a steaming hot towel. "Would you like anything to drink?"

"Can I get a glass of water and some hot green tea as well?" I asked as I cleaned my hands with the towel.

She left without saying anything, but I assumed she was getting my drinks.

Akio leaned over, brandishing the first plate. "So for the first course, we have flounder sashimi served with green onions and mo-miji oroshi, or daikon radish with chili pepper."

The fish was delicate and subtle, with a nice, firm texture. What followed after this opening course was an onslaught of fantastic ni-giri, small balls of pressed sushi rice with various toppings, served two at a time so I could fully appreciate each perfect morsel.

Sea bream was followed by sweet shrimp, tamago, yellowtail, salmon, soy sauce-braised octopus, crab, grilled eel, and the final two pieces were otoro, or tuna belly. The richest, fattiest, most melt-in-your-mouth pieces of tuna I'd ever had.

Between the tamago and yellowtail courses, the chef's daughter (he'd told me who she was after she'd left so abruptly) returned with my water but no tea. "Oh excuse me, I also ordered some green tea?"

She glared at her father, as if it were his fault she'd forgotten, then said, "OK. I'll be back."

She left and Akio placed the salmon nigiri in front of me. "I'm sorry about my daughter. Both she and my wife are grieving right now. A friend of theirs passed recently."

"I'm so sorry to hear that. My condolences to you and your family."

He picked up his knife and sliced the octopus with a little more force than necessary. "Save your condolences. He was no friend of mine."

I raised my eyebrows but said nothing, choosing to savor the fresh fish in front of me. When he saw I was properly enjoying my meal, he said, "You understand food. You appreciate it, I can tell. Not like him."

Ooh, was this it? Was this the opening I was hoping for? I swallowed a little too quickly and began coughing. I sipped at my water glass (still no tea) and asked, "Not like who?"

"That damned food critic or blogger or whatever he claimed to be. Started coming over a lot in the summer and I thought he loved my food. Till I saw his reviews."

I was working through the octopus, the softest, most flavorful octopus I'd had in a while, but managed to ask, "Oh no, what did he say?"

"Nothing but lies that don't bear repeating." His grip on the knife tightened briefly before he set it down. "It's fine though, he got what was coming to him."

My eyes widened. "You mean because he was murdered?"

Akio looked confused for a moment, then said, "Oh, no, not that. I mean, I'm not exactly sad he's gone, but I don't think killing him was the way to go." He set a plate in front of me. "Here's the last sushi course, lightly seared tuna belly dressed with yuzu salt."

I could tell the tuna belly deserved my full attention, so before I tasted it, I asked, "So then what did you mean 'he got what was coming to him'?"

"He beat him up," a familiar voice behind me said. Yuki stood there, holding a small pot of green tea as well as a carafe of warm sake. "Sorry for the wait. The sake is on the house."

I eyed the offering, wondering what her game was.

She snickered. "I haven't poisoned it, if that's what you're wondering. I understand my daughter wasn't being the most attentive server, and we pride ourselves on our service."

I nodded and sipped at the sake, feeling the warmth course all the way down to the tips of my toes. "This is delicious! And I'm sorry, did you say your husband beat up Derek?"

Akio lifted one disinterested shoulder. "He shouldn't have lied about my food like that. I take those kinds of comments very seriously."

"Yes, your food. All you care about is your precious food," Yuki said with disgust. "Never mind your family. He would've pressed charges if I hadn't smoothed things over with him. You got lucky."

I raised an eyebrow. "Smoothed things over? How?"

Akio grunted and walked away to the kitchen without answering. Yuki's hand went to her hair, which she patted nervously. "Oh, nothing special. Just promised him a few free meals. He wasn't so bad once you got to know him. After he helped with the health inspector, we started chatting over sake almost every night last summer."

She looked sad, then scared when her husband marched back, a scowl still darkening his features. "But you two stopped talking soon after that, right, Yuki? You never saw him again?"

Yuki nodded slowly, saying, "Yes, of course. I never saw him again," before drifting away.

Akio placed a plate containing three pieces of mochi ice cream in front of me. "Here. Dessert."

Compared to the rest of the meal, the ice cream was clearly an afterthought, bought from the supermarket and slightly freezer burnt. Not terrible, but nowhere near on par with the rest of the meal. Still, I'd gotten one heck of a meal and plenty of food for thought. I just wished Yuki was easier to pin down.

I paid the bill, which was shockingly low for omakase. The same meal in Chicago would've cost twice the price. Probably better service and dessert though. I thanked Akio (Yuki had disappeared into the back and seemed content to stay there till I left) and promised to be back soon.

The delicious meal had done a good job of placating me over Janet's absence. Still, the fact she supposedly knew something that could save me from jail, and was not only choosing to withhold it from me but had done something as childish as stand me up, was infuriating. What was her endgame? To humiliate me? Make me beg for her help? So much for turning over a new leaf for Terrence.

Emboldened by a tummy full of yummy fish and free alcohol, I decided to pay Janet a visit. She probably thought I'd be too chicken to go confront her, and usually she'd be right.

But not today.

Chapter Twenty-three

I marched into the hospital, then saw an elderly woman at the front desk and made a conscious effort to slow down and appear less pissed off. Doubted she'd want to help me if I started shouting demands.

"Hello, I'd like to speak to Janet Spinelli, please. We had a lunch meeting scheduled, but she never showed up."

"Oh dear, that won't do. Let me give her a call, make sure she's in her office." The volunteer overseeing the desk looked over the directory list, then punched the number into the phone. She listened for a moment, then shook her head and hung up. "I'm sorry, she's not answering. Maybe she had to run some errands?"

"Would it be possible for me to wait in her office? I really need to talk to her."

"Well . . ." She glanced over at the security guard sitting next to her, who shrugged and went back to his phone. "Maybe you could sign in? And just wait here in the lobby? I don't think I can let you into her . . . Oh, Miss Stanton! Perfect timing."

A stocky White woman wearing an ill-fitting pencil skirt and suit jacket with white gym shoes joined us at the desk. "Hi, Avis. What can I do for you?"

"Miss Stanton here is Miss Spinelli's assistant," Avis the volunteer explained, addressing me. "She can help you out."

I thanked Avis and turned to Miss Stanton, holding out my hand. "Nice to meet you. I'm Lila Macapagal, and I had a lunch meeting scheduled with Janet, but she never showed up. She's not answering her phone, so I was wondering if you knew when she'd be back."

She returned my firm handshake, then pulled out her phone to consult her calendar. "That's odd. I have you on the schedule for lunch at one thirty p.m. and have the reminder set as well. She never showed up?"

I shook my head. "I waited for half an hour before ordering lunch for myself. I just finished and decided to stop by to see if there was some kind of mix-up."

Miss Stanton pulled her lips into a thin line. "Let's go upstairs and see if she left a note or something. This is rather unlike her."

We rode the elevator in silence while I texted Adeena what I'd learned and Miss Stanton also thumbed through her phone. Once we reached their floor, we hurried over to Janet's office, Miss Stanton pulling her keys out of her purse.

It was unnecessary.

The door to Janet's office was slightly ajar, so after a quick glance at her assistant, I pushed it open. Her office was fairly small, with a tiny workspace shunted off toward the side and an enormous mahogany desk dominating the room. My eyes couldn't help but be drawn to it, and Miss Stanton and I made the discovery at the same time.

Or at least, she screamed at the same time I noticed the blood pooling on the floor and the figure lying behind the desk. As she ran out to the hallway calling for help, I moved toward the figure, careful not to disturb any of the surrounding area. Luckily, the room was neat and tidy, with everything in its place.

Except for Janet, of course.

She lay behind the desk, curled almost into a fetal position. Her eyes were closed, and I couldn't see her chest moving, but as I reached my hand out toward her, debating if I should feel for a pulse, I was rewarded with a tiny flutter of breath against my skin.

"She's still alive!" I called out.

A doctor rushed into the room, followed by two nurses pulling a stretcher. The doctor did a cursory check on Janet, then barked instructions to the nurses, who quickly yet gently lifted her onto the stretcher. Before I could fully process what was happening, she was whisked away and a security guard entered the room to hold us for questioning.

Time passed slowly as we waited for the cops to arrive. The security guard glared at me when I pulled out my phone, so I focused on comforting Miss Stanton, who'd started crying. Finally, a uniformed police officer made his way over to us. After a brief introduction, he got right to the questions.

"What were you two doing in here?" he asked.

Miss Stanton explained she was Janet's assistant, gesturing to the ID card hanging on her lanyard and pointing toward the matching placard on her desk. "Janet missed a scheduled appointment with Miss . . . Lila, so we came up here together to talk to her."

"What did you need to talk to Miss Spinelli about, Miss Lila?" the cop asked.

Detective Park appeared at the doorway. "Yes, Ms. Macapagal, what did you need to speak to her about?"

I took a step back. "Detective Park! What are you doing here?"

"We got a call about an assault victim at the hospital, and I come here to find you stomping around my crime scene." He gestured around the room. "What exactly is your connection to the victim?"

"I was supposed to meet her for lunch. She'd called me saying she had information that could help me out."

He nodded, jotting this down on his tablet. "Regarding?"

I swallowed. "The, uh, the Derek Winter case."

He raised an eyebrow, but kept writing. "What kind of information?"

"She wouldn't say. Just told me I owed her a decent lunch in return. We were supposed to meet at Sushi-ya at one thirty."

"What time did you arrive?"

"At the restaurant or here at the hospital?"

"Both."

"I walked into the restaurant at one thirty on the dot. Janet's not the most patient person, and I was worried she'd leave if I was late. But she wasn't there. I waited half an hour for her, but she never showed. So I treated myself to an excellent lunch, then came here to the hospital."

Remembering the conversation at the restaurant, I added, "Oh, and did you know that Akio Sato assaulted Derek? And that Yuki was having an affair with him?"

He continued writing without missing a beat. "So you had lunch, a bit of gossip, and then what?"

Upset he wasn't taking my sleuthing seriously, I crossed my arms and frowned. "And everything else you can get from her," I said, motioning to Miss Stanton, who was being interviewed by the cop who'd arrived before Detective Park. "She arrived a couple minutes after I did and we came up to the room together."

"You didn't touch anything, did you?"

I shook my head.

"What do you think Miss Spinelli wanted to tell you?"

"I wish I knew, Detective." I glanced over at her desk, wishing I'd had time to look for clues before the cops had arrived. "Her assistant might know. Or maybe Terrence, her fiancé. He was the one who urged her to call me."

He stopped writing. "Why would he do that?"

I shrugged. He wasn't going to get much more out of me on that matter. It was none of his business.

"All right, you can go for now, but be available for more questioning if anything comes up." He sighed and put his tablet away. "How's Rosie doing, by the way?"

Record scratch moment. "Excuse me? What do you care?"

He frowned. "I consider her a friend and want to make sure she's doing OK."

"She's in fear of losing her restaurant, her home, and now me. How do you think she's doing?"

Now it was his turn to cross his arms and get defensive. "You act like I'm gunning for you. Just because I don't tell you who or what I'm investigating doesn't mean that I'm twiddling my thumbs while I sit on my ass at the station. I don't need to clear my actions with you. I go where the evidence points me."

At this point, the shock of finding Janet and frustration with the case overrode my "don't antagonize the cops" survival instincts. "Yeah, well, evidence can be falsified. I bet you just want to wrap this up quick and neat, add another notch to your belt. Who cares that you're literally ruining the lives of innocent people?"

His eyes flashed, but when he responded, his voice was calm and even. "Could you please tell your aunt I asked about her? I'd like to stop by some time to check up on her. You seem to be too busy running all over town interrogating people to be much help to her. Oh, and one more thing," he added. "'Innocent people' don't usually have a record. You think I wouldn't check what you'd been up to when you were in Chicago?"

And with that parting shot, he was gone.

Chapter Twenty-four

What a low blow from Detective Park, bringing up the second stupidest thing I'd done in my life. It hadn't gone down the way it seemed, though. I'd seen the police records and they left out some crucial parts of the story.

What had happened was, I'd been helping my then-fiancé, Sam, set up his restaurant. He'd been getting supplies at amazing prices, and when I asked him about it, all he'd say was, "I know a guy."

It was Chicago—I just kind of assumed everybody knew a guy.

Turned out Sam's guy wasn't on the up-and-up and had acquired these supplies in less-than-legal ways. Because I was the one who had signed for the supplies, it was my name on all the documents, and so it was my name that went into the Chicago PD database when the guy finally got caught. The police thought I was involved in some weird restaurant-supply smuggling ring. The only thing that saved me was Sam paying off his connection so that he'd claim I had no idea the goods were illegal—which was true. But Sam was a little rich boy and didn't want his name to get dragged into the case, so it was easier for him to make me the sacrificial lamb.

The number one stupidest thing I'd ever done in my life? I'd stayed with him after that whole mess. It had taken his cheating for me to finally realize how terrible he was and cut him loose.

Whatever. Forget him and forget Derek and forget Detective Park. He was trying to shake me off the case and I wasn't going to let him.

I stopped by Janet's room to check on her, but the cop guarding her room informed me that only family was allowed inside. No exceptions.

I texted Terrence, asking him to get in touch whenever he had a chance. I hoped the hospital had already contacted him because I didn't want to be the one to break the news about Janet, and we really needed to talk. When he didn't get back to me right away, I decided to swing by Java Jo's, hoping to catch Adeena at the end of her shift. The coffee shop was packed and both she and Kevin were in panic mode trying to accommodate the crowd.

"Whoa, what's going on?" I asked, once I finally got to the front. I'd been waiting in line for almost twenty minutes—most days there wasn't even a line.

"Remember how Kevin gave me full control of the Sunday menu? Well, I guess our customers really like what I came up with, because it's been like this all day." Adeena raised her voice. "Guess he should've listened to me when I first asked him about the Sunday specials. Looks like I do know what I'm doing, even without fancy barista training."

Kevin called out, "Yeah, yeah, we get it. You're good at this. Now get back to work!"

She laughed, and I stepped aside so she could help the next customer. As she prepared their order, she said over her shoulder, "By the way, your baked goods absolutely flew off the shelves! Luckily, we had some cookie dough and scones in the freezer from last week, but those are almost gone, too. You wouldn't happen to have more treats you could bring us, would you?"

I laughed, too. Despite all that had just transpired, Adeena's happiness and excitement were contagious. About time Kevin realized what a treasure she was. Besides, after the stress from everything that had happened earlier, I really wanted to lose myself in some baking.

"I have the dough for ube crinkles and the coconut shortbread crust in my freezer. Can I bake them here? The restaurant kitchen is off-limits and it's definitely some kind of health code violation if I baked them at home because of Nisa."

She handed the customer their latte, told them to have a nice day, and immediately began ringing up the next customer. "Yeah, of course. You have full control of our ovens. Not like Kevin ever puts them to good use anyway. Besides, the smell of fresh-baked cookies is sure to draw in more customers."

I rubbed my hands together. I'd been wanting to play with Kevin's industrial ovens forever, but he mostly used them to reheat junk he'd bought from the wholesale store. This was going to be fun.

Noticing the look on my face, Adeena giggled and said, "Hey, Kevin! Thank Lila for saving our butts."

He stuck his tongue out. "I'll thank her when those cookies are ready and not a moment before. Now let's switch out. You can make your fancy drinks and I'll man the register since you can't seem to stop chatting with our customers."

Adeena rolled her eyes, but did what he said. I turned to leave, but he stopped me and handed over a coconut milk latte, my lactose intolerant drink of choice and usual order, in a to-go cup. I hadn't actually ordered anything since, as he'd pointed out, Adeena and I had been too busy chatting, but he said, "It's on the house. And seriously, thank you. I really appreciate it."

Kevin may not have been the best businessman—not to mention a pretty horrendous baker—but he was a good guy overall, and he put up with a lot from Adeena and me. Maybe we should cut him some slack.

Once he gave Adeena a huge raise, that is. Then we'd talk.

With the thought of Kevin and his shoddy baked goods still on my mind, I remembered I never got back the signed paperwork for the dentist. Kevin retrieved it from the backroom and I headed over to Dr. Jae's Dental Clinic.

Not going to lie, I hoped to catch a peek of Jae before I had to run off. I might not have been looking for romance, but I appreciated eye candy as much as the next person. And OK, I'd gotten some interested vibes from him at dinner the other night, but maybe I was reading too much into it? I hadn't exactly been the best judge of character lately. We were supposed to have dinner again tonight, which would be a great chance to get to know him better. Just a nice, friendly, investigative outing. Right?

As I stood in front of the clinic, overthinking everything as usual, I heard someone clear their throat behind me.

"Lila? Are you waiting for someone?"

I whirled around and looked into Jae's quizzical (and beautiful) face.

"Oh! Hi, I was just, uh, bringing back the signed paperwork. I was just at the cafe and just remembered I hadn't returned the paperwork, so I thought I'd just stop by real quick."

Oh my gulay, Lila, stop saying "just!" I could practically hear Lola Flor admonishing me. "All that time and money for your fancy education, you'd think your vocabulary would've improved by now. English isn't even my first language and I'm practically Shakespeare compared to you."

OK, that's not how my grandmother really talks, but I couldn't help it. In my mind, the voice of criticism always came to me in the voice of Lola Flor. Make of that what you will.

Either he didn't notice or kindly chose to overlook it. "That's great. Would you like to come in for a minute? It's freezing out here."

It was, in fact, freezing outside. But my face was burning so hot I didn't notice, and even though all I had wanted earlier was a chance to chat with him, I realized if I stayed around him any longer, I'd probably end up humiliating myself beyond repair.

I thrust the signed paperwork at him. "Actually, I'm in a bit of a hurry. I need to run home and grab my cookie dough since the cafe ran out."

He laughed. "Another pastry emergency at Java Jo's? Well, considering their usual offerings, I thank you on behalf of all their customers. I'll try to stop by in an hour or so. I could use a pick-me-up after my next patient."

"Cool, see you there!" I scurried over to my car before I could do any more damage, but I couldn't wipe the grin off my face.

Maybe this town wasn't so bad after all.

Over four dozen cookies and several jars of calamansi curd later, the weight of the last few days had lightened considerably, and Adeena and I were ready to call it a day. The cookies had sold out within the first hour, as had the hot chocolate I'd sampled earlier in the week. The chai-spiced coffee had also proved surprisingly popular, despite not being one of Adeena's more creative offerings. It sure was tasty though. The floral monstrosity, thank goodness, hadn't made the cut.

We closed up shop a little after six, way later than their usual Sunday hours. Kevin took off his apron. "Great job, you two. We sold out of everything we made, so yes, Adeena, I'm glad you're in charge of the Sunday menu. Lila, from now on, your drinks are on the house and you have a standing order to bake for us every Sunday. Whatever you want, as much as you want. That cool?"

"Heck yeah, that's cool. Thanks, Kevin!"

"No man, thank you. Can you two clean up the tables while I take a quick break? I'll finish closing up once you're done."

We nodded as he grabbed his vape pen and headed to the break room.

"I can't believe we sold out! And so quickly, too. We make a great team, yeah? Together we could give Java Jo's some real competition." Adeena freed her waves from the Java Jo's hat she wore while working (I think one of the reasons we're so tight is our connection to unflattering baseball caps) and shook it out.

I removed mine as well and loosened my hair from its ponytail. I wasn't sure how to answer the question Adeena was really asking, so I just said, "Your drinks were fantastic. I'm telling you, that hot chocolate is gold. And even though the spiced latte is a bit basic in concept, it's like the Desi answer to pumpkin spice lattes. Very cool, very tasty."

She ran her hand over the shaved side of her head as she mulled that over. "The Desi answer to PSLs . . . I like it! And you're right, it felt like something was missing, but I think I know what to do. Wish we weren't all out so I could see if it worked now."

Jae's voice rumbled behind me, a not unpleasant tingling spreading throughout my body at the sound. "Oh no, you're already sold out? I was with a patient and couldn't break away until now."

"Jae! I didn't know you were open on Sundays." Adeena reached under the counter for a small to-go cup of coffee she'd stashed earlier. "I was saving this for myself but you look like you need it more."

He grasped the cup, chugging down at least half of it in one swallow. "Oh man, I really did need that." He grabbed a napkin from the dispenser to wipe his mouth. "And I'm usually not open on Sundays, but my mom convinced me to make an exception for a family friend. And then another family friend called and another . . . and here we are."

I pulled a baggie of cookies, two of each kind, from my purse and handed them over as well. "I was going to give these to you at dinner, but that's not for another couple of hours and these are best when fresh. Eat up."

Jae obediently pulled out an ube crinkle and took a large bite. "Whoa, what is this? It's delicious!"

"It's made with ube, a purple yam that we use in tons of desserts in the Philippines. Sorta similar to taro, if you've ever had taro boba tea, though not exactly the same," I explained.

He snapped his fingers. "That's what it reminded me of! Taro is my favorite flavor of boba tea." He scarfed down the second ube crinkle. "God, these are good. Do you take personal orders? I think my mom would like them, too."

Lord, was this guy for real? I thought Amir was the perfect guy (even the fact that he was off-limits made him extra desirable), but he was facing some stiff competition in Dr. Jae Park.

As if sensing my thoughts, my phone rang, and who should it be but Amir?

"Hey, what's up?" I answered.

"Why didn't you tell me about Janet?" he demanded.

"Oh shoot. Sorry, I meant to text you, but I got caught up helping your sister at the cafe. How did you hear about it?"

"Never mind that, you need to get home. Now."

I glanced over at Adeena and Jae, who were clearly listening in. "Why?"

"Marcus called to warn us that Detective Park wants to charge you with Janet's assault."

"What?!"

"I know, but he's wary of all these coincidences happening around you. We need to move fast, Lila. Get over here now."

Then he hung up on me, leaving me with a half-formed response on my lips and a million questions running through my mind.

Chapter Twenty-five

"I can't believe you didn't tell me that Janet was attacked! Why am I just now finding out about this?" Adeena said.

After explaining that I had an urgent meeting with Amir and breaking off my dinner plans with Jae, Adeena insisted on riding with me to my house. I appreciated her support, though I could've done without all the screaming.

"It's not like I did it on purpose! You were so busy and I got distracted, and there just wasn't a good time to talk about it. Not like I could tell you I found Janet Spinelli lying in a pool of blood in front of all your customers, you know."

"Fair enough."

We rode the rest of the way in silence.

Tita Rosie greeted us at the door. "Oh anak, I can't believe this! Is Janet OK? Have you heard from Terrence?"

Oh jeez, I really was a terrible friend, wasn't I? Other than that brief text I'd sent earlier, I'd completely forgotten about Janet's fiancé, who was not only my close friend, but Derek's best friend from high school. I wasn't the only one having a terrible week. My phone showed a missed call from him and I made a mental note to reach out when I got the chance.

I peeled off my coat and hung it up, then unzipped my boots. "Since I'm not family, I wasn't allowed to see her or ask for any details on her condition. Has Ate Bernie or Ninang June heard anything?"

"Not yet, but Marcus told us there's a guard outside her door in case whoever attacked her comes back to finish the job," Amir said, walking in with a tray of snacks, followed closely by my grandmother and godmothers.

"Detective Park seems to think that someone is you," Ninang April announced unceremoniously as she helped herself to a mug of coffee and piece of ensaymada. "What did you do this time, Lila?"

"That's enough, April," Lola Flor said. She lowered herself slowly to her seat at the head of the coffee table, then pushed the tray of goodies toward me, taking nothing for herself. "Now tell us everything."

So I did.

Amir listened carefully, jotting down notes as he did, occasionally shaking his head or grunting, but never actually interrupting me. Wish I could say the same for my godmothers. Finally my story wound down. "And yeah, that's pretty much it. Detective Park questioned me, I told him everything I told you, though I didn't go in-depth about the Satos. Then I helped Adeena and Kevin at Java Jo's for a couple of hours and here we are."

Lola Flor voiced what we were all thinking. "I don't know what that detective's playing at. The hospital is bound to have security cameras and it'll be easy to figure out who attacked Janet. Or if the criminal was smart enough to hide their face, the cameras in the lobby will prove Lila's alibi."

Amir frowned. "Unfortunately, several of the hospital's security cameras have been broken for months, including the one in that hallway. But you're right, his behavior as of late has been strange. He must really want to wrap up the Derek Winter case fast. Or at the very least, have your bail revoked."

"Why would he want to do that? And what happens if my bail's revoked?"

Amir stared thoughtfully at his notes. "Detective Park didn't work homicides till he came to Shady Palms. We don't really have a detective force here, so he's kind of a jack-of-all-trades now. But before coming here, he worked Vice. Busting up drug rings was how he made his name back in Chicago. It's starting to feel like a personal vendetta against you, Lila. He thinks you're messing things up in his quiet little town."

"But why me? I get that he doesn't know me so he can't vouch for my character, but I just got back here a few months ago. How could I suddenly have a drug empire?" I threw up my hands in exasperation. "Plus, doesn't anyone else think it's strange that the murder doesn't seem to be bothering him, but the drugs have him practically kicking down our door?"

He shrugged. "Didn't say it was logical. Just my theory. It might be something as simple as Sheriff Lamb riding him to wrap up the case ASAP. The sheriff and Mr. Long are friends, after all."

Nobody else had much to add after that, so we sipped at our drinks in sullen silence until Detective Park arrived.

He glanced at all of us arrayed around the living room. "Gang's all here, huh? Although the Gossip Trio seems to be missing."

"No, just in the kitchen," Ninang April said as they entered the room with more snacks.

I didn't appreciate his attempt at humor. "Detective Park, why are you here?"

"What, the local grapevine hasn't informed you yet?" I stared at him stone-faced, so he said, "We have good reason to believe it was you who attacked Janet Spinelli."

"And what reason would that be?" Adeena asked before Amir or I could. Amir glared at his sister, but repeated her question.

"Yes, Detective, what possible evidence could you have against her? Are you telling us that you've viewed the security footage and spotted my client committing the act? Because if not, this is starting to feel an awful lot like harassment. Which I will be pursuing in court."

Detective Park waved his hand. "We're still sifting through the footage. But we have it on good authority that you recently got into an argument with the victim. Is this true?"

I snorted. "That's your ironclad evidence? Everybody knows Janet and I don't get along. We got into an argument outside her office a few days ago because she wants to act like we're still in high school. You can ask anyone at the hospital what we argued about. I'm sure it's spread far and wide by now."

He looked taken aback. "Is that so? Then why didn't you share this information with me when I questioned you earlier?"

I shrugged. "I wasn't trying to hide anything. What we argued about wasn't connected to her attack or anything else that's been going on."

"See, that's where I think you're wrong. You want to paint me as some bumbling small-town detective, but I've been working this Derek Winters case for a long time now. You think I didn't know that at one point he was the main drug dealer for this county? That he'd been faking prescriptions for years?"

Detective Park leaned forward, trying to get into my face, but Amir stood in his way. "Derek had turned informant for me. His suppliers were the ones I wanted, and the big-time distributors as well. He was trying to get out of that life, but was afraid of what would happen to him and his mom. We were trying to take them down little by little so they wouldn't get wise to him. And then a mere two weeks before we were supposed to do our big bust, Derek gets murdered. You don't find that suspicious?"

"Don't answer that," Amir told me. Which was just fine since none of what Detective Park had said made sense to me. I couldn't have responded even if Amir begged me to. "Detective, you're dancing around the issue. What does my client have to do with the assault on Janet Spinelli or Derek Winters's criminal activities? I'm still liable to charge you with harassment."

Detective Park studied Amir. "How much do you know about your client's criminal record in Chicago?"

Oh, that son of a—

"What criminal record?" Lola Flor demanded. My family had done a good job of listening quietly and not interrupting (for once) but this latest revelation was just too much.

"Would you like to be the one to tell them, or should I?" Detective Park asked me.

I sighed. "Sam had been stocking his restaurant with goods that were . . . not acquired legally. It started small, with cheese that he'd smuggled over because U.S. regulations didn't allow certain types to be imported or sold here. But then he also started getting top-range kitchen equipment for extremely low prices. He told me it was because the supplier was a friend of his dad who wanted to help him out. I believed him. Since I was in charge of all the stock, I ordered through the suppliers he gave me and signed for all the deliveries. Which meant my name was the one on all the documents, not his."

I paused, not wanting to relive this difficult time. Part of the reason I hadn't been home in so long was because I'd been dealing with this. I didn't want anyone back home to know what I'd been involved in. Not even Adeena.

But Detective Park wasn't going to let me end the story there. "Long story short, she got caught. Her rich boyfriend hired a lawyer who got her off on a technicality, so she probably thought she was safe hiding this from you all. But what I'm seeing is a pattern. I don't believe that you knew nothing about what your ex-fiancé was doing. I also believe you knew about Derek's criminal enterprises and helped him out. Then when you found out he was going to flip, you killed him so he wouldn't sell you out."

Dear Lord, I was getting whiplash from all the twists and turns coming out of Detective Park's mouth. Is this why he was coming after me so hard? He thought I was some girl who lived dangerously by shacking up with pseudocriminals and helping them rule their enterprises?

I glanced over at my aunt, who had the most heartbreaking expression on her face. "Tita, I swear it's not like that."

"Not now, Lila. Don't give him any ammunition," Amir warned me. "OK, Detective, you seem to have drawn a pretty clear picture of how you think Lila and Derek are connected. But you're here about Janet Spinelli. Why would my client attack her?"

"I'm hoping Miss Spinelli will wake up and confirm this, but I believe she's the one who supplied Derek with the signed prescription pads. If I'm correct, which I usually am, and Miss Spinelli was the source, it's very likely your client went to tie up loose ends. Either convince Miss Spinelli to continue being her supplier or shut her up the way she did with Derek. Isn't that what your argument was about, Ms. Macapagal?"

Out of nowhere, Ninang June burst out laughing. "Detective, is that really what you thought they'd argued about? Didn't any of the staff tell you what they overheard?"

He frowned at her. "They all claimed it sounded like personal business but couldn't hear the details. Why? What do you know?"

"The argument was over the same silly thing they've been fighting about since they were kids. A boy."

"Ninang June!" I said.

"No," Amir said. "It's fine. Go ahead and clear this up so he knows how ridiculous he's being."

I sighed. "Janet accused me, yet again, of going after her fiancé, who I briefly dated in high school. Terrence was also Derek's best friend, which is why I tried to talk to her, but she wasn't interested. She still blames me for their breakup, even though they're engaged now." I rolled my eyes. "Like I said, high school stuff."

Detective Park grunted. "Well, I'll be checking out your story with some of the hospital employees. As well as this Terrence you're so fond of. Is this the Terrence Howell Miss Spinelli had listed as her emergency contact?"

"That's him," I said. "Are we done here, Detective?"

He stood up and put away his tablet. "For now, yes. But we'll be speaking again soon, Ms. Macapagal." He nodded at my aunt and grandmother. "Sorry to impose. Hope to see you again soon, Rosie."

My aunt shook her head sadly. "I'm sorry, Jonathan, but I don't. You bring nothing but bad news and accusations against my family. Until you catch the real criminals, I hope I don't see you again."

For the first time, a glimmer of actual human emotion emerged on Detective Park's face. "I'm sorry, too, Rosie. But I'm just doing my job."

Lola Flor snorted. "What, by coming into our home and accusing my granddaughter of disgusting crimes?" She held up her hand to stop his retort. "I don't care. Get out of my house."

He looked over at my aunt one last time and said, "Of course. Until next time, ladies. Counselor."

Detective Park departed, leaving a hollow victory and strange sense of unease behind him.

Chapter Twenty-six

I woke up Monday morning with the feeling it was going to be a big day. Well, even bigger than usual.

One, the health inspector was finally coming over to clear us. Two, I was meeting Terrence (old friend, ex-lover, Derek's ex–best friend, and Janet's fiancé) for lunch at our old high school hangout. I was not in the mood for "Hey isn't it weird that my ex is dead, your fiancée is in a coma, both of them were possibly involved in the drug trade, and now I'm being accused of murder, assault, and drug trafficking? Wild, right? Anyway, what's been going on with you these past few years?" but I couldn't put it off any longer. And three, Jae had called to reschedule our nondate, so our dinnertime reconnaissance was back on for tonight. He even mentioned his brother calling to warn him away, which seemed to strengthen Jae's resolve to spend time with me. Figured I'd deal with that weird family dynamic some other time.

"Good morning, Tita Rosie." I greeted my aunt with a quick

squeeze on the shoulder—it was the most physical affection my family could tolerate.

"Oh, anak, did you sleep well?" She ladled garlic fried rice onto a plate and topped it with a fried egg. She slid the plate, along with a platter of Filipino breakfast meat, toward me. "Kain tayo. We have a long day ahead of us."

I was too anxious to eat, but she was right, I needed the sustenance to get through what was going to be a long day. I helped myself to a few slices of tocino, the slightly sweet cured pork pairing perfectly with the strong, salty flavors on my plate. "Where's Lola? Usually she's up before us."

"What, I can't sleep in a little? Not like we're actually working today." Lola Flor's voice sounded behind me, making me jump. She'd been doing that a lot lately.

"Nay, we need to get ready for dinner service after we pass the inspection. Lila, you're in charge of letting everyone know we're open. Post on our Facebook and . . . Tweeter?"

I bit back a giggle. "Twitter, Tita. I'll update all our social media accounts. Maybe we can even do a promo. First ten customers receive a free dessert or something like that?"

"That's a great idea! Everybody loves your lola's sweets. We should get a lot of customers with a promotion like that."

Lola Flor snorted. "Hmph. Not bad."

And with what constituted as high praise from my grandmother, the day began.

We got to the restaurant about half an hour before the health inspector was due to arrive, but he still managed to beat us there. And with him was an unexpected guest.

"Mr. Long?" my aunt asked. "What are you doing here?"

"It's my property, isn't it? I have a right to know what's going on in my buildings. Especially," he said, eyeing my grandmother warily, who was staring daggers at him, "when my son was killed on the premises, and the police are calling in favors so you can open up again."

Lola Flor made a dismissive noise with her lips. "He wasn't your son, so stop pretending like you care. Spend more time comforting your wife, who just lost her only child. Also, everyone knows this man is your friend, so now who's trying to call in a favor?"

Mr. Long's jaw dropped and his face flushed an ugly, deep red. "Wha— How dare you imply—"

"Rosie, open up the door. Let's get this over with. If we want to be ready in time for dinner, we have a lot of shopping and prep to do." Lola Flor muttered a few more things under her breath in Tagalog, but nothing I could translate in polite company.

The health inspector, who introduced himself as Mr. Nelson, cleared his throat. "Yes, that would be best. I have other establishments to visit today, Mrs. Macapagal."

Tita Rosie was so flustered, she didn't bother correcting him on her title. "Of course, Mr. Nelson." She opened the front door and gestured inside. "After you, sir."

We all stepped into the dining area and I tried to look at the restaurant with fresh eyes, analyzing the space the way the health inspector probably was. Our restaurant was always spotlessly clean, but the space itself was a little rough around the edges. Not a hygiene problem, more of a "we haven't updated the space in twenty years 'cause we're broke" kind of an issue.

Back in December, when I had gotten the call that the restaurant was failing and my aunt needed me to step up, the first things I did were set up a social media presence and change the decor. We didn't have the money to make any real alterations, but we did what we could. Adeena helped us paint the walls a lovely shade of terra-cotta to cover up the dingy white it was before. We hung family pictures and mementos and scattered Philippine memorabilia throughout the space: a giant wooden fork and spoon set hanging by the kitchen, hand-woven table runners, a print of *Prayer Before Meal* by the cubist artist Vicente Manansala, and several Barrel men figurines posed on a high shelf.

A painting of the Last Supper graced the wall where we seated large parties, so our diners could eat awkwardly below it as they contemplated their sins. I'd tried to get rid of it more than once, but that painting was the one thing my aunt refused to budge on. I'd already convinced her to remove the Santo Niño statue that used to watch creepily from the corner, so I figured a compromise was in order.

Mr. Long paused in front of the painting long enough to give a derisive snort before following the rest of us to the kitchen.

My aunt wasn't having any of that. As she flicked on the kitchen lights, she said, "Sir, you don't have to agree with my choices, but I ask you not to insult the Lord in my—Susmaryosep, what is this?!"

Smashed dishes and bent-up cutlery littered the floor. Pots and pans were strewn around the room, far from their usual resting places. One of the windows was broken, shards of glass littering the sink and windowsill. Worst of all, the food stored in the fridge and freezer had been pulled out and left to rot in the open air. The food hadn't been out long enough to begin to smell, luckily, but long enough that we'd have to throw it out.

All that food—and money—wasted.

My eyes swept over our beloved kitchen, my horror and nausea building as I took in the destruction. "I think I'm going to be sick."

But before I could run off to the bathroom, Tita Rosie wailed and started to fall to her knees. I caught her and we both sank to the floor.

I held her as she cried, as she screamed, "Bakit?" over and over again. Why indeed. What had our family done to deserve this?

Meanwhile, Lola Flor was screaming at Mr. Long and the health inspector. "You had something to do with this, didn't you? You've been wanting to kick us out for years! If you think this is your chance . . ." She trailed off, clearly thinking about a threat strong enough. She couldn't seem to find one to convey her true meaning in English, so she switched to Tagalog to berate him.

Mr. Long went from barely concealing his pleased smile to alarm as my tiny grandmother advanced on him. "Get away from me, lady, or I'm calling the cops!"

Sensing a task that could occupy my aunt, I said, "That's right, the cops! Tita Rosie, you need to call the police and report this. They'll need to investigate, find out who did this to us."

She waved her hand helplessly at the mess. "What's the point? We don't have the money to replace this. We're done."

This caught my grandmother's attention. She marched over to us and yanked my aunt up with one hand. That old woman was *strong*. "I won't have any daughter of mine talking like that. You are a Macapagal and we do not give up. Now go call that detective and tell him to do his job. I'll start cleaning up."

Tita Rosie wiped her face with a napkin I handed her. "You're right, Nay. Let's get to work."

She scurried off to her office to make the call, but I stopped Lola Flor from walking into the kitchen. "Wait, Lola! We can't disrupt the crime scene." At her huff of impatience, I said, "We need to keep it preserved so the cops can document it for our insurance claim. We do have insurance on this place, right?"

Reluctantly, she nodded and stepped away. "Fine. But call your lawyer friend and tell him to get here right away. If the police are coming, we'll need him."

The health inspector sidled away as I waited for Amir to answer. "I'm obviously not needed today, so maybe we should—"

"Hey, you're not going anywhere," I said just as Amir picked up. "No, not you, Amir. I'm talking to the health inspector."

I explained what had happened and he promised to head over immediately. "Don't touch anything, make sure nobody leaves, and take pictures of everything for the insurance. Be there soon."

Mr. Long and the health inspector tried to leave while I was distracted, but my grandmother planted herself in their way and refused to move. Detective Park and his team arrived just in time to witness these middle-aged men get crossed over by a woman in her seventies.

"Mr. Long and Mr. Nelson, are you trying to leave a crime scene? You should know I'd have questions for anyone involved," Detective Park said, watching the tableau before him with amusement.

Mr. Long huffed. "I'm not involved and have nothing to say. Everything was like this when we got here. Also, why are you here? Does Shady Palms PD usually send a high-ranking detective to investigate vandalism? Or is this another favor being called in?"

"I'm here because this is still a crime scene in an ongoing investigation. I need to make sure these events are not connected in any way. If you're not involved, then you'll have no problem telling an officer what you saw when you got here." Detective Park waved one of his men over to interrogate Mr. Long and the health inspector. "Talk to these two separately, will you?"

The officer nodded and led Mr. Long away first for questioning. Detective Park turned his attention back to my grandmother and me. "So what happened here? Where's Rosie?"

Lola Flor pursed her lips. "We're not talking until our lawyer gets here."

Detective Park raised an eyebrow and looked at me. I shrugged. "What she said."

A police photographer moved through the wreckage of the kitchen, taking quick shots of everything. I did the same from the doorway, careful not to enter. Not only did I not want to contaminate the scene in any way, it no longer felt like a safe space. It was no longer our kitchen.

"You don't have to do that, you know. We could send copies of the photos to your insurance company," Detective Park said.

"And we'll of course be requesting those official photographs, Detective. But it never hurts to have a backup," Amir said, the tinkling of the door chimes announcing his arrival seconds before his voice did.

The look on Detective Park's face was difficult to read as he watched Amir make his way toward us. "Mr. Awan, come to save the day again. I sure hope this family is paying you well since you seem to be at their beck and call."

"And I hope you find out who is so obviously trying to put my clients out of business that they're willing to not only trash their restaurant, but also frame one of them for murder." Amir's smile was so sharp and cold I flinched, even though it wasn't directed at me. "We've both got a lot of work to do, Detective, so why don't you cut to the chase. Lila will go grab her aunt and the family can answer your questions."

"With you present, of course."

"Of course." Amir's expression relaxed a bit as he turned to me. "Can you call Auntie so we can get started?"

"It's OK, I'm here." Tita Rosie plodded toward us, her face still filled with grief but her voice clear and strong. She smiled at Amir and nodded at Detective Park. "Jonathan. Let's get this over with. I want to start cleaning as soon as your men are done in my kitchen."

Detective Park's face softened as he looked at her. "Rosie, I'm sure you don't believe me, but I'm very sorry about all that's happened. I just need your statement and I can assign some men to this case."

"You're not going to look into it yourself?" she asked.

He shook his head. "Already have my hands full with the Winter case and now the Spinelli assault. But don't worry, I trust—"

"Wait, don't you think this vandalism and your case are connected?" I asked.

"No comment," he said, readying his tablet. "Now, on to the questions."

We walked him through everything we'd seen and done, starting from when we got home last night until the cops arrived at the restaurant this morning.

Other than the questions he asked, Detective Park made no additional comments, just noted down the information as we gave it. When we finished the interview, he said, "OK, give me a moment while I go check on something."

We watched him converse with another officer, who pulled out his own tablet and seemed to be comparing notes with Detective Park. The detective nodded, seemingly satisfied, and made his way back to us.

"OK, your story checks out. The officer tailing Ms. Macapagal confirmed your alibis for last night."

Wait, someone was tailing me yesterday and I never even noticed?

My hands balled into fists. "You had someone spying on me? How dare you!"

"Ms. Macapagal, forgive me, but you're a suspect in both a homicide and a narcotics case. On top of that, you were also found at the scene of an assault. Only a fool would've let you out of their sight after that series of events. At the very least, we can clear you of vandalism. Judging by the lack of smell, the earliest this could've happened was last night. Your tail confirmed your whereabouts early Sunday. Also, the patrols were adamant neither you nor any member of your family left the house after our talk yesterday."

"Oh, goody for us." My initial instinct to react with sarcasm was quickly brushed aside when what he said sank in. "Wait, did you just say I was cleared of vandalism? You thought I destroyed my own restaurant? Me? Ruin the years of hard work that my aunt and grandmother put into this place? How could you even think such a thing?"

He shrugged. "It's not unheard of. You could've done it to throw us off your scent. Make your family out to be the victim, so that we focus on some phantom vandal instead of you. Or maybe you did it for insurance reasons."

I thought Lola Flor was going to spit in his face, she looked so disgusted with him. I put a hand on her arm and almost shook my head at her, but that would make her more likely to act out of spite.

Amir stepped between my grandmother and the detective. "Well, unfortunately for the Macapagal family, they are the victims." He gestured toward me. "My client is innocent of all these heinous crimes you seem desperate to pin on her, and I hope your department works quickly to find the true culprits."

Detective Park ignored him, closing his tablet with a snap. "Our interviews are done and we have the pictures we need. You might want to talk to Mr. Nelson and reschedule that health inspection, Rosie. Hate seeing this place closed down for so long."

My aunt didn't answer him, just turned around and marched back to her office. Lola Flor followed her. I stayed put, watching the cops pack up and leave as a unit.

Detective Park lingered for a moment before saying, "I was serious about hating to see this place closed down. Rosie is a good woman. You need to take better care of her. I don't think she's handling this well."

How dare he accuse me of not taking care of my aunt when he was one of the main reasons she was so stressed out?

The fury in my eyes must've been palpable because he took a step back. "Look, I'm just saying . . . call a cleaning service. Have it charged to the insurance. Don't let her put everything on her shoulders, OK?"

I didn't give a response and he didn't seem to be waiting for one. He turned his attention to Mr. Long and the health inspector, and I watched, confused, as Detective Park issued a warning to them. Something about not pulling any of that "funny business" here. What the heck was he talking about? Was Detective Park also investigating the scam Derek seemed to be pulling on local restaurants? That dude had his fingers in a lot of pies.

After the detective left, Amir cleared his throat and handed his business card to the health inspector. "I'll be contacting you with some concerns I have about your business practices, Mr. Nelson. You too, Mr. Long."

The health inspector nodded and hurried away without a word, but Mr. Long narrowed his eyes at us. "We're not done here. Not by a long shot."

Chapter Twenty-seven

Mr. Long's not-so-cryptic threat hung in the air long after he left, making me wonder what else was in store for my family. Was he trying to hint that the destroyed kitchen was only the beginning of our problems? Was that a confession?

I asked Amir as much.

He frowned. "I don't know, Lila. He definitely has it in for your family, but I have a hard time picturing him taking that kind of risk. He already knows you're having trouble with your bills. He could just wait for you to default on your payments and close you down without dirtying his hands."

"Well then feel free to brainstorm with me because I'm all out of ideas." I chewed on a fingernail, not even caring that I was getting a mouthful of glitter polish. Usually that was enough to deter me from this old habit, but today was a special occasion.

Tita Rosie and Lola Flor approached us, arms loaded down with cleaning supplies. "We're going to start cleaning up, Amir," my aunt said. "I'm sorry, but can we talk about how to file insurance claims and everything else later? I want to get this done as soon as possible."

"Of course, Auntie Rosie. But shouldn't you call a cleaning service for this? It's a lot of work and you'll probably be reimbursed by your insurance, if you're worried about the money."

Lola Flor dismissed that with a quick *psh*. "Pay good money for something we can do better ourselves? Forget it."

Knowing better than to argue with my grandmother, he said, "OK, I'll handle things on my end and be back soon." He gave a quick squeeze of my hand, nodded at my aunt and grandmother, and hurried out.

I went to the office to change into the spare clothes I kept around for cleaning, then walked back to the kitchen, hesitating at the doorway. I watched my aunt stoop over as she swept up the debris while my grandmother threw out everything that was left in the fridge, keeping up a steady stream of complaints and Tagalog curse words as she did so.

As I stood there, a silent observer of this tragedy, Tita Rosie straightened slowly, groaning as she rubbed the kinks out of her back. The fluorescent lighting picked up flecks of gray in her beautiful black hair, gray strands that weren't there when I first left for college. A collage of images overlaid themselves in my mind like a photo reel as I remembered watching this same sight year after year, her spirited movements becoming slower as time passed. It was there that it hit me: My aunt was getting old. Old and tired and massively overworked.

Detective Park was right. Tita Rosie needed looking after and there was no one else up to the job but me.

So I rolled up my sleeves and got to work.

I was hauling out yet another bag of trash when Amir and Adeena showed up. Bernadette, Marcus, and the Calendar Crew pulled up next to them, followed by Kevin.

"What are you all doing here?" I asked, nearly dropping the bag.

"Did you think we were going to let you handle this mess alone? Amir told us what happened. We're here to help." Adeena held up a bucket with cleaning supplies and rubber gloves.

"Just like Rosie and Flor not to say anything," Ninang April said as she pushed past me to enter through the back door of the kitchen. "What are they trying to prove?"

As expected, my aunt made a big fuss, thanking everyone for their time but insisting we didn't need help. "Besides, don't you all have work?"

"The coffee shop's closed on Mondays," Adeena said.

Kevin nodded. "Plus you've been so helpful lately, I figured it was time I extended a neighborly hand."

The Calendar Crew spent most of their time helping Ninang June run her late husband's business and had a side hustle selling things on eBay, so their schedules were extremely flexible.

"Well, what about you three?" Tita Rosie asked, looking at Amir, Bernadette, and Marcus. "You have a career. Very important jobs, diba?"

"We're both working the midafternoon shift," Bernadette said, gesturing to her and Marcus. "So as long as we leave before two, it's not a problem."

Amir shrugged. "You're my client, aren't you? So I'm technically working. And my prices are very steep."

My aunt bit her lip. "Oh Amir, I don't think I can—"

"A home-cooked dinner, including soup, a main dish, and one of Grandma Flor's fantastic desserts." He held out his hand. "Do we have a deal?"

Amazingly, it was my grandmother who responded. "You drive a hard bargain, young man. I like you." She shook his hand. "I expect everyone here at our house for dinner tonight at six. Now come on, we have a lot of work to do."

W e all attacked the place with vigor, only taking a brief break for lunch, which the aunties provided. After we ate, everyone went back to cleaning except for Bernadette and me, since I needed to take her to work. As I gathered my things, I noticed I had five missed calls and a bunch of texts. Mostly from Terrence.

"Oh, sugar," I said.

"'Sugar'?" Bernadette raised an eyebrow.

"Shut up, you know what it's like if you swear around Tita Rosie." I grabbed my stuff and hustled out to the car. "Let's make this quick. I was supposed to meet Terrence for lunch but forgot about it after all this mess."

As I eased the car onto the icy road, I figured now was the time to pump my cousin for information. After all, we were alone, so we didn't have to worry about anyone eavesdropping. Plus I could play the sympathy card since she saw how messed up Tita Rosie was about the restaurant.

I cleared my throat. "Speaking of Terrence, how's Janet doing?"

Bernadette twisted her lips, as if chewing on the words before deciding to speak them. "She seems responsive, so I think she'll be OK. The doctors are cautiously optimistic."

"That's great! I really wanted to see her, but they wouldn't let me. Do you think you could get me in?"

This time her lips thinned. She knew exactly what she wanted to say. "No, it's still family only. Besides, she's in a coma. There's nothing you can get from her."

My grip tightened on the wheel as the truth of that hit me. Why did I want to get in and see her so badly? What did I think I could accomplish?

"You feel guilty," Bernadette said, as if reading my thoughts.

I kept my eyes on the road.

"Look, Lila, from what I hear, she contacted you, right? She was the one who was trying to blackmail or negotiate or Lord knows what with her supposed info. She's a grown woman and she knew what she was doing."

Oh my gulay, was Bernadette actually trying to comfort me?

She must've read my expression because she said, "Don't get it twisted. You're still pretentious and full of yourself. But you're not like, a bad person or anything. And you are not the reason Janet's in a hospital bed. So stop pitying yourself and figure out who put her there."

I pulled in front of the hospital. Before exiting the car, she left one last barb. "Get over yourself, Lila. Tita Rosie needs you. She's needed you for a long time."

Chapter Twenty-eight

I thought about swinging by Adeena and Amir's place to go over what just happened, but Bernadette's remarks about my aunt played over and over in my head. She'd spent her entire life taking care of people, and it was my job now to pick up the slack. After all, wasn't that why I had come home?

Well, one of the reasons, anyway.

I called my aunt's cell to see where she was. "Hey, Tita Rosie. Are you still at the restaurant?"

"Oh hi, anak. No, I dropped off Marcus at work and now I'm at the grocery store picking up a few things for dinner. Do you want anything?"

"No, I'm OK. Just make sure to have at least one vegetarian option for Adeena, please. Oh, and no pork dishes since the Awans can't eat it."

She chuckled. "You act like this is the first time I've cooked for them. I'm not your lola, I remember these things."

I laughed, too. My grandmother, old school to the core, wasn't very sensitive or receptive when it came to people's dietary restrictions. I'd had to swoop in more than once when I knew she was pushing a dish on a customer that they couldn't or wouldn't eat. I should've known my aunt would understand.

"Thanks, Tita. I'll call Lola and ask if she needs a ride, then come home to tidy up a bit. You just focus on the cooking, OK?"

After we hung up, I called my grandmother. I figured she'd still be at the restaurant, so might as well play the filial granddaughter and offer her a ride. I lucked out—when she answered, she informed me she was already at home, which meant I didn't have to endure a car ride with just the two of us.

"OK Lola, I'm heading home to help clean. Tita Rosie should be back from the store soon, but do you need me to pick anything up?"

"No, just come home and start cleaning. This place is filthy!"

My grandmother's idea of "filthy" was the same as Marie Kondo's idea of "impeccably clean," but I hurried home anyway. I knew better than to question her.

An hour later, the house was gleaming, my grandmother's desserts were cooling on the counter, and the house was blessedly quiet since she wanted to nap before dinner. My aunt had called earlier to say she had another errand to run and was going to be back late.

So the kitchen was all mine, just the way I liked it.

My lola had made a few jars of her specialty, matamis na bao, or coconut jam, to spread on our pandesal and kakanin. The fragrant smell of coconut cream, caramelized sugar, and pandan leaves wafted through the room, the intoxicating aroma of the dark, sticky jam making my mouth water.

I scanned the contents of the fridge, waiting for inspiration to strike. Whatever I made had to be small and snack-y, so as to complement but not draw attention from my grandmother's sweet, sticky rice cakes.

Maybe some kind of cookie to go with our after-dinner tea and coffee? Coco jam sandwiched between shortbread would be great, but sandwich cookies were a little heavier and more fiddly than what I was looking for. Maybe if they were open-faced?

As I thought of a way to make that work, my eyes fell on the pandan extract in the cabinet and everything clicked into place. Pandan thumbprint cookies with a dollop of coconut jam! Pandan and coconut were commonly used together, plus the buttery and lightly floral flavor of the cookies would balance well against the rich, intense sweetness of the jam.

I had just removed the butter from the fridge when I heard the front door open and someone stomping in the hallway.

"Tita Rosie, is that you?"

"Lila, come help me with these bags!" was the response to my question.

I hurried out into the hall to bring the grocery bags into the kitchen while my aunt went back to her car for one more load. From the looks of things, she'd bought enough food to feed the entire neighborhood, let alone the dozen or so people expected to show up tonight. Her greatest nightmare was holding a party and not having enough food for everyone.

The horror.

After putting all the perishable items away into their respective compartments, I started washing and peeling the vegetables my aunt planned to use. "So what's on the menu?"

"Amir said he wanted soup and there's snow in the forecast, so I thought sopas would be a good starter since it's his favorite."

The creamy chicken soup with macaroni noodles was pure comfort in a bowl, yet light enough to leave room for more courses. Great choice, but . . .

"No soup for Adeena?"

"I've been experimenting with meat substitutes, and I actually found a great replacement for chicken. I also have some vegetable stock in the freezer. You won't even notice the difference. Just don't tell your lola, ha?"

Whoa, I knew she was conscientious, but I had no idea she was spending this much time making sure my best friend had something to eat. "Thank you, Tita. That's very thoughtful of you, and I'm sure we'll all love it. Everything you make is fantastic."

My aunt smiled and continued with her menu. "I'm also making lumpiang togue, adobong tokwa, pinakbet, and monggo guisado."

I breathed a sigh of relief. "Perfect."

My aunt was kind and loving and nurturing, but she had no head for finance. Her love of feeding and entertaining people usually rang up one heck of a grocery bill, but tonight's menu was not only delicious, it was downright frugal and vegetarian to boot.

The egg rolls were time-consuming to make, but the bean sprout filling was cheap and tasty. Besides, a party just isn't a party without lumpia. Fried tofu braised with soy sauce, vinegar, garlic, and peppercorns wouldn't exactly break the bank, and neither would the bitter melon and vegetable stir-fry. The mung bean stew was traditionally made with pork and topped with chicharon, but knowing Tita Rosie, she'd use some kind of pork substitute and leave the pork rinds on the side.

As I prepped the veggies for the stir-fry, she got started on the bean sprout filling. It needed plenty of time to cool, or else the spring roll wrappers would get soggy before we even fried them.

"So, Tita, you dropped Marcus off at work, right? Did he tell you anything more about the case?"

She stiffened, then went back to pulling the strings out of the bean sprouts as if I hadn't said anything.

I laid the knife down. "Tita? What did he say?"

She finished the bean sprouts and moved on to chopping the garlic and firm tofu. "Can you get the patis? I forgot to set it out."

I grabbed the bottle of fish sauce, one of the few strictly nonvegetarian things Adeena allowed herself, and handed it to her. "Tita Rosie, what did you talk about? Was it about the vandalism? Does he know more about Derek and the drugs?"

"Ay, Lila, stop worrying so much. Amir will handle everything when we go to court. It's fine."

I dropped the large piece of kalabasa I was peeling back onto the cutting board with a clatter. "Tita, we are not fine! I'm not a child anymore. You asked me to come back, you wanted my help with the business, fine. I'm here. The least you could do is tell me the truth."

My aunt stepped back, shock written all over her face. I never talked back. Even when I was a teenager, my biggest concession to a rebellious phase was perfecting my eye roll and heavy sigh. Oh, and my fashion choices, but that was more to bother Lola than her.

My stomach churned with guilt, but I stood my ground. I upended my life to move back home and save our family business (Which, OK, wasn't going so well, but still. My point stands.) Maybe I shouldn't have raised my voice to her, but I couldn't help out if I didn't have the truth.

My aunt seemed to have reached the same conclusion. "I don't appreciate your tone, but you're right. If I want your help, I have to be honest about our situation. But we can talk and work at the same time."

I picked up the squash I'd dropped onto the cutting board and finished peeling it before moving on to the carrots. "How bad is it?"

"Marcus told me he'd been talking to Joseph."

"Well, they are brothers. What's wrong with that?"

"They were talking about you getting arrested and Joseph told him about our financial situation."

"Oh." I forgot Joseph was also our accountant. "Is he allowed to do that?"

She shrugged. "Does it matter? Not like anything is a secret around your ninang. Anyway, our finances were already in trouble, but the bail money was supposed to cover this month's rent, and with Mr. Long after us . . ."

I did some quick mental math. "OK, we're about three months behind, but if I halt my student loan payments, we should be able to pay him off—"

"Lila, he wants everything paid in full by the first of the month."

It was already the eighteenth. "Oh my god, are you serious?"

Tita Rosie slammed her hand on the counter, making me jump. "In this house, we do not take the Lord's name in vain!"

"Sorry, Tita. But if we can't pay him back by the first . . ."

She nodded. "We lose the restaurant, even if you win your court case. The only reason we've been able to hold on to it so long is because his wife wouldn't let him kick us out. But I doubt she's going to intervene on our behalf if she thinks we killed her son."

My heart clenched. "Mrs. Winter thinks we killed Derek?"

"She's Mrs. Long now," she reminded me. "I don't think she knows what to believe. But she's grieving and her husband is insisting we're to blame. She'll probably take any explanation as to why she's lost her only child."

Oh man, I totally forgot Derek was an only child. It was one of the things we'd bonded over, though he didn't have the extended family that I did. I should probably visit Mrs. Winter, I mean Long, at home later to pay my respects. Or would that be awkward? Maybe I should just wait for his funeral? What was the etiquette when you were suspected of killing someone's only child?

"So what are our options?" I asked.

"Get the restaurant open ASAP and earn enough money to pay him back. There are no other options."

"That's not very encouraging, Tita."

"It's only a problem if we fail. And we're not going to fail because we have you now, diba."

Oh great. So calling me back home was our Hail Mary play?

Yeah, no pressure.

Chapter Twenty-nine

After Tita Rosie dropped the bombshell that she was counting on me to somehow make the restaurant (our currently closed and trashed restaurant, by the way) turn enough profit to pay back three months' worth of rent in less than two weeks, Lola Flor decided to make her grand entrance. This meant all talk of money went out the window and we spent the next hour and a half bickering about the "lazy" way I chopped vegetables.

My aunt, in an attempt to redirect the conversation, asked, "So how did your lunch with Terrence go? You were supposed to meet him today, weren't you?"

Oh no, I totally forgot to call Terrence back after dropping off Bernadette. My conversation with her had turned my attention to my aunt and I completely blanked on him. And my non-date with Jae was supposed to be happening in a couple of hours, too. "Oh sh—shoot, I forgot about Terrence! I'm supposed to meet Dr. Jae tonight, too. I have to make a couple calls."

I washed my hands and dashed out to the living room. I really hated the phone, but considering I had stood up Terrence and was canceling on Jae at the last minute, again, I should do them both the courtesy of a phone call rather than a text.

Terrence, thankfully, didn't pick up. Nobody actually listened to their voice mails anymore, so I sent him a quick text explaining what'd happened and begging his forgiveness. His response came less than a minute later, meaning he'd been screening my call. All he said was,

I understand. See you tomorrow.

Oof, that period after 'see you tomorrow' felt super aggressive. Also, see me tomorrow? Was he trying to reschedule? Before I could text back, Jae messaged me.

My brother just told me about your restaurant.
You OK?

I smiled. How thoughtful of him! Not just that he was checking on me, but that he texted first instead of calling. I selected the "Call" option on his contact and he picked up right away.

"Lila! How are you? I'm guessing we should postpone dinner again?"

"Hey, Jae. Yeah, I'm sorry to ditch you again, but—"

"No worries, I understand. Your family needs you. You still busy cleaning up? I can stop by to help."

"Aww, that's sweet, but we had a bunch of people volunteer to help us clean. We got the place in great shape, but to thank them, my aunt and grandma are cooking up a big meal for everyone. They're insisting I be here to show my appreciation for everyone."

"Wow, that . . . that sounds really nice. It's great that you have so many friends willing to help you out."

He sounded so wistful, I wondered what his deal was. Then I remembered how happy he was to be out at dinner with me and Adeena. That he lived alone and didn't have many friends in town.

"Hey, I hope this isn't too weird, but would you like to join us for dinner? My family always makes way too much food, and my aunt really likes your brother. I'm sure she'd love to meet you as well."

"Yes! What time? Should I bring anything?"

Pretty sure his eagerness was because he couldn't stomach another night alone or with his parents, but I still flattered myself that I was part of the draw.

"Hold on, let me ask."

I wandered into the kitchen. "Tita, what time are people coming over? I invited Detective Park's brother to dinner and he wants to know if he should bring anything."

"Why? Does he think we won't feed him properly?" my grandmother asked. "What would he need to bring?"

"Lola, he's just being polite. People usually bring like, wine or dessert or something."

"Bring dessert? Into my house?"

Tita Rosie cut in. "Tell him that we don't need anything, but thanks for the offer. And everyone's coming over at six o'clock."

I went into the other room and relayed the information. "Don't you dare bring food or dessert into this house or my grandma will kill you. Wine is a possibility, but my aunt doesn't drink and we don't even own wineglasses."

He laughed. "Yeah, I overheard. I'm looking forward to meeting your grandmother. I'll just bring flowers or something. And did I hear your aunt say six o'clock?"

"Yeah, but we all run on Brown People Time. Do not come at six, you'll just stress everyone out. Any time after seven should be safe."

He chuckled. "Sure are a lot of rules when coming over to your place."

I laughed. "Just be glad we're not dating. The level of scrutiny you'd be under has made tougher men than you crack under the pressure."

He was silent for a moment. "I bet I could handle it."

That was . . . not the response I was expecting. "Oh, um, I'm sure you could." A beat passed. "Anyway, see you tonight?"

"After seven o'clock, bearing zero edible items, and ready to run through the gauntlet. See you later, Lila."

Chapter Thirty

Jae was still the first person to arrive.

At seven o'clock on the dot, the doorbell rang and there he was on my doorstep bearing a gorgeous bouquet of lilacs. "Hey, Lila! Thanks again for inviting me. I didn't even think to ask if it would be awkward of me to come since my brother . . . you know . . ."

"Don't worry about it. You did say that he can't tell you who to be friends with, right? Though, if you could throw a good word about me his way, I wouldn't complain." I buried my face in the purple petals perfuming the room with their sweet scent. "Anyway, how did you know lilacs were my favorite?"

He grinned. "I got lucky. Purple is my favorite color and 'lilac' is pretty close to 'Lila,' so they reminded me of you." He sniffed the air. "Man, it smells good in here. Where's the rest of your family? I should probably say hi, right?"

"My aunt and grandmother are still cooking, so I'll introduce you when they're done. Take off your shoes and have a seat in the living room while I find a vase for these."

Longganisa waddled in from the kitchen and made herself comfortable at Jae's feet. "Oh sorry, I forgot to tell you I had a dog. You're not allergic or anything, are you?"

Jae reached down to scratch Nisa's head, and she responded by flopping on her back for a good belly rub, which he obliged. "Don't worry about it. I've always wanted a dog, but my mom never let me have one. What's his name?"

"Her name is Nisa, short for Longganisa."

"Like the sausage?"

At my nod, he said, "That is adorable! I think I'll have to call her by her full name because it's too cute." Jae rubbed her belly and addressed her in a baby voice. "Isn't that right, Longganisa?"

Be still my heart.

While they played together, I continued my search for a vase. The doorbell rang as I climbed on a chair to grab one out of the top cabinet in the kitchen. I called out, "Jae, sorry, but could you get that for me?"

I heard the door open and an exchange of male voices, then silence after the door closed.

Curious, I headed into the living room with the vase in one hand and the flowers in another. Amir and Jae sat across the room from each other, each sizing up the other in silence. Strange. Amir could charm a wall and Jae was so friendly. I was sure they'd be chatting away.

Amir spotted me and jumped up for a quick hug, made rather awkward since I was still holding the vase and flowers.

"Hey, Amir, you made it! Where's Adeena?" I asked.

"She said she'd be riding over with her new friend. She didn't tell you?"

I looked at my phone notifying me I had seven unread messages.

"Oh, she probably did, but I missed her texts. I put my phone on silent earlier and forgot to turn the sound back on."

Jae, still stroking Nisa, who was perched on his lap, joined in our conversation. "Ah, that explains why you never answered if your family preferred coffee or tea. I figured those were safe beverages to bring, but when you didn't respond, I decided to get the flowers."

"Oh, that reminds me, can you arrange these for me?" I asked Jae, handing him the flowers and vase. "I need to put Nisa in my room since Amir's allergic to dogs."

Amir eyed the bouquet, then Jae. "You got Lila her favorite flowers."

Jae met his gaze. "Seems that way."

The silence that stretched out after that statement seemed to last five hours, but was probably only five seconds. I cleared my throat, excusing myself to put Nisa in my room and wash my hands. When I returned, the men were still silent, so I did my best to resume the conversation.

"Sorry about not answering your text, Jae. I love beverages of all kinds. I'm usually a coffee person, but I can appreciate a nice cup of tea. It depends on what I'm pairing the drink with."

"Which reminds me . . ." Amir went over to the bag he'd left on the couch. "Mom just got back from visiting her sister in Turkey. She brought back that apple tea you love, as well as the Arabic coffee you tried last time you visited."

"Ooh, with the cardamom?"

He nodded. "She knows you like to grind the beans yourself, so it's just the roasted coffee with a packet of cardamom pods and instructions. She said she also likes to toss in a pinch of saffron or rosewater for special occasions."

I read over the instructions, which included a note on the variations Amir mentioned and insisted Arabic coffee be served with dates or a sweet treat. "Very decadent. I love it! I'll have to come over some-time and thank her personally."

He smiled. "You know you're always welcome in our home."

Jae had moved away and was examining the pictures on our walls, but noticeably stiffened up when Amir said that. I decided to lighten the mood.

I forced a laugh. "Well, I'm not always welcome, if you'll recall. Your dad has feelings about me 'corrupting' your poor, unsuspecting sister."

Jae wandered back toward us. "Really? You corrupted Adeena? I always figured it was the other way around."

"You know my sister?" Amir turned his attention to Jae.

"Yeah, the cafe is in the same plaza as my dental office, so I stop by pretty often."

"Oh, so is that how you met Lila, too? Eating at Auntie Rosie's restaurant?"

Jae's cheeks flushed. "No, I, uh, haven't had time."

Sensing Jae's embarrassment, Amir pushed harder. "Why not? Auntie Rosie makes some of the best food in town and it's right by your office. You have time for a hipster cafe but not to support a family restaurant? Your brother visits all the time."

I glared at him. "Amir, it is none of your business where this man does and does not eat. Leave him alone."

Perhaps spurred on by my defense, Jae put his hand on my arm. "Lila, it's OK. I'm sure you wondered, too, but were too polite to ask." He sighed. "My mom stops by the office and drops off lunch for me every day. Then I usually go over to my parents' for dinner after work."

He glanced at Amir, who, to his credit, wasn't laughing, though he clearly wanted to. "I've asked her to stop making extra work for herself, but then she gets mad at me."

My aunt entered the room at that moment. "Of course she does.

She's doing that because she loves you and you don't appreciate all the effort that goes into it." She held out her hand. "Dr. Park, right? I've heard a lot about you from Jonathan."

Jae shook her hand. "I'm Jae. And I've heard a lot about you, too. I've been wanting to come over to thank you for that delicious tray of noodles you dropped off when I first arrived but, well . . ."

She smiled at him. "Try not to get too frustrated with your mother. She's just showing her love the way she knows how. It doesn't matter that you're an adult and can take care of yourself. In her eyes, you'll always be the bunso, the baby of the family."

He groaned. "Trust me, I know. They never let me forget I'm the maknae."

The doorbell rang again, and Tita Rosie went to go answer it.

"Does your family really call you maknae?"

"No, we don't speak a ton of Korean at home. But my mom makes sure we use all the correct honorifics and things like that with our elders."

"Oh, that's similar to me. I understand Tagalog but don't speak it much."

"Of course you don't. Your generation has no respect for tradition. No interest in learning about your heritage." My grandmother hobbled into the room at that moment with a tray of drinks in her hand. "Lila, our guests have been here how long and you haven't given them any refreshments?"

I bit back a retort. It was bad manners on my part to have Amir and Jae over without offering them anything, but I didn't have to agree with her.

Before I could get their drink requests, Jae asked, "Wait, is your name pronounced LY-la or LEE-la? Because I've been saying LY-la, but your grandmother just called you . . ."

I smiled at him. "Yeah, I know. Technically, it's 'LEE-la,' but only my family pronounces it that way. In school, the teachers would always pronounce it the other way and I got tired of correcting them. I just started introducing myself that way since it was easier."

Lola Flor shook her head. "How could you let other people tell you how to pronounce your own name? It's not even difficult."

OK, now my grandmother was sounding like Adeena. Also, I did not appreciate her being right about two things in a row.

Luckily, my aunt came back in the room at that moment with the Calendar Crew, plus Adeena, Elena, Bernadette, and Kevin. "Seems like everyone's here. Marcus can't make it, so remind me to set aside a plate for him. Should we get started?"

Chapter Thirty-one

"That was amazing! And it was all vegetarian?" Jae asked, scraping the last bits of rice off his plate. When my aunt nodded, he said, "I'm going to make it a point to stop by for dinner once you open back up."

"Wait till you try my sweets," Lola Flor said, sizing him up. "Good-looking, but you need a little meat on your bones. Don't you want to be strong like your brother?" She stood up without waiting for his answer. "Lila, help me serve."

I followed her into the kitchen, dreading what was about to come. And sure enough . . .

"So, he's a dentist? Good job. Means he's smart and very stable."

I made a noncommittal noise as I helped her set out the plates of various kakanin, sweet sticky rice cakes served with the coconut caramel spread she'd made earlier. On a separate tray, I laid out my thumbprint cookies as well as the mugs for the coffee and tea.

My grandmother watched me work, eyes narrowed at the cookies. After a beat, she asked, "He's your new boyfriend?"

"What?" Even though I knew it was coming, the question startled me enough that I missed the handle when reaching for the electric kettle and burned myself on the hot steel. Running my aching fingers under cool water, I said, "Of course not, Lola, why would you ask that?"

"He wasn't part of the restaurant cleanup, which means you invited him separately. Then he shows up with your favorite flowers. What am I supposed to think?"

The Calendar Crew came in at that moment, on the pretense of seeing if we needed help. Catching the last bit of what Lola Flor said, they all jumped in with their own observations.

"And do you see how he looks at Lila? Diyos ko, I think he's in love already!"

"Never mind Lila. Do you see how Amir and Jae looked at each other? I sense a love triangle!"

"Hmm, a lawyer or a dentist. Both very good choices. I mean, since Lila decided my Marcus and Joseph weren't good enough for her," Ninang Mae added with a sniff.

All four of them stood in a semicircle in front of me, staring in a way that I could only describe as ravenous. Not for blood, but for some good ol' tsismis.

I pulled a tube of antibacterial ointment out of one of the drawers and carefully rubbed some on my burnt fingers, avoiding everyone's eyes. "Everybody's waiting for dessert, so I think we should go back out there. Can you three please help me with the drinks?"

Ninang June winked at me as she picked up the teapot. "OK, but you can't avoid the question forever. You know we don't forget."

With that slightly ominous proclamation, we headed back to the dining room, where everyone was chatting in twos: Adeena and Elena, Amir and Kevin, and Jae and Bernadette, with Tita Rosie piling extra helpings on everyone's plates.

Ninang June sidled up to me. "Better move fast or Bernie will be the one with the doctor husband."

Sighing deeply but somehow refraining from rolling my eyes, I set my tray of cookies on the table and started toward Adeena and Elena, then realized I should give them some time to get to know each other. I veered over toward Amir and Kevin instead.

"Hey guys, can I interest you in a beverage and some sweets?" I waved my hand toward the kakanin and coco jam thumbprint cookies. I poured Amir his usual cup of coffee with two sugars and a big glug of cream, then some Darjeeling for myself. "Kevin?"

Kevin looked intimidated by the array of sweet rice cakes in different shapes and colors. "Some coffee would be great. Black, please. And can I try a little of everything?"

"Of course." I served him, then dished up some kakanin and several cookies to share with Amir. I was so used to sharing dishes with the Awans that I thought nothing of it till Kevin asked, "So how long have you two been dating?"

I choked on my tea. "What? We're not dating."

Kevin scratched the back of his head. "Sorry, I just thought it was real sweet that you know how he takes his coffee without asking him. And how you're sharing a dessert plate."

"Oh, well..." I glanced around the table and saw that we had everyone's attention. My godmothers were all grinning, but both Adeena and Jae wore frowns.

Kevin tried to cover up his gaffe by gushing over the food. He popped a cookie in his mouth and said, "Whoa, these are fantastic! I better be careful, between Adeena's drinks and your desserts, the two of you are going to put me out of business."

Adeena responded, "That's right!" at the same time I laughed, saying, "You have nothing to worry about there."

We both stopped and stared at each other, trying to figure out how serious the other one was about what we'd just said.

Amir swooped in to smooth over the situation. "Adeena and Lila have joked around about opening their own place someday, but we all know that's a pipe dream, right?" He glanced over at his sister, noting her expression. "What's wrong?"

"Nothing," she said in a way that meant, "Oh you know *exactly* what's wrong."

Amir was usually pretty attuned to people's emotions, but his ability didn't extend to his sister. Funny how one's self-awareness went totally out the window when it came to family. "Really? Then why are you making that face?"

"This is just my face, Amir Bhai. Now drop it." Adeena turned her back to us and resumed her conversation with Elena, who (bless her) continued talking to Adeena as if the whole exchange hadn't happened.

"So, Kevin," I said, desperate to change the subject. "Tell me about yourself. I don't know much about you, other than your terrible taste in pastry companies. What brought you to Shady Palms?"

He played with the crumbs on his plate. "Not too much to tell. I was adopted when I was a baby by a family in Minneapolis, but my mom told me that my biological parents were originally from Shady Palms. Stopped by last year to try and learn more about them and just really fell in love with the small-town vibe. I was a barista back home, so when I saw the coffee shop going for so cheap, it felt like kismet. I was meant to stay here."

I couldn't imagine anyone falling in love with Shady Palms, but I understood the pull of reconnecting with your roots. I was lucky to have Tita Rosie (and I guess Lola Flor and the Calendar Crew) around to talk to me about my parents. "Were you able to find your family?"

"Sort of. They cut out years ago. But from what I learned, giving me up for adoption was the kindest thing they could've done."

Ninang Mae frowned. "How could you say that? They were your family, doesn't that mean anything? Anyway, who are your people? I probably know them."

Before he could answer, Jae, who'd been trapped in conversation with a Bernadette on the prowl, leaned over toward us. "So have you always wanted to run a small-town cafe? Seems like a pretty big decision to make on a whim. I mean, there are coffee shops in Minneapolis, right?"

I smiled at Jae, glad to find someone who agreed with me. "Seriously. You're not much older than I am. This is one of the last places I'd think to open a high-end cafe."

Bernadette, pouting a little at losing Jae's attention, said, "Who cares why he did it? Thanks to him, we finally have a cool place to hang out and get some decent coffee in this town."

Adeena smiled at Kevin, but there was a tinge of sadness to it that I didn't understand. "I'm glad that Lila is *clearly* wrong and there's *obviously* a demand for a nice cafe here in Shady Palms. We're lucky to have you. Especially after . . ." She shook her head. "Anyway, thanks to you I'm learning a lot. You must be the only person in town who provided something that Derek deemed worthy."

Kevin shifted in his seat. "I don't know about that. I mean, it's not like I really knew the guy."

"What are you talking about? He came in every day and would only let you make his drink." She rolled her eyes at the rest of the table. "According to Derek, Kevin was the only one who could brew it right."

Bernadette agreed, smiling down the table at Kevin. "I'm addicted to the drinks at Java Jo's. Every other place in this town serves that cheap, burned sh—um, stuff, that doesn't deserve to be called coffee. Or that gross instant junk. No offense, Tita," she quickly added.

Lola Flor snorted. "We can't all have such refined tastes as you,

Little Miss Prinsesa. You go ahead and pay five dollars for a cup of coffee with a silly name that tastes like every other cup of coffee. Ridiculous."

Tita Rosie shook her head at her mother, then asked Kevin, "What about your family in Minneapolis? Do they ever come visit you here?"

Kevin squirmed in his chair, probably wondering why dinner had turned into an interrogation. "Not really. It was just my adoptive mom and sister. And me. They're both gone now," he added, with a note of finality.

After that, it was hard to go back to the levity of the previous conversations. I tried to engage with Adeena and Elena several times, asking Elena to tell us about her family since Kevin shared about his, but Adeena kept boxing me out. Eventually, Elena and I both shrugged and stopped trying to force it.

The dinner party broke up soon after that, with people packing up leftovers to take home with them. Jae thought he was being polite by refusing to take anything, but that just made my grandmother extra fierce about loading him down with plastic takeout containers. He looked over at me to save him, so I said, "Lola, don't forget to pack some baon for Marcus."

Tita Rosie said, "Oh no, I forgot about him!" and flew around gathering the last of the food to give to Ninang Mae.

Jae mouthed, "Thanks" to me and I winked at him. Or at least tried to. I wasn't sure how successful the maneuver was because Amir caught the exchange and looked at me funny. I probably wasn't smooth enough to pull off winking.

"Amir Bhai, let's go. I have work in the morning." Adeena waited by the entrance, already suited up for the wintry outdoors.

"Huh?" Amir pulled his gaze away from me and Jae. "I thought you were riding with Elena?"

"Nope. I'm riding with you and we have to leave now," she said, heavy emphasis on the last word. "Thanks for dinner, Auntie Rosie and Grandma Flor! Everything was delicious."

"Yeah, I'll definitely have to stop by once your restaurant is open," Elena said. "Thanks for having me over. And, Lila, great seeing you again," she said, giving me a quick hug.

"Of course. Hope we can hang out soon."

She glanced over at Adeena, who was making a big show of not listening in, and said, "Come by the restaurant. You know we'll feed you good."

And with that, the three of them left, Adeena pushing a protesting Amir out the door. "Wait, I wanted to stay longer! OK, thanks, bye!" he called over his shoulder as she hustled him out.

"That was strange," Bernadette said. "She mad at you?"

I rubbed my right temple. "Yeah, probably."

Jae raised his eyebrows. "What for?"

"For something I've been avoiding for a really long time." At his confused look, I added, "Our dreams seem to have gone in different directions. I thought she was just joking, but now I don't know. We probably need to have a talk."

He nodded, still slightly confused but hanging in there. "OK, so I guess that's my cue to leave as well. Thanks for the lovely dinner and for inviting me into your home. You'll have to come over sometime so I can return the favor."

Bernadette glared at him for a moment before shaking her head. "Seriously, Jae? You, too? Ugh, I'm out." She grabbed her leftovers. "See you later, titas. Lola." She nodded at me and Jae, then headed out the door.

Jae stared after her. "Wait, is she mad at me? What did I do?"

I sighed. The men in my life were denser than my grandmother's rice cakes. "Good night, Jae. Let's do this again sometime."

Then I pushed him out the door before my family made the situation even more awkward than it already was.

I went back into the dining room, where my godmothers were cleaning up. "So Lila, did you learn anything about the case tonight?" Ninang Mae asked.

Once they removed all the dishes, I began wiping down the table. "What was there to learn? Nobody talked about the case. They were all just here to have a good time."

My godmothers exchanged glances. "I see," Ninang June said. "You really weren't paying attention, were you?"

"Well, it's to be expected. Jae and Amir were very distracting," Ninang Mae said with a wink. "Though, honestly, you invited the brother of the detective on your case and didn't think to ask him anything about it?"

"She's still got a lot to learn," Ninang April added as she put on her coat.

After the day I'd just had, my godmothers' nonsense was extra frustrating. I threw up my hands. "A lot to learn about what?"

"Life," Lola Flor said, sneaking up behind me. "She's right. But enough about that, you better get ready for bed. Another big day tomorrow."

"Yeah? What's so special about tomorrow?"

"Derek's wake."

Chapter Thirty-two

Despite my best intentions to follow Lola's advice and sleep early, I couldn't. I spent half the night sending texts to Adeena that went unanswered while avoiding Amir's suddenly pressing need to talk to me. He called no fewer than three times, but didn't leave a message or send any texts, so it couldn't be anything too urgent. Besides, I did not have the bandwidth to deal with him after the day I'd just had.

I woke up foggy-headed and grumpy, so after a light breakfast of coffee, pandesal, and coco jam, Nisa and I went out for a run. But even that provided no relief, as my steps became more and more plodding and Nisa seemed more interested in marking various banks of snow than helping me get out of my funk. I called Adeena when I got back home, but still no answer. Thought about leaving a voice mail but decided against it. While showering, I formulated the next steps of my investigation.

Derek's wake wasn't until one p.m., so I thought I'd swing by another place on the suspect list for an early lunch. I'd originally planned on staying home and spending time with Tita Rosie, but she was busy preparing food and refreshments for the service. I would've helped her, but she waved me away, happier than I'd seen in a while—Mrs. Long had assigned her the task and my aunt wanted to give it her all. Strange that Mrs. Long would solicit the help of an accused murderer—according to her husband—but she knew us well enough to know my aunt was innocent. After all, Mrs. Long had spent quite a bit of time at our restaurant back when Derek and I were dating. Tita Rosie still visited her to drop off food since her chronic pain sometimes kept her in bed for days at a time.

So either she trusted us completely or Derek's death had left her even more lost and helpless than I thought.

Pierogi Palace was next on the list, but when I got there, a sign stated they were closed "indefinitely." I was sitting in the car, staring at that sign and wondering what my next move should be, when I got a text.

> **Hey its elena**
>
> **Can you come by the restaurant**
>
> **We need to talk**

Well that sounded ominous. It did solve my problem of what to do next though, and I needed to talk to her about last night. Might be a good chance to pump her for info without Adeena hovering over my shoulder.

As soon as I got to El Gato Negro, Elena hustled me toward a secluded table in the corner. "Thanks for coming on such short notice. I'll be back in a minute to take your order."

The place was bustling and it took awhile before she could make her way back to me. I placed my order (the goat taco special and agua de jamaica to drink) and when she came back with my food, she sat down with her own plate.

"It's my lunch break, so I thought we could talk and eat at the same time. Cool?"

I nodded and we both dug in, focusing on our food rather than conversation for the next few minutes. I made quick work of the first two tacos on my plate and was starting on my third when Elena cleared her throat.

"So you're probably wondering why I asked you to come over. And how I got your number."

Understatement, but OK. "I'm assuming you got my number from Adeena."

She shook her head. "Adeena got really pissed when I asked her, actually. That's part of what I want to talk to you about."

I sipped at my iced hibiscus tea, wondering where this was going.

"Amir was the one who gave me your number. He also gave me his card last night, saying he heard my family was a suspect in Derek's murder. Wanted me to contact him if anything happened, or if I remembered something that could help your case." She crumbled a chip into little pieces on her plate. "Is it true you're investigating Derek's death?"

Way to alert our suspects, Awan family.

"Not exactly. Just asking a few questions here and there. The sooner they wrap up the case, the sooner my family's life goes back to normal."

Elena crossed her arms and glared at me. "And you think my family had something to do with his death?"

I clutched at my cup. "It's not like that. I'd heard rumors about your aunt and uncle having to close up shop and I wanted to see if they might've targeted him for revenge. Then it turns out they're not even around anymore and you and your mom took over and Adeena really likes you and I don't know what to think about anything."

I let out the breath I'd been holding and threw back the last of my agua de jamaica as if it were a shot of tequila. Oh, I wish, I wish.

Elena softened. "I totally understand your instinct to protect your family. And after meeting them last night, I also know there's no way your family had anything to do with Derek's death. I want to help. That's why I called you over."

I'd been staring into my empty glass feeling sorry for myself, but looked up at that last line. "Really? Why?"

She ran her hand through her gorgeous hair, which was even thicker and unrulier than Adeena's. "I like Adeena, too. But whatever problems you have are between the two of you. Derek, however? Totally involves me. He messed with my family and I'm not letting him mess with another one."

I took out my phone and pulled up my Notes app. "Don't get mad, but I'm going to ask some really personal questions. I'm not judging you or anything, just looking for the truth and how it all fits together." She nodded, so I started with, "You said you went on a few dates with Derek. What happened?"

"Ugh, of all the places to start." Now she was the one clutching her glass as if it were a shot. "He started coming around the restaurant last fall. My uncle and his family had already left, but my mom was determined to get everything back for him. Even called me to come back home and help out."

"You're not from around here?"

"I'm from Cicero, but my mom moved here after I went away to college. U of I," she said, answering my unasked question. "I'd already graduated, but had planned on sticking around for the summer to finish my internship then find a job in the city. But family came first."

How she said that without a hint of sarcasm or bitterness, I had no idea. There was more than a touch of sadness though. The two of us needed to have a night out with Jae where we drowned our sorrows and family expectations in booze and karaoke.

She toyed with the straw in her glass. "I was happy to help at first. I thought my mom had the right idea in fighting for my Tío Hector and his family. But I had no clue how much work it was to run your own restaurant. I was a server and hostess through most of college, so I knew it wasn't easy. Still didn't prepare me for the stress of having to run it all with just my mom to rely on instead of a full staff."

"I get that, but in the reverse. I grew up in the restaurant biz, so I've never known anything else. It wasn't until I went away to school and worked at places that weren't my aunt's that I saw the responsibility she carried and really appreciated all the work she'd put in. It's how I knew I wanted a place of my own someday, rather than running someone else's dream."

She smiled. "My mami would like you. All that ambition. Anyway, the first month of getting this place up and running was a nightmare. Barely any sleep. No days off. Even when we were closed, we were working. And my mom knows how to run small businesses, but a restaurant is a completely different beast. Figuring how much to order and of what and from who, and what all the regulations are and trying to remember that what works in a home kitchen absolutely does not work the same in a professional one. Things like that."

Like with Yuki, the vibes I got from Elena told me more about her relationship with Derek than she was letting on. "I'm guessing this is where Derek comes in? You saw him as a stress-reliever, a way to have some fun in this tiny town?"

Her jaw dropped. "How did you know? He started coming around and was so cute! And sweet and charming and I should've known he was up to no good."

"You didn't know who he was? Your mom never told you?"

"She did, actually, but not till after we'd already gone out a few times. She works the back of the house, doing all the cooking and paperwork, so she doesn't interact with our customers. She only saw us together 'cause he came by to pick me up one day after we'd closed."

I grinned. "How'd she take it?"

She groaned. "You got that look on your face, you know exactly how she took it. My sweet, hippie, makes-her-own-soap-and-insists-on-organic-products mother went off on him. She actually took off her shoe and threatened him with it. It was intense."

Ah, the power of the chancla/tsinelas. I sipped at the water glass I had ignored earlier in favor of my hibiscus tea. "I'm surprised you didn't go all star-crossed lovers and insist that you wanted to be together."

"Eww, first of all, Romeo and Juliet are not relationship goals. Second, in that story, it was the parents who did all the shady stuff. Romeo and Juliet were innocent. But Derek? He was one hundred percent to blame when it came to what happened to my uncle. He chose to write those lies. He chose not to correct the rumors that started going around because of his reviews. And I'm sure it was him who sicced that crooked-ass health inspector on us. So eff that dude."

The health inspector again. Interesting. "What makes you think Derek had anything to do with the health inspector?"

"Because the health inspector is best friends with his stepdad. And you don't find it suspicious that just when those negative reviews came out, the health inspector suddenly decided to pay us a visit? I don't know what their deal was, but there's something more going on there."

I filed that away to talk about with the other restaurant owners later. "Did you accuse him of any of this?"

"No, I just slapped the shit out of him after my mom let me know who he was. Told him never to come near my family again or he'd regret it. And I know how that sounds. But I didn't kill him and neither did anyone else in my family."

I nodded, wondering how to phrase my next question without making it seem like I didn't believe her. "When was the last time you saw him?"

"He never came by the restaurant again, I can tell you that. My mom hired a couple of my guy cousins to bus tables and keep an eye out for him. I ran into him a few times at Java Jo's, so I stopped going there. Nice to know I can go back there for my caffeine fix. Especially now that I know Adeena."

She had a sweet, goofy look on her face as she thought about Adeena, but my next question wiped the smile off her face. "What about your cousins? Where were they when Derek died? Did they have beef with him?"

She shook her head. "They knew better than that. It's one thing if Derek were to come into our restaurant and they needed to throw him out. But they're not foolish enough to go looking for him. Two Mexican boys from Cicero beating up a White boy from Shady Palms? How you think that'd go for them?"

Good point. And yet I had to say, "True. If he'd been beaten to death, it'd make more sense for it to be them. But he was poisoned. And you and your mom work with all kinds of stuff that could be toxic if ingested or used in large amounts."

I'd looked up details on making your own soap and cosmetics and was surprised at how many people dabbled with potentially dangerous substances. On top of their organic cosmetics and bath products, they offered herbal teas and supplements, as well as both fresh and dried herbal arrangements. It was a stunning array, but what interested me most were the various warnings attached to the products. And when I looked up the individual plants that were listed as ingredients, it was like a laundry list of poisons growing in their own personal greenhouse.

She clenched her jaw. "You're one step behind, Lila. You think the cops didn't come check out our greenhouse after finding out Derek was poisoned? They said nothing we had matched what was in his system."

"Oh."

"'Oh' is right. Plus how would we even get him to ingest it? You'd know if we were anywhere near your place. When could we have put it in his food?"

Oh, sugar. It just kept coming back to that point, didn't it? We were the ones with the most access to his food when he died. What did they say cops looked for? Means, motive, and opportunity? Based on what the police found, we easily fit all three. If only Adeena's friend in the lab would hurry up with the results, we might be able to shift the focus away from us.

I buried my face in my hands. "Sorry. I'm so bad at this. It's way easier when I have Adeena with me since we can play off each other. I just sound like a jerk when I try to question people."

Elena put her hand on my arm. "It's OK. Not like you have a ton of experience doing this kind of thing. But you need to make up with Adeena. For your friendship, and because it's safer with the two of you together. What if I hadn't had good intentions? I just texted you to come over here with no explanation. What if I was the killer? Did you tell anyone you were coming here?"

I bit my lip and shook my head, my cheeks flushing a deep red.

"See? Talk to Adeena. Or get any of the people I met last night to go with you. They seem to care about you a lot."

That seemed excessive. I mean, I'd lived on my own in Chicago for years, it wasn't like I needed a chaperone now. I was perfectly capable of running around solo during the day at least.

These mutinous thoughts must've shown on my face because she said, "Doesn't matter that it's daytime. Derek died during the day, right? His killer is still out there. And you haven't exactly been subtle with your questions. Watch yourself."

I didn't know what to say to that, so I made a big show of looking at the time on my phone. "Thanks, Elena. I appreciate you reaching out. Got to get ready for the wake though, so can I get the check?"

She stood up and began clearing the table. "It's on me." When I started to protest, she said, "I expect you to respond in kind once Tita Rosie's Kitchen opens again, OK? This isn't charity."

Instinctively, I reached over and gave her a big hug. She hesitated, then wrapped her arms around me. "We got your back, chica." She pulled away but took my hands in hers. "Be safe, OK? And go catch that killer."

Chapter Thirty-three

The Johannsen Funeral Home was the only funeral home in Shady Palms. While there were a good handful of places of worship scattered throughout the town, the Johannsen family held the monopoly on death. Housed in a sober, nondescript gray building, everything about the premises screamed "Death and loss!" But in a very dignified way, of course.

It had been a long time since I'd had to attend a wake, so the changes that had taken place inside were a pleasant surprise. Despite the age of the building, everything was well maintained and tastefully decorated in shades of black, gray, and white. Yet the effect was neither plain nor oppressive, instead exuding a sense of elegant melancholy. I needed to snag whoever did the decorating because they'd done a fabulous job. Though it was missing the requisite bits of flair to really liven up the place, no pun intended.

What was not so fabulous was the overwhelming scent of lilies scattered around Derek's casket. Beautiful, but their sickly sweet scent always reminded me of death. I could never smell lilies without remembering my parents' funeral, young as I was. The fragrance ensured I would never forget it.

Derek was laid out in the main viewing room, a blown-up headshot from his high school graduation mounted behind his casket. His mom, Mr. Long, and a woman I'd never seen before lined up next to him so that the procession had to greet each of them in turn before paying respects to Derek.

I wasn't ready for this.

The Calendar Crew had already gone ahead to give their condolences and Tita Rosie and Lola Flor approached the family after leaving the food they'd prepared with the funeral director. The mystery woman shook their hands perfunctorily, but Mr. Long refused to extend his hand. Mrs. Long elbowed him and I heard her say, "We talked about this. No scenes."

She intended it to be a whisper, but in the empty space her voice rang out as clearly as if she were announcing it to the room. Other than the Longs and my family, nobody else was there. It was still early, but I panicked at the thought that no one but us would show.

Looking at Mrs. Long, the premature lines etched on her face, the makeup she had caked on for the occasion, the handkerchief she wrung in her hands, the rigid way she held her body when her husband touched her, I knew I couldn't face her. I just couldn't.

I started to back away, but bumped into what felt like a brick wall. I glanced behind me and exclaimed, "Terrence!" much too loudly for this solemn space. Clapping my hand over my mouth, I glanced toward the front of the room. Sure enough, everyone was staring at us.

Luckily, Terrence Howell was well-known to both families and he smoothed things over by walking over to Mrs. Long and giving her a big hug. "I'm so sorry for your loss, Nancy. I know I haven't come over in a while, but Derek and I used to be close. Let me know if there's anything I can do."

He glanced back and gestured for me to move forward. I walked up next to him and said, "My condolences as well, Mrs. Long. Please let me know if there's anything my family and I can do to help."

Mr. Long muttered something that sounded suspiciously like "Go to jail," but the look Mrs. Long threw him shut him up.

"Thank you so much, both of you." She clasped Terrence's hands. "It means a lot to see you here. You were such an important part of his life."

I gathered my courage. "Mrs. Long, I hope you don't think—"

"Nancy, I just remembered we need to talk to the funeral director." Mr. Long literally elbowed me aside as he addressed his wife. He turned to the unknown woman standing next to him. "Cate, can you keep an eye on things till we're back?" He jerked his head in a not-so-subtle manner toward me and my family.

Cate, whoever she was, rolled her eyes but agreed. I tried to telegraph a message to one of my godmothers to figure out who this lady was and if she'd be a good source of information since Mr. Long didn't seem too eager to let me talk to his wife.

Ninang Mae, always the quickest on the draw when it came to ferreting out information, came over toward us and held out her hand. "Cate, I think I heard Mr. Long call you? I'm Mae. So sorry for your tragic loss."

Cate fidgeted a bit as she gave Ninang Mae a dead-fish handshake. "Nice to meet you."

Ninang Mae tipped her head. "I'm sorry, I thought I knew everyone in this town, but I can't seem to place you. Have we met before?"

Cate shook her head. "I'm Ed's sister. Our parents divorced when we were teens, so I've lived in Joliet most of my life. When I heard what happened, I wanted to be here for Nancy. She's such a dear."

"Oh that's so kind of you. How strange though, you're here for Nancy, not Ed?" Ninang Mae asked.

Cate looked uncomfortable again. "Nancy was my best friend when we were kids. She's always been a little fragile, in need of a soft touch. Besides, Ed, well, let's just say he wouldn't appreciate me making a fuss. I'm sure he has his own way of coping."

Seemed like a good time to introduce myself as well, so I held my hand out. "Hi, I'm Lila. That's my Aunt Rosie and Grandma Flor." I waved them over. "Cate is Mr. Long's sister," I said, making the introductions. "She's here to keep Mrs. Long company."

"Oh, that's so kind of you, Cate. Please let us know if there's anything we can do," Tita Rosie said, clasping Cate's hand briefly.

Lola Flor nodded at her. "We'll stop by later with some food. Nancy looks like she's losing weight. It's important for her to keep her strength up at a time like this." She looked Cate up and down. "You, too. You look tired. Take care of yourself as well as others, ha? What good are you if you get sick?"

Cate raised her eyebrows. "Thanks, I guess. Are you—" The ring of a cell phone cut her off, and she frowned at the ID display. "Excuse me, I have to take this." She answered the phone. "Ed? What do you ... yeah, I was just talking to them. What?" She sighed, rolling her eyes. "You're being ridiculous. Fine. I said fine!" She hung up, muttering under her breath.

"Sorry, it seems I'm needed," she said to us. "It was very nice meeting you."

Then she swept away before we could respond, leaving me, my aunt and grandmother, and the Calendar Crew alone with Derek's body. Or at least I thought so. A movement out of the corner of my eye caught my attention, and I realized Terrence was still there. He stood in front of Derek's high school graduation photo, frowning down at it.

I walked over to him and leaned my head on his shoulder so we could both contemplate the picture together. Derek was two years ahead of me in school and a very different guy back then. Looking at his picture, it was hard to reconcile my high school sweetheart with the man he became. The man who ended up in a casket with few people to mourn him or care.

"How you holdin' up, Lil' Mac?" Terrence's deep, reassuring voice rumbled through his chest, the vibrations against my cheek strange yet calming. His nickname for me, a shortening of my first and last name as well as a callback to a character in a retro video game he loved, brought a wave of nostalgia that was so sudden and intense I worried I'd drown in the memories and emotions it evoked in me.

"Not great," I admitted. "You?"

"Same."

I looked up at him to ask another question, but the grief etched across his features stopped me. I knew he and Derek were close once, but the depth of his sorrow surprised me.

Then I remembered Janet.

Janet, his fiancée, currently in a coma because she had information about Derek's death. Did he know she was supposed to meet me the day she was attacked? Did he blame me?

As if sensing my thoughts, he looked down and said, "Can we talk? Maybe grab some food? We got a lot to catch up on."

I smiled, a little sadly. What an understatement. "Sure. Just let me tell my aunt. Meet you at the usual spot?"

"See you in twenty."

George and Nettie Bishop were a Shady Palms institution. Adeena and I would hang out at Big Bishop's BBQ almost every day after school. The food was cheap and delicious, and their extensive side-dish menu meant Adeena didn't have to starve while

I consumed mounds of charred animal flesh. Derek and Terrence were usually with us as well, plus whoever Terrence happened to be dating at the time. Growing up, I didn't really have many friends. Just extended family that I was forced to spend time with, but who never really got me. This little group was all I had. Until Derek changed.

When I got to the restaurant, Terrence was already at our usual booth chatting with Nettie. I hadn't been there since I'd first left for college, and watching such a familiar scene playing out in front of me felt like I was in a time warp. Had it really been more than five years since I'd been here? What had I been doing all this time?

Terrence saw me watching them and motioned me over. Nettie turned to see who he was gesturing at and the smile that lit her face was as warm and inviting as a slice of her sweet potato pie.

"Well, well, well, if it ain't little Miss Lila!" Nettie swept me up in a big Bishop hug, pulling me into her softness and warmth in a way my aunt and grandmother never did. I smelled cocoa butter, the scent I always associated with her, and breathed in deeply.

"Lord, Miss Nettie, I've missed you so much." I tried to keep the tears out of my voice, as well as off my face, as I hugged her back.

"Then maybe you should come visit more often, hmm?" She pulled back and chucked me under the chin. "Now go sit with Terry and I'll be back for your order. You still drink sweet tea?" She looked at me sternly, as if that one thing would be the final tipping point between us.

"Only if you make it, Miss Nettie. Nobody can do it like you do, especially not in Chicago."

Nettie lowered her voice. "Is it true they drink their tea unsweetened?"

I nodded. "And if you ask for sweet tea, they'll bring you the tea with ice and a bunch of sugar packets. It's horrible."

She shuddered. "You poor thing. OK then, two sweet teas, coming right up."

I watched her walk away with the usual spring in her step. Her black, tightly curled hair had always been shot with premature grays, and her dark brown skin remained soft and smooth. All that cocoa butter, I assumed, the familiar smell enveloping me like one of her hugs. I'd only been away a few years, but it seemed like so much had changed while I was gone. The fact that Nettie remained steadfast was an anchor, a blessing.

I joined Terrence at our booth. His hands were folded in front of him, resting next to the unopened menu I saw Nettie place on the table.

I grabbed the one at my seat. "You're not eating?"

"Already know what I want. Come here often enough to have the menu memorized by now."

I smiled. He was right. As I looked over the options, the only thing that had changed was that the once-flimsy paper menus had been replaced with a laminated version rocking a fun, funky cover design.

"They changed up their logo! Wow, it's really good. I should ask them who their graphic designer was. Our restaurant could really use a rebrand."

Terrence frowned. "I did it. I do freelance graphic design as well as my construction work. You don't remember?"

I flushed. "Oh. Right. Well, after all this is over, maybe we can talk concepts and prices and whatnot. Assuming we still have a restaurant after this whole mess is over."

"Yeah, maybe."

Silence settled over the two of us, as heavy and leaden as a weighted blanket. I took the opportunity to see the differences that time had brought to my friend. Terrence's gray-green eyes still sparkled with humor and warmth and his full lips were still distractingly perfect. But deep lines around those features marred his otherwise smooth, deep brown skin. And though he kept his hair shaved down to a number-two fade, I could see hints of gray threaded throughout. He wasn't quite thirty yet, but the truth was staring me in the face. My friend wasn't the sweet, goofy teenager I had once known. We were both adults now. The way his eyes swept over me, I could tell he was analyzing me the same way. What changes had he noticed that I hadn't? Hope I passed muster.

Nettie stopped by, order pad in hand, interrupting our silent evaluations. "You two OK?"

I picked up the menu and pretended to look over it again. "Yeah, we're fine. You order first, Terrence. Having trouble making up my mind."

He ordered the brisket platter with hush puppies, collard greens, and mac and cheese as sides. I'd been eyeing the same thing, but knowing that I could steal some of his made my decision easier.

"Can I have the fried catfish special, but fries instead of the hush puppies?"

"Of course, sweetie. Back in a bit."

As she hustled off to the kitchen, Terrence shook his head. "You're making a mistake. Their hush puppies are the best."

"It's cool, I'll just steal one of yours."

He laughed. "Good luck with that."

The laughter erased the lines I'd seen earlier and made it easier for me to say what I had to say. I put my hand on top of his. "You probably don't want to talk about this, but I need to get this off my chest. I'm so sorry about Janet."

He pulled his hand back and wrapped them around his glass of sweet tea.

I mimicked his movement. "Sorry. This probably isn't the place."

"No, it's not that. I'm sorry. I've been trying to work up the nerve to talk about her. Her and Derek and what the hell is going on. So go ahead. Ask me anything. I know you want to."

Outside of Adeena, Terrence had been my best friend, but we drifted apart after high school. Not because of the distance, but out of respect for his relationship with Janet and to acknowledge how things were different now that Derek and I weren't together. It was amazing how well he knew me, even after all this time. I should've known though. We'd never been the type to have to chat every day to feel close—that's not the kind of friendship we had.

I sipped at my sweet tea, the golden nectar as comforting and syrupy sweet as it had always been. "How is she? Have the doctors said anything?"

His hands gripped the glass so tightly, they started trembling. "Not much. She's in a coma. They did some test and said there's brain activity and it was a good sign, but that's all. No idea on when she'll wake up. Or if."

He'd already pulled away from my grasp, so I didn't want to force my physical comfort on him. Instead, I stretched my hand out to the middle of the table and left it there in case he changed his mind.

"Hey, I don't want to be that person trying to comfort you with sappy greeting card phrases. But we both know that Janet is one of the strongest, most stubborn people to ever grace Shady Palms. If anyone can pull through, it's her."

He laughed, finally loosening his grip on the glass, and reached out to give my fingers a quick squeeze. "Too true. Thanks, Lil' Mac. I know you two don't have the best relationship, so I appreciate how positive you're being."

I sighed. "High school was a long time ago. I'm a different person now, and I hope she is, too. For your sake."

His face grew serious. "Just 'cause I love her doesn't mean I don't recognize her flaws. I've seen how much she's tried to be better. She even told me she was real petty to you at the hospital and wanted to apologize."

Ha, could've fooled me. "Really? When was this?"

He thought back. "That day she first saw you outside her office. Said she wanted to be the bigger person, so she promised me she'd help you. She called after you two arranged that lunch date, though. Told me she not only didn't apologize, but basically forced you into meeting for lunch." He shook his head. "I don't know what it is about you, but you bring out the worst in her. I told her to bring you a small peace offering. When she heard you were back in town, she made a dachshund sculpture. It reminded me of your dog, so she was going to give it to you as a gift." At my surprised look he said, "I guess you never got it."

I shook my head. "We never got to meet. I thought she stood me up, so I ate lunch by myself then went to the hospital to confront her. I was the one who found her in her office. Well, me and her assistant, since we went up together. I don't remember seeing a sculpture, but I could've missed it with everything that happened."

We both sat in silence until Nettie came by with our lunch platters. We tore into our meals and the food was every bit as good as I remembered. Chicago may have Luella's Southern Kitchen—which was boss—but Shady Palms had Nettie in the kitchen and George at the grill, bless them both.

Once the edges of hunger were gone and I could eat at a more leisurely pace, I asked Terrence, "Do you have any idea what Janet wanted to talk to me about?"

He swiped a fry off my plate. "Don't get too excited. I asked her to tell me what was going on with Derek's case, but she said patient confidentiality prevented her from sharing that info with me."

"Even though he's dead?"

"That's what I said! Supposedly it lasts for fifty years after the person's death or something like that. Anyway, all she'd say is that she got real curious after you'd come to visit and she went to go schmooze the medical examiner. Said he told her something interesting and she needed to talk to you immediately."

"I don't understand though. Why me? If there was something strange in the tests, why didn't she just tell Amir? Or better yet, the cops?"

Terrence popped the hush puppy into his mouth and chewed slowly, whether to fully savor it or to delay answering, I didn't know.

I put my elbow on the table and chin in my hand to wait out his response. When he didn't answer right away, I sipped at my sweet tea without breaking eye contact. I was in no hurry and could wait him out, no problem.

Luckily, he wasn't a stubborn person and always caved pretty quickly.

"Look, I love her with all my heart. But we both know how she is. She's not going to do something that doesn't benefit her in some way, especially if she could get in trouble for it. Telling the cops might make her feel important, but she doesn't get anything out of it. With Amir, she wouldn't even get that satisfaction. But you? You needed that info, would likely do anything to get it. You were the clear choice for her."

My mouth hung open so long Terrence was probably thinking of balling up a piece of bread and using it for target practice. "So what? She wanted to blackmail me for the information? Over sushi?"

"Blackmail is such a strong word. It was like, a business lunch. She wanted to negotiate with you."

"Dude, I remember the phone call. She made it very clear that lunch was on me, and from what I remember of her, that was just the beginning of her demands."

Terrence, with the weakest, most pathetic protest, said, "She's a good person, I swear."

"Yeah, well, I thought Derek was a good person and he proved me wrong."

Terrence looked at me sharply. "How much do you know about what he was up to?"

"You mean with his food reviews? All I know is that we weren't the only restaurant he attacked, but we were definitely his biggest obsession. I mean, with the other places, he'd eat there a bunch of times, release a couple of nasty reviews, then move on. For us, it was one nasty post after another. Why? What do you know?"

"Not much," he said cautiously. "At least, nothing for sure. But I think he had a hustle going with the health inspector."

Interesting. This backed up my suspicions. "What makes you say that?"

"The health inspector is Mr. Long's best friend. Every place that Derek went after got a visit from the health inspector, and there was talk of 'big fines' that had to be paid. Or else."

"This isn't the first time I've heard these claims, but how do you know about it?"

Terrence shrugged, looking uneasy. "After Janet and I got engaged, she urged me to reach out to him. Mend walls or whatever. She thought he was the only person who deserved to be my best man. And honestly, I hoped she was right. Despite all his BS when we were in college, I still missed him."

"So what, you two went fishing and hashed out your problems or whatever?"

He laughed. "We smoked weed and played video games like the old days. It was great at first. But then he started talking about some of his, uh, shadier side hustles. Tried to get me involved. It wasn't long before I saw that even though we were doing what we'd always done, we were now very different people. So I told him that he'd always be my boy, but I didn't see us doing this again. Made me sad, but I wasn't prepared for Derek's reaction."

"Let me guess, he accused you of thinking you're too good for him?"

He nodded. "Went on a huge rant about how everyone thinks they're too good for him now. He brought you up and uh, it wasn't all that flattering. Also he's still pissed that we went on those dates."

I groaned. "Him and Janet both. Did you explain to them that it was weird and felt wrong and like kissing a sibling?"

He grimaced. "Damn, you don't have to put it like that. Anyway, he called me a liar. Said I'd always been jealous of you and him and that he'd show us all."

"That's a pretty vague threat. Do you think he meant it? Like he actually had some kind of revenge planned against us?"

"It's hard to say, honestly. Old Derek, of course not. But New Derek, well . . ." He eyed me, wondering how to continue. "Look, you keep saying Derek was a completely different person, but I don't think you really get how much he'd changed. The year you two broke up, you didn't notice him becoming . . . moodier? More short-tempered?"

I'd put that time in my life behind me and didn't enjoy dredging it up again. "Um, I guess? There was a lot wrong with him at the time. He became more possessive, needier. I thought he just didn't like the idea of me going away to Chicago while he was stuck at Shelbyville Community College. Why? Was there something more to it?"

Terrence bit his lip. "There's no way to ease into this, so I'm just gonna say it. He had a drug problem."

I scoffed. "That's ridiculous. We smoked weed like, once or twice in high school. He refused to try anything stronger since he knew how I felt about that stuff after my cousin."

"Yeah, well, he fell in with a bad crowd from Shelbyville. We were in different programs, and I was busy with the track team and the Black Student Union. He was always after me to hang out, but I told him to join a club or get a job if he was so bored. I regret that now. Should've seen that he wasn't adjusting to college life as well as I was. I mean, Janet and I had just broken up, and I was free, you know? I wanted to see what else was out there, what the world had to offer. I was having the time of my life. I thought it was just a stoner crowd he fell in with. Turned out to be much more than that."

I didn't know what to say, so I just stared at him, hoping things would start making sense.

He continued. "And then Derek's mom got sick again. He stopped hanging out with those fools and got a job on campus, but it wasn't enough, so he dropped out and got a full-time job."

"At Callahan's Pharmacy. I remember that."

"Yeah, but it still wasn't enough. So he started dealing on the side."

I gasped. "That's ridiculous. I would've known."

"How would you have known? You think he would've told you? If you didn't notice, why would he tell you something he knew you'd disapprove of?" He let a beat pass. "Seriously though, how could you not have known?"

I buried my face in my hands. "I don't know! I don't know anything about anyone, it seems. We were so close and I loved him so much and then suddenly I just . . . didn't. I had just started my senior year when our relationship imploded. I was busy studying for exams, applying for scholarships, researching the best schools for restaurant management in Chicago. He didn't want to hear about any of that. He didn't want to be there while I was stressing out about my future. Everything was always about him! His worries, his needs, his dreams. You remember how he was. It was his way or nothing. I couldn't live like that anymore."

Terrence frowned. "He used to complain that you were abandoning him when he needed you the most. I kinda agreed with him."

"What? I thought you were on my side! You were the one who told me I needed to see what else was out there before settling down with Derek."

"Yeah well, I always thought you'd come back. And that you and Derek would work things out when you did. Kinda like me and Janet. But you never came back. Not really. And Derek just got worse and worse. I couldn't stand seeing him like that, but he wouldn't stop and he wouldn't get help. Then after that girl OD'd last year, I knew he and I were done. I wasn't involved in any of his dealings, but knew if I stuck around, I'd get dragged into it."

"The girl that OD'd? What girl?"

Terrence's forehead furrowed as he stared at me in disbelief. "You didn't hear about that? It was all over the news. Plus, I figured your family would've told you about it. Don't your aunties live for gossip?"

Vague recollections of my grandmother on a tirade about idiots with drug problems came back to me, but I assumed she was talking about my Tito Jeff, Tita Rosie's estranged husband. Besides, I was deep into my problems with Sam, and small-town gossip was the least of my worries.

"Never mind that. Who was she?"

He shrugged. "She wasn't from here. She didn't have any people here, either, as far as I know. You wanna know more about her, you should ask Adeena."

I tilted my head in confusion. "What? Why her?"

"Because Adeena used to work for her." At my blank look, he said, "The dead girl was the original owner of Java Jo's."

Chapter Thirty-four

When it became obvious that I had no idea what he was talking about and that my best friend in the whole wide world had kept this enormous secret from me, he quickly changed the subject. But every attempt to continue the conversation died as thoughts like *How could Adeena not tell me about this? Sure, it's not like I was ever begging her for news from home, but this was huge. This was definitely something she would've told me. Right?* ran through my head.

Flashbacks to her discomfort and anger when I spoke dismissively about substance abusers after the cops found those pills in my locker. How strange she'd been when I asked about school. Her sudden need to settle down in Shady Palms instead of breaking out in the world.

". . . Lil' Mac? You listening?"

Terrence's voice broke into my thoughts.

"Hmm? Sorry, yeah, totally listening."

His expression drooped and it took me a minute to piece together that he had asked if I thought Janet would ever wake up again. Oh man, what an insensitive time to space out.

Luckily, Nettie swooped in at that moment to save the day. "How is everything?"

"Just as delicious as I remembered! Now that I'm back in town, expect to see me here all the time."

"It really has been like old home week lately. Although with Derek…" She shook her head and exchanged a look with Terrence. "I cannot believe the stunt that boy pulled. I thought Big George was going to knock his block off."

I gasped. Big George Bishop wouldn't hurt a fly. For him to almost turn to violence…

"What happened?"

She frowned. "He started coming round again a month or two ago. We were so happy to see him at first. It'd been awhile and even though we heard about what he was doing with those other restaurants, we never dreamed he'd do that to us. He was like family! But nobody lets you down like family, I guess."

Ain't that the truth. "Let me guess, he wrote nasty reviews about your food and sicced the health inspector on you?"

She nodded, eyes widening. "How'd you know about that? He wanted us to hire a specific contractor to fix the problems, or he'd shut us down. But my brother does all our repairs, so I told him we'd pay the fine but hire our own workers. He did not like that, I can tell you."

Seemed like every restaurant owner on that list had the same story. So Derek had a hustle going with the health inspector, but was that enough to kill him? If they couldn't afford those fees and were forced to shut down, maybe. You take away a person's livelihood, and in some cases their life's work, there's no telling what they'd do.

I looked around the shop, trying to spot Big George. "Where is Big George, anyway? I wanted to say hi to him, too."

Nettie cleared her throat. "I don't think that's a good idea right now, honey. This whole mess with Derek really hurt Big George and he's still sensitive about it."

"But . . . what does that have to do with me? Why wouldn't he want to see me?"

"For better or worse, you and Derek were always a pair in our minds. Big George made the mistake of asking him about you, and we think that's what set Derek off. Plus now with his death . . . just too many sad memories." She put her hand on my shoulder. "I hope you understand, sweetie. We know you had nothing to do with it. And as mad as we were, we wouldn't wish this on anyone. I was hoping we could fix things between us. But now it's too late."

She shook her head. "Make sure you fix things when you can. Sometimes you don't get another chance."

After Nettie left, Terrence and I silently finished the last of our meal. She seemed to have given us both a lot to think about.

Finally, Terrence cleared his throat. "Speaking of old home week, where's Adeena? I know she hated Derek, but I thought she'd at least go to the wake with you."

I fiddled with the untouched bread on my plate. Why did barbecue joints always include that slice of cheap white bread? "She's not talking to me at the moment."

"Oh. Sorry about that. It's none of my business, but is there anything I can do?"

"Doubt it. I think she finally realized Amir and I have a thing for each other."

Terrence choked on his sweet tea. "You serious? Just now she's realizing this? You two have been making eyes at each other since what, freshman year? Derek was so sure you were seeing him behind his back. Part of the reason he picked that fight with you when you broke up."

I groaned, burying my face in my hands. "Were we really so obvious? I've been fighting this for years, Terrence. *Years.* You know Adeena has a weird complex when it comes to her brother."

Terrence stole a fry off my plate. "Yeah, but I figured since you were her best friend, she'd be happy for the two of you. You know, a girl who's finally good enough for Mr. Perfect?"

I swiped a hush puppy in retaliation. Whoa, Terrence was right. The fries were a mistake. "You've met Adeena. You've seen how she reacts when a girl even mentions that Amir's cute. It's never going to happen."

He frowned. "Even though you and Amir clearly care about each other?"

"It's not just the Amir thing. I mean, she's definitely not happy about it, but it goes way deeper than that." I rearranged the silverware, lining it up carefully on the paper napkin. "She's been dropping major hints that she wants us to open up a place together here in Shady Palms. At first I thought she was joking, but it's become obvious that this is something she's serious about. And I'm not."

"Still not ready to settle down in Shady Palms?"

"I don't know that I belong here, Terrence. I know I got people here, but there's a whole world out there, and Shady Palms just stays the same. There's got to be more than this. I thought Adeena felt the same, but I guess not."

"You ever think the reason Shady Palms stays the same is 'cause that's how you picture it in your mind? You haven't actually been here in years, how would you know what we're about now?" He shook his head. "You ever bother asking Adeena why she feels this way? Why the sudden change?"

Now it was my turn to shake my head.

"So then why are you telling me all this instead of her?"

He was right. As usual. Terrence had always been the voice of reason back in high school. The calm and steady good influence that the rest of us never listened to. Yet he was kind enough to never rub it in our faces that he was right.

Maybe it was time for me to start listening to him. And to the advice that Nettie had given us, to make things right when you had the chance. I just had one more stop to make before I did.

Chapter Thirty-five

After catching up with Terrence, I felt the overwhelming urge to talk to Derek's mom. Before I could make up with Adeena, I needed to put the past to rest. At the wake, I was too much of a coward to really deal with her pain, but hearing about the way Derek had changed—and reminiscing with Terrence about who he used to be—made me realize I needed to hear his mom's side. Maybe together we could figure out where it had all gone wrong.

Besides, I still didn't know if Adeena would talk to me and I didn't want to get iced in front of a crowd at Java Jo's. Needed to kill time till she got off work.

I pulled up in front of the Longs' house, which used to be the Winters' house. I'd spent quite a bit of my youth there. After finding out what Derek was doing to my family, I'd pushed away the memories we'd shared and the feelings that had started to crop up once again. But now, faced with the reality of the house that had once been a second home for me, I couldn't run away from them.

I hadn't been there since we broke up my senior year. It was such a typical small-town breakup. I wanted to go to Chicago for school. He wanted me to stay in Shady Palms, where we'd get married, have kids, and live blandly ever after. At the time, staying in Shady Palms for the rest of my life had felt like death. So I left him behind. Him and everyone else I cared about. Selfish? Maybe. But it got to the point where I felt like I couldn't breathe. Where I started having panic attacks when I thought about my future here. Why was it selfish to try to save myself?

Even now, the thought of staying here forever felt like a hand squeezing me tighter and tighter—this phantom hand molding me into the shape everyone else wanted me to be.

Why couldn't Adeena understand that?

I mentally shook myself. Sitting in the car staring at the house wasn't going to solve anything. Also, it was super creepy. I was lucky no nosy neighbor had called the cops on me yet. Most people in this town had the cops on speed dial, as if the police department were customer service meant to deal with their every complaint.

I reached back to grab the box of ube crinkles that I'd picked up from the house before driving over. I remembered Mrs. Long sharing my love of ube, and my aunt had raised me better than to arrive at someone's house empty-handed. I marched up the steps and rang the doorbell, eager to get this over with. I heard the clanging of the bell within the house, but nobody answered. I rang it again. And again. Nothing.

I was about to ring one last time before realizing my blunder. Everyone was probably still at the wake. How could I forget they usually went all day? To be fair, it'd been awhile since someone I'd known had died, but still.

Should I leave the box of cookies on the porch? No, I'd hate for them to get stolen, or worse, have mice picking at them. Maybe I could just slip a note in her mailbox and come again tomorrow? Decision made, I hurried down the steps to grab a pen and paper from the car when someone rounded the side of the house and slammed into me.

"Ope!" I yelped as I grabbed the person to stop myself from falling. "I'm so sorry, I didn't see you there."

"Lila?" The hooded figure peered closely at me. "What are you doing here?"

The voice was Mrs. Long's.

I held up the box of cookies. "I didn't have a chance to truly express my condolences. I remembered you liked my baking, so I wanted to stop by for a bit with my ube crinkles."

She lowered her hood, eyes flickering to the treats I held out, then back to meet my eyes. "I was wondering if you were ever going to come over."

I bit my lip. "Wasn't sure if I was welcome. Your husband certainly doesn't want me around."

"Yes, well . . ." She turned away and stomped toward the front door. "It's my home, too, and I'd like a chance to talk to you. So come on in."

I followed her through the open door, expecting the usual warmth of a Midwestern home but was met with the chill of an unheated house. Guess they'd lowered the temperature before heading out to the funeral home. I took off my boots, but kept my coat on, trying—and failing—to suppress a shudder.

Noting my involuntary gesture, Mrs. Long hurried over to the thermostat. "Sorry about the cold. Ed likes to keep the heat as low as possible to cut costs."

I smiled to reassure her. "Don't worry, my grandmother's the same way." I mimicked my Lola Flor's stern voice. "'If you're cold, put on a sweater, ha? You think it's cheap heating up this old house?'"

I left out the part where she'd make some crack about how all my excess fat should be keeping me warm. And people wondered why I wanted to leave so bad.

Mrs. Long smiled. "That sounds like her all right. But your house is always so lovely and warm when I stop by."

"That's because Tita Rosie turns the heat back up to normal human temperatures." Realizing what she said, I frowned. "Wait, you've been by recently?"

Her hands fluttered up toward her permed blonde hair, fingers fluffing up the curls. "N-no, I wouldn't say recently. Maybe a few months ago? I stopped by to pick something up for a church function and your aunt invited me in. She fed me enough food to constitute a three-course meal even though I said I'd already eaten. Insisted it was just coffee and snacks."

I smiled, slightly embarrassed. Tita Rosie's warmth was genuine, but my family's hospitality could be a little on the pushy side. "Yeah, sorry about that. Her innate need to feed the world can be a little overwhelming at times."

She laughed. "It was the best meal I'd had in a long time, so I didn't mind. Ed keeps me on a pretty limited budget when it comes to buying groceries, and I'm not very creative in the kitchen, so . . ."

She trailed off and glanced at the kitchen, eyes widening suddenly. "How rude of me, having you stand around without even offering you a drink! Let me just pop into the kitchen and I can make some coffee to go with those, um, how do you pronounce it?"

I held out the box to her. "Oo-beh. It's like a mild sweet potato that we use for desserts in the Philippines."

She picked one up clumsily in her gloved hands and took a small, timid bite. Her eyes bugged out and she popped the rest of it into her mouth, chewing vigorously. "Ohh, I remember the taste of these now! Subtle and sweet, and such a lovely color."

I nodded. "Thanks. I love them, too."

"They're quite addictive." She ate two more in rapid succession and urged me to have one as well, so I helped myself to a few.

They worked up quite a thirst, but I didn't know how to signal to Mrs. Long that I was really craving that coffee she'd offered. I cleared my throat a few times as she worked on another cookie, but it took a fake cough to draw her attention.

"Are you OK, dear?"

"Sorry, winter doesn't really agree with me. The cold gets into my chest and makes my throat so dry."

"Oh, right, the coffee! Coming right up. Just wait here a moment." She put the box down on a side table and scurried off to the kitchen.

I followed her, figuring it was time to stop stalling and talk to her about Derek. "Mrs. Long, I'm sorry but—"

For the second time that day, I bumped into her. She was barely my height, which wasn't all that impressive to begin with, and a wisp of a thing, but the rigidity of her body and the shock of the sudden stop nearly knocked me down.

"Whoa! Mrs. Long, what's—" I peered past her into the kitchen and gasped as I saw what had caused the abrupt motion.

There on the floor lay Mr. Long. If the pool of blood that had inched its way toward the kitchen entrance wasn't proof enough that something was wrong, the knife embedded in his chest was.

"Oh, dear Lord," I said, crossing myself. What in the world was going on?

"Lila," Mrs. Long said, keeping her eyes on her husband's still form, "would you be a dear and call the police?"

Chapter Thirty-six

I have to say, Ms. Macapagal, you either have the greatest intuition or worst luck when it comes to stumbling across crime scenes," Detective Park observed as he finished taking down my witness account.

After years of living in Chicago, I still wasn't used to the speed at which the Shady Palms Police Department arrived. I'd called less than ten minutes ago, and in that time, a full team had arrived to take pictures of the crime scene, search for evidence, and take down my and Mrs. Long's statements.

I was going to make a flippant remark about some girls having all the luck, sarcasm being my preferred defense mechanism, but bit my tongue when I caught the look on Mrs. Long's face. She still hadn't taken off her winter coat, scarf, or gloves, and all that puffy black material seemed to swallow her up as if it were a physical manifestation of her grief. This woman had lost her only child as well as her husband in less than a week.

No, "lost" wasn't a strong enough word to describe the unfairness of it all. It wasn't some freak accident that took these men away from her. Their lives had been stolen.

My mind swirled with questions at this revelation. Was the person who stabbed Mr. Long the same one who poisoned Derek? Bludgeoned Janet in her office? Vandalized our restaurant? How many would-be killers and criminals were running around quiet little Shady Palms? And if the Long family was being targeted, did that mean Mrs. Long was next?

I asked Detective Park as much. He nodded, not in agreement, but to acknowledge he'd been thinking along the same lines. "So you noticed that connection as well. Don't worry, Mr. Long's sister is staying with her, so she won't be alone in the house. And we'll have patrol cars coming by every hour."

I looked around the room but didn't see the woman from the wake. "Where is his sister? What's her name again? Cate?"

"Yes, Cate Long. According to Mrs. Long, Cate stayed at the funeral parlor to greet anyone who stopped by to pay their respects."

"That's strange. She didn't seem particularly close to Derek. Why wasn't Mrs. Long the one to stay behind?"

Detective Park cleared his throat. "Seems she needed to get away and clear her head for a while. I can't blame her. Couldn't have been easy for her to have to stare at the body of her son for hours on end."

I winced, catching the rebuke in his voice. "That makes sense. What about Mr. Long though? Did he leave around the same time as her? I could understand her needing some time alone, but you'd think he'd be there in case anyone else showed up for the wake. He knows the people in this town; his sister doesn't."

He checked his notes. "According to Mrs. Long, she wanted to be alone but her husband insisted on accompanying her home. The last time she saw him alive was when he dropped her off at the house. He told her he was going to see his friend Craig Nelson and he'd pick her up in an hour. After he left, she went for a long walk to clear her head and bumped into you."

"Was Mrs. Long actually walking for an hour? Or did Mr. Long get home early? Maybe he surprised a burglar who thought the family would be out at Derek's wake and killed him in a panic? Is it silly to think everything that's happened recently all ties to Derek's case?" I spat out these questions as they came to me, one after another, not sure if Detective Park would actually answer me, but needing to get them out.

"Mrs. Long isn't sure how long she was out for. She's not wearing a watch and she didn't have her phone during her walk. Until we talk to Mr. Nelson, we won't know what time he headed back home or if that's even where he went."

"What about the murder weapon?"

A raised eyebrow was the only response I got. Fair enough, he'd already shared more than he needed to with me. I couldn't expect him to tell me everything. Maybe if I played up my fear about constantly being so close to death, I could get his sympathies on my side. It's not like I'd be lying anyway. This latest encounter had me shook. And then I remembered something Terrence had said.

"Oh, Detective, did you find a dachshund statue in Janet's office? Her fiancé mentioned it to me."

He glanced through his notes and shook his head. "Sorry, it's not on the list. You sure it was there?"

"I never saw it but Terrence said she was planning on giving it to me. It seemed important to him, so I wanted to check."

"I'll ask my team in case they missed anything, but it's doubtful."

I couldn't ask for more than that, so I thanked him. "You haven't told my family about what happened here, have you?"

"I called Rosie once I got here and was able to ascertain your safety. She should be here any minute." A frown creased the space between his eyebrows. "Is that a problem?"

"No . . ." I said, dragging that single syllable out. "I just, I was hoping to be the one to tell her. After all that's gone on, a call from the cops is enough to trigger her anxiety."

Detective Park swore loudly, surprising the heck out of me. "You're right. I didn't even think of that."

I sighed and sat down. "I know you were just joking earlier, but this is starting to feel like too much. I don't like that I'm always the one who's around when these bad things happen. Like, am I being set up? Or what if something happens again, but this time I walk into the situation? Am I in danger, too?"

"We've already got patrols watching your home and restaurant. I don't think you've got anything to worry about."

I wasn't sure if that made me feel better or worse. "Because you were worried about our safety?"

Detective Park rubbed the stubble on the back of his head. "Among other reasons, yes."

I remembered that he still considered me his prime suspect and was likely counting down the days till he could arrest me. So, worse. The knowledge that my family was under constant surveillance definitely made me feel worse. At least I knew Tita Rosie and Lola Flor were safe.

As if on cue, the two of them dashed into the room.

Tita Rosie went straight to Mrs. Long and grasped her hands. "Oh, Nancy. I'm so, so sorry."

Lola Flor marched over as well, ignoring Detective Park and me. "Nancy, you can't stay here tonight. The police will be all over this place and it's not good for you to be here."

Mrs. Long protested faintly, eyes on the space between my grandmother and aunt. "No, it's fine. I'm fine. Cate will be here later to stay with me. We're fine."

"Cate can come over, too. Just for tonight."

Mrs. Long didn't respond.

Tita Rosie squeezed Mrs. Long's hand. "Would you like to go back to the funeral home? Maybe talking to Cate will make you feel better. Then you can say goodbye to your son."

That seemed to wake Mrs. Long up. "That's a good idea. I need to clear my head. If Cate wants to stay with you, we can. I'll leave it up to her."

Cate agreed immediately. "I'm sorry, Nancy, but the idea of staying in the place where Ed was just killed . . ." She shuddered. "I'd never be able to sleep." She turned to my aunt. "The funeral director said you were the one who provided the food for the wake."

Under normal circumstances, my aunt would've beamed and asked what Cate had thought. But this whole Derek thing had left her more cautious, undermined her confidence. Her response was hesitant, as if she wasn't sure what Cate was going to do with this information.

"Yes, my mother and I made the food. We own a restaurant here in town."

Cate grinned, brightening her previously dour expression. That simple motion lit up her face, highlighting her kind, keen eyes. "Your food is unlike anything I've ever tried before. So delicious! If you're going to feed us like that, maybe we can spend more than one night."

Mrs. Long's eyes widened. "Cate! Tonight is fine because Ed was just—it's too soon to stay in that house. But we will not trespass on their hospitality."

Cate took one of Mrs. Long's hands into hers and patted the top of it. "I'm joking, Nancy. I'm here as long as you need me, wherever you choose to stay." She paused. "And I'm sorry about Ed, I really am. I wish to God you didn't have to go through this."

She looked at us. "You probably think I'm cold, making jokes like this after my brother's death. But this is how I deal with things. And right now, I'm more worried about Nancy's safety and well-being, so thank you for opening your home to us. If it gets to be a problem, we can always check into a hotel."

I chewed on a fingernail as I watched this scene, torn between pleasure at helping Mrs. Long in her time of need and discomfort at the thought of the difficult conversations I knew we'd have soon. At the very least, giving my aunt someone to take care of seemed to take her mind off our restaurant problems and my legal troubles, so this tragedy had one bright spot.

With that taken care of, there was one last thing I had to do. Swallow my pride and go talk to Adeena.

Chapter Thirty-seven

When I walked into Java Jo's, Adeena was at the counter. She laughed and chatted with each customer until she saw me in line. The smile melted off her face like a bowl of halo-halo on a Midwestern summer day. She finished serving the customer in front of me, but when I stepped up, she called out, "Kevin! Time to switch!" then headed over to the espresso machine. She didn't make eye contact with me once.

Kevin came to take my order, frowning, but chose not to ask any questions. "Hey, Lila. Coconut milk latte, right? You want that hot or iced today?"

Without taking my eyes off Adeena's back, I said, "Give me a Java Jocinno."

As a jab at the people who kept asking him if he served Frappuccinos, Kevin started selling "Java Jocinnos" with the tagline "Are you really going to keep pretending this is actually coffee?" They were basically milkshakes with a shot of espresso and super delicious, but very obviously not coffee. Coffee snobbery at its finest, and I was all about it.

Kevin blinked, but again chose not to question it. "Wow, mixing it up today, huh? So you wanna stick with your usual coconut or try one of our other alternative milks? We got almond, soy, rice, oat—"

"Nope. Give me the real stuff, Kev. And no messing around with that two percent. I want whole milk. One scoop each of double fudge and sea salt caramel. Triple shot of espresso."

"You want whipped cream on top?"

I raised an eyebrow. "Kevin. You know I want whipped cream on top. And actual whipped cream, not the coconut cream kind."

He sighed. "Lila, do you need to talk? Because I really don't think—"

I slapped some cash on the counter. "I'll be sitting in my usual spot. Call me when it's ready."

He shook his head but rang up my order and handed me the receipt. "Should be up in five."

I nodded and headed over to my table, catching up on all the social media stuff I've been ignoring for the past week. I scrolled through my personal accounts, but nothing really caught my eye, so I switched over to the Instagram account I'd made for Longganisa. She was way more popular than I was, but I hadn't uploaded a new pic in a week and her fans were not pleased. I made a quick post of her splayed out on the sidewalk the day she gave up mid-run. A quick caption of "My human is mad I stopped running to sploot, but doesn't she know it's important to stretch?" and there we go. Enough to appease her fans for a couple of days, at least.

Finally, I switched over to the business account I'd created for Tita Rosie's Kitchen. Other than a quick post I made the day Derek died, explaining we were closed until further notice, I hadn't bothered checking the account. So I didn't notice the DM sitting in our in-box.

It was from Yuki, Derek's former paramour if I'd guessed correctly. She'd sent it the day I visited her and her husband at Sushi-ya.

> We need to talk. But not at the restaurant. Contact
> me here if you can meet me.

Hoping I hadn't missed the window of opportunity, I messaged her back.

> *I'm at Java Jo's right now. Could you meet me here?*
> *If not now, sometime today or tomorrow?*

She answered back almost immediately.

> Too public

That was it. No other suggestions or a hint of what she needed to talk about. Not even a ". . ." appearing to show she was composing another message.

> *Where are you? I could come to you*
> I'm at the funeral home
> *For Derek's wake?*
> Yes
> *How long will you be there?*
> I don't know. No one else is here, so get here soon

I calculated how long it'd take me to get there.

> *Gimme 20 min. Don't leave before I get there*
> I'll try but no promises

I started to message back, telling her to be patient, when my Java Jocinno was plunked down in front of me, sticky-sweet liquid trailing down the large fountain drink glass.

"Oh, shoot, sorry, Kevin. Can you make that to go?" I asked without looking up from my phone.

"Why are you doing this?"

I glanced up at Adeena's voice to see her glowering at me. Ten minutes ago, I'd wanted nothing more than to finally have our heart-to-heart where I'd lay all my cards on the table. But now I had a lead with a time limit and did *not* have time to deal with her brotherly insecurities and demands on my future.

"You're going to have to be a little clearer. Got a lot of stuff going on that you seem to disapprove of, so you'll have to narrow it down. Oh, and can I get a to-go cup, please?"

She didn't budge. "You're super lactose intolerant. You only order something with this much dairy to punish yourself."

I took a quick sip and holy sugar, was it ever delicious. "I also get it when I need a bit of cheering up. Don't know if you noticed, but I could do with some cheer."

"Don't give me that. You order stuff like this when you're depressed, thinking it'll cheer you up, but again, you're really just punishing yourself."

I closed my eyes and counted to ten before saying, "Adeena, are you going to get me that to-go cup or not? 'Cause I'm in a bit of a hurry."

"Oh, I'm sorry. Are you running away again? Because that seems to be your go-to move."

"Oh my *God*, are you serious right now? Why does everyone accuse me of running away?! Why can't you all accept that I'm just trying to do what's best for me?"

Adeena gave me a pitying look. "How long you going to keep lying to yourself?"

"You know what, I'm tired of all this high school drama. When you're ready to talk to me, come find me. I got enough to deal with right now." I pushed up from the table and put my coat back on. "Forget the to-go cup. I've lost my appetite."

"Lila." Adeena's voice was so strained, I could almost feel it snap in the air between us.

Usually that tone of voice would have me bending over backward to accommodate her, but I couldn't deal with her right now.

"Sorry, gotta go talk to a possible murder suspect while sitting next to my ex-boyfriend's dead body. Come find me once you've gotten over yourself."

"Lila—"

"Oh, and Mr. Long's dead, too. Mrs. Long and I both found him. Knife stuck in his chest, lots of blood everywhere, that whole thing. Just so you know the kind of day I'm having. OK, bye!"

I waved cheerily at her as I got in my car and delighted in how she stood staring at me, mouth agape, even as I started backing out of my spot. Petty? Yes. Cruel? Well, maybe a little. But because of her, I not only had to deal with the uncomfortable feeling that she was right, I was also going to face a potential murder suspect alone and uncaffeinated.

That had to count for something, right?

Chapter Thirty-eight

Running inside a funeral home was probably frowned upon, but I couldn't help sprinting toward the main viewing room to make sure Yuki hadn't left yet. I'd DM'ed her my phone number in the car and told her to call if she left before I got there. So far no phone call, but you never know.

I darted past the scowling funeral director and skidded into the mostly empty viewing room. Cate and Mrs. Long were already at my place (Tita Rosie texted me earlier saying I'd better be home in time for dinner), so none of the family was there to greet visitors.

Yuki stood alone beside Derek's casket, a black-clad figure silhouetted against the light wood finish of the casket and spray of white lilies surrounding it. One hand rested on the edge of the casket as she stared down at Derek's handsome, still face. Though when I got closer to her, I realized "rested" wasn't the correct word to describe her. The knuckles on her hand were white and shaking—the hand clutching the casket was the only thing keeping her upright.

"Yuki?" I said, hating to intrude into what must've been a very private moment of grief. "It's Lila. You wanted to talk?"

Yuki nodded, her movements slow and measured, as if even that routine movement required concentration and effort. "Yes. I wanted to talk."

I waited for her to continue, but she stayed silent. "OK . . . what did you want to talk about? And why here?"

"How did you know Derek?" she asked, without turning around.

All this cloak and dagger was so she could ask me about my dating history with a dead guy?

"We grew up in this town. Dated for a while in high school. Why?"

"Why did you break up?"

I shrugged, then realized she couldn't see my gestures. "We were young. We wanted different things in life. Typical high school stuff. It was all a long time ago."

She shook her head, still not facing me. "Not for him it wasn't. He still loved you."

"He said that?"

"He didn't have to say it. I just knew. He thought I didn't, but I knew."

I edged closer to her, the strain in her voice pulling me toward her like a magnet. "What was your relationship with Derek? He wasn't just a jerk food critic to you, was he?"

She finally turned around, tears coursing down her face. "We were having an affair."

Ha! I knew it! It wouldn't do to gloat over my ability to read people, so I said, "I'm sorry. You obviously cared about him."

"I did. Or at least, I think I did." She glanced toward the casket, then back at me. "It started off innocently. You know? I just wanted to improve the public image of our restaurant, so I had to talk to Derek to figure out where we went wrong. Akio is such a . . . Well, you saw how he is. I knew he'd just get in another fight. I was able to talk Derek into not pressing charges, but then Akio tried to fight the health inspector, too. There was no talking things out with him, so I had to pay him off."

She looked down. "I had to pay him to change our score, too. Akio thought it was because the inspector realized he'd made a mistake, but no. Derek told me he knew how the inspector worked and this was the only way to make things OK for us."

I appreciated Yuki confirming what I had already pieced together, but I sensed there was more she wasn't telling me.

"OK, so that explains your situation with the health inspector, but what about Derek?"

"It had been a couple of weeks since he wrote his nasty review. After tipping me off about the health inspector, his column stopped focusing on our restaurant. I guess he had moved on to his next target. I wanted to thank him, but also to slap him for putting us through all that. So I told him I needed to see him again. And it just . . . happened. I can't explain it."

I could. Derek could be dazzlingly charming when he wanted to be. How else could I have stayed with him so long? How else could I have been tricked into getting back together with him, ever so briefly, when I came back to Shady Palms? Which reminded me . . .

"Wait, so if you've been messing around since summertime, you were together when I came back to town, right?"

Her face tightened. "How else would I know he was still in love with you? But it's not like I could say anything to him. I couldn't exactly demand loyalty when I go home to the man I've been married to for over a decade and have no intention of leaving."

I bit my lip. "Did . . . did he talk about me?"

"He wanted to ruin you," she said. "That's how I knew he wasn't over you. And why I thought you were the one that killed him."

I rubbed at my temple. "OK, you're going to have to explain that, because those are two giant leaps you're making right there."

"I knew he was seeing you because out of nowhere he started avoiding me. I asked around and found out his ex was back in town. I was actually relieved. I'd been feeling guilty and wondering if there was a graceful way to break it off, but suddenly I didn't have to. Then he called me one night and demanded I meet with him. Went on and on about uppity women and how I was the only one who understood him."

I stared at her. "And that wasn't a red flag for you to get out?"

"I cared about him. The madder he was at you, the sweeter he was to me. And if he focused on your restaurant, it meant he'd leave mine alone." Yuki shrugged. "I'm not proud of it. But we had struggled long enough and I didn't know you. Seemed easier to mind my own business and hope he'd lose interest in me again."

"Did he?"

She laughed, the sound amazingly bitter despite its light, tinkly quality. "Just the opposite. Said that he was finally going to get away from that life and leave Shady Palms behind. And he wanted me to come with him."

Could this be a reference to the drug-dealing Detective Park had mentioned?

"When did he say this? And what did he mean by 'that life'?"

"Not sure, but it might have something to do with the con he was pulling with the health inspector. I was supposed to meet him the day he died to give him an answer."

I hesitated. "Did you love him? Would you have gone with him?"

Yuki toyed with the ring on her left finger. "I love my husband. We have a beautiful daughter together. A good life, though it's quieter than I'd like. So no, I wouldn't have gone with him."

"You realize that makes you look even guiltier, right? Not only were you having an affair with him, but you were afraid to break it off in case there was retaliation. It'd be easy to build a case saying you tried to end it, he threatened to destroy your business, and you killed him. Or maybe your husband found out about you two and did the deed himself."

Yuki laughed again. "Akio? Poison someone? No, for all his faults, he would never resort to something like that. He's all about the idea of a fair fight."

"Then what about you?"

"Me? You already know I was nowhere near your restaurant the day he was killed. In fact, I hadn't seen him in days. How could I have slipped him poison?"

I was grasping at straws now. "Maybe you paid someone to do it?"

Yuki smiled that same smile I saw when we shared a cell. The one that spread soft and slow across her face, never quite reaching her eyes. "So now I'm hiring a contract killer? And who is this mystery assassin?"

"Um . . ."

Before I could stun her with a brilliant deduction, Marcus's number flashed across my screen. He'd gone silent on me after he'd helped clean the restaurant, so I wondered if this was a social call or if there was a big enough break in the case to risk Detective Park's wrath.

I held up a finger to signal to Yuki that I needed to answer it. "Hey, Marcus, what's up?"

His words came in a rush, no pauses or breaths taken between words, and I struggled to follow along.

"You gotta get over here now. Tita Rosie's been brought in for questioning but I can't tell you any more since someone's watching me gotta go bye!"

It took me a few seconds to realize he'd hung up before my brain could even give context to his words. Tita Rosie? Being questioned? Oh Lord, what now?

I looked at Yuki. "Gotta go. Thanks for meeting with me. If you remember anything—"

She nodded, then turned back toward Derek's casket. "I've got your number."

I ran out to my car, dialing Amir on the way. He picked up on the first ring. "I know, I'm heading to the station right now. See you there."

I gripped the wheel but took care not to push the speed limit too much. There were more cops here than you'd expect for a town of our size and they were only too happy to slap you with a ticket over any little infraction. As much trouble as my family seemed to be in, legally and financially, I figured adding a speeding ticket on top of it was not going to do me any favors.

Still, I made it to the station in record time. I burst through the doors, looking around wildly for Amir and my aunt.

"Lila!"

I whirled around at the sound of Marcus's voice. "What's going on? Where's Tita Rosie? Why is she even here?"

He held his hands out, trying to get me to lower my voice. "Hey, chill, Amir's with her right now, so she should be OK."

I took a deep breath to force down the panic that had been rising since his phone call. "OK, but why is she here? Why does she even need a lawyer?"

Marcus put a hand on my shoulder and leaned down to be eye level with me. It was a gesture meant to convey support and empathy, but it only filled me with dread. Marcus, little It-Wasn't-Me Marcus Marcelo who, when caught stealing a pack of cookies from the store tried to pin it on me, was risking his job for my sake. Which meant that whatever he was about to tell me was going to hurt. A lot.

"Don't freak out, but . . . the knife that killed Mr. Long? It belonged to Tita Rosie. They're holding her on suspicion of his murder."

I didn't realize I was slipping to the floor till Marcus grabbed me and guided me to a seat. "I'm sorry, what? That doesn't make any sense."

Marcus helped me sit then took a seat farther down to give me some space. "I know. And trust me, Detective Park was not happy about it. The sheriff's gotten involved. Been riding him hard to close this case. Seems he was poker buddies with Mr. Long and wants justice. Plans on holding a 'press conference' soon."

We both snorted since the only press we had was the local newspaper staffed by three or four people and whatever high school intern they could trick into free labor by claiming it'd look good on their college applications. A town of fewer than twenty thousand didn't yield a ton of newsworthy events, so they'd been going hard on the Derek Winters case. I would've canceled our subscription long ago, since any publication that allowed Derek to write that garbage wasn't worth reading, but the pages were great for cleaning windows and glass. Left them nice and streak-free.

I sobered up at the thought of Detective Park interrogating Tita Rosie, pushing and prodding her until he got what he wanted. Amir was good, but with Sheriff Lamb involved, it was only a matter of time before the police department got desperate. Heck, they already were if they thought Tita Rosie had anything to do with a man's death. In a twisted way, I understood their reasoning when it came to me as a suspect. I'd even understand if they thought it was Lola Flor. Enough people had been on the wrong side of a tirade from her to know what her temper was like. But my aunt? Not in a million years.

I tried to think the way Amir would, how he would ask questions to not only get information but seed doubt. "So one of Tita Rosie's knives is the murder weapon. Do they have anything else to tie her to the crime?"

"Lila, I've already told you too much. The fact that I called you to tell you she was here is enough to get me suspended."

I waved my hand. "As long as no one saw you, we can say I'm here because of Amir. I called him to ask about Adeena, and he happened to be on his way here to represent Tita Rosie. Not a problem."

He sighed. "I don't know the specifics, but I think there was a witness. Someone saw her at the Longs' house earlier today. We don't know his exact time of death yet, but she was there in that general time frame."

"Who was the witness?"

"I don't know."

"Don't know or won't tell me?"

"Lila—"

"He can't tell you because it would mean a suspension. Isn't that right, C.O. Marcelo?" Detective Park said, coming out from one of the rooms with Amir and Tita Rosie.

Marcus shot up from his seat. "Sir, I haven't told her anything. I was just trying to comfort her, I swear."

Detective Park sighed. "How kind of you. Anyway, relax, Ms. Macapagal. As you can see, your aunt is just fine. In fact, she's free to go home."

I raised an eyebrow. "Just like that?"

He shrugged. "As long as she comes back tomorrow to answer more questions. No reason to hold her here overnight."

Before I could ask anything else, Amir stepped in. "Yes, you're so magnanimous, Detective. Lila, we should go. Auntie Rosie is a bit tired."

I fought the urge to let him know he wasn't the boss of me, but he was right. Tita Rosie came first. Any arguments between us could come later.

I pulled my aunt's arm through mine and guided her toward the door. "Come on, Tita Rosie. Let's rest a bit and then I can prepare some meryenda for everyone, OK?"

"Good idea." Tita Rosie patted my hand and slowly withdrew her arm. "I'm just . . . tired. So tired, anak."

She sighed, then pulled her shoulders back, lifted her head, and marched toward the door, disappearing outside without looking back at the rest of us. Which was good because she didn't see the tears spilling down my cheeks as I watched her walk away, so strong and so alone.

Chapter Thirty-nine

After thanking Amir for his help, Tita Rosie and I went home. She headed straight to her room without talking to anyone, and was still holed up there, hours later.

I'd taken a short nap, but woke up more restless than ever. I made my way to the kitchen and witnessed a true sign that something was wrong in the Macapagal household: Cate and Mrs. Long were attempting to make their own coffee.

"Hey, Lila. Sorry for making ourselves a little too comfortable in your kitchen, but we didn't want to disturb anyone," Cate said, as she went through just about every drawer and cabinet we had.

I forced a smile. "Don't worry about it. I'm sorry our hospitality is a bit lacking at the moment. It's been a strange day."

To hide my discomfort at finding near strangers rifling around my kitchen, I made a big show of preparing some snacks since it was time for meryenda. Too tired to come up with more elaborate fare, I toasted some pandesal and set out cheese, butter, and coconut jam. In deference to our guests, I also included some store-bought jars of peanut butter and strawberry jam in case the coconut was too intense for them.

"Strange . . ." Mrs. Long repeated, tracing her finger along the wood grain of the kitchen table. "I guess that's one way to put it."

I winced and glanced at Cate apologetically. She smiled in acknowledgement, then said, "We know why your aunt was brought in. Nancy insisted it wasn't her, and that your aunt's knife was there because she'd prepared dinner for her a few nights ago, but the detective said he still had to take her in. If it gets too awkward for you, we can check into a hotel, but Nancy would rather save the money."

"Cate . . ." Mrs. Long warned.

Cate shrugged. "Anyway, we brought over these coffee beans so we could at least contribute something, but I couldn't find a coffee grinder."

I tried to process everything Cate said, but decided it was enough that neither of them thought Tita Rosie was guilty and went along with the subject change. "Yeah, my aunt and grandmother are big believers in instant coffee. I had to bring my own coffee-making equipment when I moved back."

I pulled out my coffee grinder and French press and went to work, finding comfort in the familiar ritual and rich, fortifying scent of good coffee. I let the electric kettle come to a boil, then waited thirty seconds before pouring the water into the French press, covering the contraption, and letting it all steep for a few minutes.

As it did, I set out mugs, a sugar bowl, and spoons. "I usually take my coffee black, but would either of you like sugar or creamer?"

Mrs. Long nodded, taking the sugar bowl from me. "Yes, please. I've never been able to drink it plain. I don't understand how you can deal with that bitterness. You're just like Ed and Derek."

Ignoring what felt like a slight, I opened up the fridge and surveyed the contents. "We have coconut milk, almond milk, and soy milk."

"You don't have regular milk?"

I looked in the pantry. "Evaporated and condensed. Which would you prefer?"

She blinked at me, confused. "Milk. Like in a gallon. Or half-and-half? Cream? Not even Coffee mate?" Her voice became more and more strained as she ran through these options.

I looked around and found the nondairy creamer we kept for the random aunties that stopped by all the time. Or at least they used to before this whole mess started.

I held up the jar. "Will this do?"

"Yes!" Mrs. Long clutched at the bottle of powdered Lord-knows-what like a lifeboat saving her from the storm of ethnic food and lactose intolerance.

As she doctored her cup of coffee with the creamer and tons of sugar, I took a sip of the plain coffee as a quick taste test. Seeing how much junk she was putting in hers, I expected it to taste overly bitter or burnt, like most low-grade coffee. But this was crisp and bright with delicate fruit and citrus undertones. Perfectly suited for drinking black.

I raised my eyebrows. "This is some really good coffee, Mrs. Long. It doesn't taste like grocery store coffee beans. Where did you get it?"

"Oh, this?" Mrs. Long frowned at the creamy brown liquid filling her mug. "I don't really see what all the fuss is, but Ed and Derek loved this stuff. Cate, can you pass me the bag?"

Cate, who was leaning against the kitchen counter and chowing down on buttered pandesal, handed me the bag without comment.

"Thanks." I stared down at the bag emblazoned with a familiar logo. "You got this from Java Jo's?"

"It was either Ed or Derek. They were in charge of buying the coffee since they were so picky about it. Java Jo's was one of the few things they agreed on. They went there every day even though we had perfectly good coffee at home. Said they liked to use the shop for business meetings so they could write off their tabs as business expenses."

Little alarm bells started ringing, though I couldn't figure out why. "Business expenses? Just Mr. Long though, right? Or did Derek use the cafe to write his reviews?"

Mrs. Long buttered a bit of pandesal for herself. "I'm pretty sure Derek did work on his articles there, but they mostly used it to meet with Craig and some of the people who rented our properties. Kevin, too."

It took me a minute to place the name. "Craig? As in Craig Nelson, the health inspector?"

She nodded, mouth full of buttered bread. "Ed's best friend. They had some side business that Derek helped them with."

"What kind of business?"

She shrugged. "Ed never was one for sharing details with me. Probably thought I was too stupid to understand. Anyway, it brought in steady money and let Derek and him spend time together, so I didn't much care."

She'd dropped the fact that her husband thought she was stupid so casually into the conversation, as if it were something she'd known and accepted a long time ago. Just what was their relationship like?

I decided to switch targets slightly. "That's strange. You said Kevin was one of the people he did business with? But Kevin told me he didn't know Derek all that well."

Mrs. Long's face fell. "Now, why would he say that? I know Derek kept to a very rigid schedule and went there at the same time every day. Kevin even came over once. They were friends."

Mrs. Long looked so distressed by the fact our local barista was denying his friendship with her son that I had to try to smooth it over.

"Maybe he was just saying that because he didn't want to talk about Derek with me. You know, since it'd be too painful discussing their friendship?"

She didn't look convinced. "Maybe."

Time to change the subject. "So you're not the coffee aficionado your husband and son were?"

Cate and Mrs. Long both chuckled. "That's one of the things we bonded over right away," Cate said. "Never understood their ridiculous obsession. Coffee should be hot and strong enough to get the job done. That's it."

"Amen to that," Lola Flor muttered, as she shuffled into the kitchen and poured herself a mug. "Pass the sugar and creamer, ha?"

Cate slid them over. "Rosie still napping? It's getting pretty late."

I frowned. "She deserves a bit of rest. A lot's been going on, you know."

I glanced at the kitchen clock, noting the time. "Although this is rather pushing it. I think I'll bring her some meryenda, make sure she's not sick."

I set up a tray with a plate of pandesal and cheese, then took the time to fry an egg and some SPAM to add to the platter. Finally, I prepared a cup of coffee with so little sugar and creamer you wondered what the point of adding it was. Just the way my aunt liked it.

I knocked on the door and waited for her to call out her approval before opening the door and entering. She was awake, and clearly had been for a while, but she hadn't changed out of her duster yet. The dull green rosary that had been her constant companion my entire life was in her hands, slipping through her fingers bead by bead, their surface as well-worn as the prayers Tita Rosie murmured under her breath.

I set the tray on the table next to her bed and pulled up a chair. "You OK, Tita? Are you hungry?"

She didn't answer me until she'd finished whatever bead she was on—it'd been so long since I'd last used a rosary, I couldn't remember the order or most of the prayers.

"Anak, how did you know I was ready for a bite to eat? Come, sit with me while I have my meryenda."

We sat in companionable silence as she methodically made her way around the plate. As she wiped up the last of the runny egg yolk with the pandesal, I couldn't stay quiet any longer.

"Tita, Marcus said that a witness told the police they saw you leaving the Longs' house earlier today. Is this true?"

She sighed. "Yes, it is. I should've listened to June and just stayed at the wake."

Whoa, giving Ninang June credit for something? Interesting. "Why'd you go over there?"

"Mr. Long said he wanted to see me earlier at the wake. That his wife had talked to him and he'd figured out a way to solve both our problems. I just had to meet with him and Mr. Nelson."

Coffee sloshed onto the tray as I grabbed her arm. "Mr. Nelson, the health inspector? Did Mr. Long tell you why he wanted you to meet with the inspector? Maybe mention something about a contractor?"

"Ay, Lila, be careful! I could've burned myself." She set the mug down carefully and put the tray on her bedside table. "I'm not sure why we needed to meet. Just mentioned something about the repairs that might be necessary after the vandalism."

I knew it! Mr. Long and Derek had a side hustle going with the health inspector that involved bogus claims and raking in fees from the contractors they referred.

Which, OK, reconfirmed one major suspicion, but that didn't tell me why Derek and Mr. Long were dead now. Did the health inspector kill them both? Decided that he didn't like splitting the profit three ways and got rid of his partners? Or maybe he wanted to get out, go on the straight and narrow, and the other two wouldn't let him?

My aunt interrupted my musings. "Anak, I'm a little bit tired. Could you take the tray away? And make sure our guests have plenty to eat."

I stood up, collecting the empty tray. "Are you sure, Tita? Maybe cooking will make you feel better?"

She smiled at me, but her heart wasn't in it. "I just don't think I can face them right now. They know why I was called to the police station."

"But they don't think—"

She shushed me. "It doesn't matter. I think we all need some time, diba? Just help your lola with dinner. I'll come out when I'm ready."

I wandered out to the kitchen to wash the dishes. Cate and my grandmother were no longer there, but Mrs. Long still sat at the kitchen table, swirling a teaspoon through her half-finished cup of coffee.

"How is she?" Mrs. Long asked.

"Not great," I admitted. "But the same could be said for all of us, I'm sure."

She reached out for a piece of pandesal and began tearing it to shreds. "I hope she doesn't think . . . she knows that I don't blame her for . . ."

I placed the clean dishes in the rack next to the sink. "I'm not going to lie, she's worried about what you must think of her. Knowing that she was being questioned for your husband's murder."

Finished with my task, I looked over and noticed she wasn't eating. I had no idea what happened to the cookies I'd brought her, but a loaf of banana bread sat wrapped on the counter. I cut a thick slice and placed it in front of her.

"Honestly, I'm surprised you'd want to stay here with us. I know you said you wanted to save money, but I'm being accused of killing your son. My aunt is now a suspect in your husband's murder. How could you possibly—"

"Because you didn't do it." Mrs. Long kept her eyes on her plate. "We both know that."

"But how—"

"This banana bread was Derek's favorite, did you know that?" Tears pooled in her eyes as she tried to smile at me. "I know he gave you problems. But he really did care about you. Everything that happened these last few months . . . you have to understand, it wasn't him."

I didn't know what to say to that, so I just made a noncommittal sound as I refilled my mug.

"I have a confession to make." Mrs. Long finally looked up and met my eyes. "Those drugs in your locker. I think I know how they got there."

I dropped the knife I'd used to cut the banana bread, narrowly missing my foot. "How did you know about that?"

She smiled sadly. "Honey, the newspapers have been following my son's case very closely. And they are not particularly kind to you."

I cursed the *Shady Palms News* team out in my head with every profane term I could think of, inventing some of my own when it didn't feel like enough. "Oh. I see. So, um, how did that bag end up in my locker?"

She dropped her gaze again. "After Derek . . . passed, I went through his belongings to see if there was anything I could donate. I found that bag under one of the loose floorboards in his room." She smiled to herself. "He didn't think I knew about his secret hiding spot, but of course I did. Anyway, I brought it to Ed and demanded he tell me what he knew about it."

The thudding of my heart echoed in my ears. "And? What did he say?"

"Just that he'd take care of it and to shut up and mind my own business. And when you got arrested, he seemed awfully pleased with himself. Then I remembered he must have keys to your restaurant since he owns the building. And that he's been wanting to kick your family out for a while now."

My head was spinning with all the info she was dropping on me. "Mrs. Long, why are you telling me all this? Not that I don't appreciate it, but he was your husband. And I've been accused of killing your son."

"Oh, honey. We know who killed Derek. Don't we? You must know who really killed my son." Her eyes watered as she pushed away from the table and fled the room, leaving me with nothing but unasked questions and an uneasy feeling in my heart.

Chapter Forty

Before I could follow her to question her on that parting statement, my phone rang. The number flashing across the screen made my heart beat faster.

"Adeena?"

"Lila! I heard about Auntie Rosie being taken in for questioning. Is she OK?"

I glanced over at the door that stayed steadfastly shut. "For now. But Detective Park says he needs to talk to her again tomorrow. I think he's just waiting for one more piece of evidence to become the nail in her coffin."

"That's why I called. My lab friend told me they finally got the results on what killed Derek."

She paused for a moment, driving my blood pressure up five points. "Adeena, I hope you realize I am not in the mood for a dramatic reveal. Can you just tell me what you found out?"

"Sorry about that, Kevin was asking me something. Hold on." I heard her yell in the background that she'd finish testing the new de-caf beans and would lock up when she was done. "OK, I'm back. He died from nicotine poisoning."

"Nicotine poisoning? What about the arsenic?"

"My friend said the arsenic in his system was a small amount that'd been building up for a long time, likely months. If it had con-tinued, he probably would've died from it, but the amount in his sys-tem wasn't lethal."

"But the amount of nicotine was? How is that even possible?"

"It's not common but totally possible. Not by like, smoking a ton of cigarettes and then dying from that. My friend's theory is that he either ingested liquid nicotine or received an injection."

I paced around the room, trying to figure out my next move. "Liq-uid nicotine? Where could someone even buy that? Maybe if I narrow down the possible suppliers, I can figure out who bought it."

I heard a door slam in the background as Adeena said, "It's super easy to get your hands on and I'm pretty sure I know who got it. I'm gonna call Amir in a minute. Why don't you meet me at . . . hold on a sec, I think there's someone outside." There was a brief pause and I heard Adeena's voice again, but slightly muted as if she were holding the phone away from her mouth. "Hey, what're you doing here? You're not supposed to—AAAAH!"

"Adeena? Adeena!" I screamed into the phone.

There was the sound of heavy breathing for a moment and then nothing. She was gone.

I sped over to Java Jo's, calling Adeena's phone again and again but it didn't even ring—just went straight to voice mail. Either her phone died or someone turned it off.

The first option was unlikely, the second terrifying. I pushed my ancient SUV even faster and was trying her number one last time, when suddenly my tires hit a patch of ice. My car slid across the road and I dropped my phone on the floor as I grabbed the wheel with both hands to course-correct, but my tires couldn't seem to grip the pavement. My car fishtailed for a moment before skidding into a ditch on the side of the road.

Luckily, there was no one else on the street and I was relatively unscathed. I knew I had to hurry, but I sat for a minute, my hands gripping the wheel as I struggled to get my breathing and heart rate under control. Once my hands stopped shaking, I inched the car back onto the road and headed toward Java Jo's at a safer speed.

I finally pulled into the plaza lot, not even caring that my haphazard park job cut across two parking spots. All I could focus on was hurrying over to Java Jo's and checking on Adeena. The lights were off in the main part of the shop, but I tugged on the door anyway.

Locked.

She did say she was closing up, but she also said she'd be there testing the decaf beans. So where was she? Had she been dragged away? I looked around, but most of the snow had melted over the week, leaving icy patches here and there, but no footprints to follow. I turned toward my car, ready to find my phone and call 911, when something glittered at the edge of my periphery. I glanced around and spotted a shiny object lying on the cafe floor. I cupped my hands around my eyes and leaned against the glass door to get a better look inside. A golden bangle was on the floor a few steps from where I stood.

Adeena's golden bangle. I would've recognized it anywhere.

Even though the door was locked, the lights in the back were on, which meant someone was probably inside. I knocked on the door, carefully at first, then increasing in frequency and power until I could hear the bangs of the door echoing in the mostly empty parking lot.

Finally, someone popped into view.

"Kevin!" I slammed my hands on the window until he opened the door.

"What the hell, Lila? Why're you trying to break down my door?"

I pushed him aside as I rushed in. "Have you seen Adeena?"

"Not since she finished her shift. Why?"

Heart pounding, I stooped to pick Adeena's bangle off the floor and held the familiar object in my palm, the tinkling of its bells filling me with dread. I looked around the room but could find no other trace of Adeena there. The only activity was a small pot of coffee brewing in the decaf corner. So she'd started the pot . . . and then what?

"Lila, she's not here! Mind explaining yourself? Or at least not tearing up my shop?" Kevin asked as I started going through the items behind the counter.

"I was talking to Adeena on the phone as she closed up. She'd just finished and said she wanted to meet me when she suddenly screamed and hung up. I think something happened to her."

"Whoa, you serious? I came in through the back and everything looked fine."

"Why are you here, anyway? I heard Adeena say goodbye to you before she locked up."

He pointed to the pot of coffee steaming in the background. "I forgot that we were supposed to test out these new decaf beans. I'd wanted Adeena's opinion, but she was already gone when I arrived."

I swore loudly. "Can I borrow your phone? I left mine in the car and I need to call 911. I think Adeena's been kidnapped."

He laughed shakily and took out his vape pen. "Kidnapped? That seems a bit much, don't you think? I mean, I guess you can use the landline, but I think you're being overdramatic."

As he refilled his pen, the obvious lie Kevin had just told joined all the other puzzle pieces that began clicking into place. The fear that'd been sitting in the pit of my stomach since Adeena's call grew till I was almost doubled over from the weight of my discovery.

I'd made Derek finish his coffee before coming into the restaurant the day he died. Mrs. Long said he was loyal to Java Jo's, which meant Kevin had made his drink that day. Kevin also had access to liquid nicotine, which he bought for his vape pen.

It was Kevin. Kevin killed Derek.

I came to that realization at precisely the same moment Kevin decided to drop the act. He sighed and put down his vape pen. "You really should work on your poker face, Lila. You know that I literally watched you work out everything in real time, right?"

His tone was light and conversational even as he advanced on me. "It was almost like that Winona Ryder GIF where she's onstage trying to figure out what the hell's going on. Very amusing, but extremely inconvenient."

I tried to back away and felt the hard edge of the counter against my back. I was trapped. "Where's Adeena?"

He smirked. "She was a lot faster than you, that's for sure. As soon as she got that call from her lab friend, she made the connection. She's also a better actor. She hid her discovery from me almost the whole day. I only figured it out when I heard her talking to you as she locked up. I couldn't let her meet up with you and her lawyer brother, now could I?"

At the horrified look on my face, he said, "Oh, don't worry, she's still alive. I actually like her; would've felt terrible to have her death on my hands. I just needed enough time to get the hell out of Dodge."

"But why?"

"You already know the woman who first owned this cafe died, right? Of an overdose?"

I nodded.

"That was my sister, Jo. She'd worked so hard to get clean, and once she got her life together, she moved here to Shady Palms to start over. But then she met Derek. And he got her using again. Using and selling, actually. This place was their base of operations. After she died, I moved down here to find out what happened to her. She left me this place, so I took it over to learn more."

"When did all this happen?" How could I have been so out of the loop that I didn't know about any of it?

"Over a year ago. Maybe closer to two now. That's when Derek and Ed approached me. They had a scheme going with the health inspector and they'd leave me out of it if I let them continue using the cafe as a drop-off spot. I knew Derek must've had something to do with Jo's death; he was exactly her type. So I agreed. Took the time to get to know him. He was a disgusting human being. Absolutely no remorse over her death, but I had no way of proving he was involved without implicating myself."

Remembering what Detective Park had told me, I said, "But Derek did feel remorse over her death. After she died, he flipped and became an informant for the police. He was helping them take down the drug ring."

Kevin snorted. "And what? Then he gets to be a hero because he suddenly grew a conscience? Jo would still be dead. And he gets to start a new life somewhere with that married Japanese woman."

How did he know about Yuki?

Reading my expression, he said, "Derek told me himself. That morning, he said he was getting away from Shady Palms. Was looking forward to starting over and forgetting all that bad stuff that'd happened. You see why I had to do it, right? He thought he could just pack up and pretend he hadn't killed my sister. Before he left, he admitted the only thing he'd miss about this town was my coffee, so I gave him a final cup. On the house."

As he talked, I sidled away from him, trying to find an opening.

"And what about Mr. Long? Did he figure out you killed Derek and threaten to turn you in?"

"What're you talking about? I didn— FUUU—!"

I'd made my way over to the decaf pot of coffee. I grabbed it and threw the steaming contents directly into his face. He blocked the way to the front door, so I ran toward the back, hoping Adeena was there or that I could escape out the service door and call the cops.

Adeena was lying on the floor of the backroom, duct tape covering her mouth and binding her hands and feet. She had the tape halfway off her mouth as I came into the room and her eyes widened when she saw me. I locked the door and jammed a chair under the knob, but knew it was only a temporary reprieve. Then I pulled out my keys and got to work on the tape around her ankles as she continued freeing her mouth.

The sound of Kevin cursing and screaming made its way closer to the break room, forcing Adeena and me to work faster. The tape on her legs and mouth was completely off but we hadn't had time to free her hands yet when we heard him banging on the door.

"Where's your phone?" I asked, sawing away at the tape around her wrists.

She twisted her hands around in an attempt to speed up the process. "No idea, he took it from me. Where's yours?"

"I left it in the car. And shut up, I know exactly how that sounds," I added defensively as she pulled off the last of the tape. "Anyway, that door is the only way out of here. Is there anything we can use as a weapon? Let's rush him together then make a break for the car."

She looked around the mostly empty room and snatched something off a shelf, hefting it in her hands to feel the weight. "This should work."

I only had a moment to realize it was a statue of a dog before Kevin crashed through the door. When he saw what Adeena was holding, the skin beneath the red-mottled burns turned a sickly white. "What're you doing with that?"

"What're you doing with it?" I countered. "Janet made it for me. Why do you—" My eyes widened at the revelation. "Oh my God, you were the one who attacked her?"

"She gave me no choice! She figured out how Derek died and wanted to blackmail me into keeping her secret." His eyes darted around the room, likely looking for a weapon since he was empty-handed.

Adeena clutched the statue tighter and crouched into a defensive stance. I was still holding my keys, so I put one between each finger. Reminded me of my nights out in Chicago.

I held up my fist. "What secret?"

His face contorted in anger, the effect made even more dramatic thanks to the burns crisscrossing his skin. "She was one of Derek's suppliers. Her medical connections let her funnel fake prescriptions around town. My sister OD'd on the pills that Janet and Derek were peddling." Kevin fought back tears. "Derek knew she was a recovering addict, but he didn't care. They killed her. They may not have pulled the trigger, but they sure as hell gave her the gun. And they got what they deserved."

While he was delivering this illuminating monologue, Adeena was inching toward the door. Kevin snapped out of his confessional state just as Adeena grabbed the knob.

"Where do you think you're going?" He grabbed her, but I punched him as hard as I could with my key-spiked fist. He fell to his knees, screaming and clutching at his face as the keys tore through his already damaged skin. My hand throbbed from the effort, but we shoved past him and made our way to the front of the shop.

We were almost home free when something hit me from behind, knocking me to the ground. Kevin had recovered enough to grab a chair and hurl it at me, advancing much faster than someone who had just been scalded and knocked around should probably be moving. I tried to get up, but he pounced on me, driving his knee into my back to keep me down.

"Adeena, go!" I screamed, throwing my keys at her. She froze, torn between coming to help me or running to the car to call the cops.

"Just go!" I repeated, grabbing at Kevin's ankles as he tried to get to my keys. Adeena threw the statue at him but he dodged it, slowing down enough for me to wrap my arms around his ankles and pull him down with me. Before I could get up and follow Adeena out, I got a swift boot to the face. Everything went blindingly white, my whole body going limp at the sudden shock wave of pain.

Through the haze of pain, I could see Kevin gaining on Adeena. There was no way I'd reach him in time. My eyes scanned the room, trying to find something, anything, that would save us. The dog statue! Without hesitation, I grabbed it and hurled it at him with all the strength I could muster.

Some higher power must've guided my arm because I scored a direct hit to the back of his head and he tumbled to the floor, pulling a table down with him.

Kevin lay in a crumpled heap under the table, a pool of blood slowly seeping out from underneath him.

"Oh my God, I killed him."

I crawled over to his inert body, pulled the table off him, and crossed myself. Then I kneeled beside him, reciting every prayer I could dredge up from memory, rocking back and forth as I cried.

That's how Detective Park found me, crouched by Kevin's body, hugging myself with tears streaming down my face, as I repeated that I killed him over and over again.

"Ms. Macapagal?" I didn't respond. He repeated himself. I still said nothing. "Lila?" I looked up at him.

"I need you to move so the EMTs can get to him when they arrive." I continued staring blankly at him. "You didn't kill him. Look, he's still breathing."

I didn't believe him. How could he not be dead? He was so still, and I'd heard the crack his head had made as it connected with the statue, and look at all that blood. But the ambulance arrived moments later and an EMT confirmed what the detective said before taking Kevin away.

"You should probably go to the hospital as well. You're looking a little banged up," Detective Park said.

I shook my head. "I just want to go home."

He nodded. "I'll take you there as soon as someone examines you. An officer can bring your car around. And when you're ready . . . I have some questions for you."

"Lucky for you, I've got the answers, Detective."

Chapter Forty-one

It was the grand reopening of Tita Rosie's Kitchen, and I'd never seen the place so packed. Nothing like getting cleared of a double homicide for some free publicity.

On top of the usual suspects, I'd also extended invitations to all the restaurant owners who'd been burned by Derek but had helped me clear my name. Stan and Martha, George and Nettie, Elena and her mom, even the Satos were there, though they left after a brief appearance. I made a note to visit Yuki again soon—something told me she could really use a friend.

When Terrence and Janet arrived, I surprised everybody by running up to Janet and giving her a hug. She surprised everyone else by squeezing me back and giving a heartfelt thank-you. She'd woken up a few days after the incident with Kevin and was finally able to come clean about her involvement in the whole sordid mess.

Kevin had been telling the truth when he said Janet was one of Derek's suppliers. But after Jo overdosed, both Janet and Derek real-

ized the irreparable damage they had done and tried to get out. Derek
was in too deep to make a clean break, which is why he started passing
information to Detective Park. It was also why he started the restaurant con with Mr. Long and the health inspector—if he was going to
stop dealing, he needed to come up with a scheme that'd replace that
lost income. He'd been with that drug syndicate since his college
days, and he couldn't have them getting suspicious about why the
money was drying up.

"He really was doing his best to try and go straight," Janet had told
me the day after she'd woken up. I'd come to visit her in the hospital
at Terrence's request—she was being kept in the hospital for observa-
tion, but was technically under police custody and facing some hefty
charges. "He also tried to keep my name out of it. No one else knew I
was involved and he wanted me to have a normal life with Terrence."
Her face crumpled. "I guess there's no chance of that now. But it's my
own fault. I'm just getting what I deserve."

Terrence had been at her side the whole time at the hospital and
he was at her side now, but I could see the effort all of this was costing
him. Amir had gotten Janet off on bail, but he'd warned them that
even with a plea deal, she was going to have to serve time for her
crimes. Terrence had vowed to stay by her side throughout the whole
ordeal, but whether or not marriage was still in their future remained to be seen. He was another one I had to keep a close eye on. I
couldn't continue letting these important relationships slip through
the cracks.

As for Kevin, he had yet to wake up from the coma I'd put him in
but was also facing some serious charges. Not only did he admit to
killing Derek, Craig Nelson had rolled on him after Janet admitted
her part of the scheme. Mr. Nelson had been brought in for questioning after Janet woke up and he confessed to everything: the restaurant
con, the countywide drug dealing, even the fact that Mr. Long had

been poisoning Derek with arsenic for months since he'd suspected Derek had turned on them.

When Derek and Mr. Long had met for that fateful lunch, Mr. Long had planned on giving him a large enough dose to kill him and blame it on the restaurant, but couldn't since Tita Rosie and I were so solicitous. Then when Derek passed out, he panicked and wanted to dump the evidence, so he put it in Derek's dessert dishes. Mr. Long was also the one who destroyed our kitchen and tainted the rice to put the cops on our trail.

The only thing Mr. Nelson didn't confess to was Mr. Long's murder. He had an airtight alibi for the night his best friend was killed, but pointed the finger at Kevin. In their last conversation together, Mr. Long told Mr. Nelson he knew it was Kevin who killed Derek and wanted to figure out a way to work that knowledge in his favor.

Kevin was going to have a lot to deal with when he woke up.

If he woke up.

I knew that I'd acted in self-defense. I also knew that if I had the chance to do it again, and it came down to choosing between mine and Adeena's lives or his, I'd make the same choice every time.

But knowing something logically doesn't take away the guilt.

Which was something Detective Park, of all people, made sure to talk to me about when he found me at the restaurant. "You made the only choice you could, Lila. Maybe it doesn't feel like a good choice. But it was the right one. I have no doubt in my mind he would've killed both you and Adeena to get away."

He put his hand on my shoulder and looked me in the eye. "I also know that this is something that never really goes away. It gets easier. With time. And therapy. And the right people around you."

He waved his hand around the restaurant, gesturing toward my aunt, grandmother, and the Calendar Crew circling the room to make sure everyone was being fed properly. Bernadette and Marcus laughing it up with Adeena and Elena. Amir and Jae working behind the buffet table, doling out food and chitchat with our patrons.

Those last two caught me looking at them and broke into goofy grins and waved at me. I waved back, knowing sooner or later I'd have to deal with them. But not today. Or anytime soon, really. I'd come back to this town to nurse a broken heart and had immediately jumped back into a relationship with my ex, as if I were in a 90s rom-com and that was the solution to my problems. Maybe it was time to focus on the relationships I'd let fall by the wayside, like my family and Adeena and Terrence.

And I knew exactly how my new start would begin.

Earlier that morning, when my aunt and grandmother were already at the restaurant preparing for the reopening, Mrs. Long and Cate had called me into the dining room. Their bags were packed in Cate's car and ready to go. I handed Mrs. Long a loaf of fresh-baked, salabat-spiced banana bread. She handed me a manila envelope.

"This is my way of thanking you. Don't worry, it's not money," she said, sensing my protest. "I just want to make sure you're taken care of. You've done so much for me, and . . ."

She trailed off, searching my face. "You know, don't you? What I did?"

I nodded. I didn't have to say anything else. We all knew. I guess it was finally time to have it out.

She nodded. "Of course you do. You were always so smart." She started wringing her hands. "I never would've let your aunt get taken away. And I swear I wasn't trying to pin the blame on your family. It's just that Rosie had left the knife there the last time she made dinner for me, and it was so sharp and Ed . . . I overheard him talking to Craig about what he did to my son. What he was trying to do to you and your family. And I just couldn't let him ruin anymore lives. So I confronted him. And he, he grabbed me and—"

She started crying and Cate put her arm around Mrs. Long. "We know, Nancy. Ed was a brute and a greedy, selfish bastard. I just wish I had come sooner. That I could've saved you from all this."

Cate glanced at me. "What are you going to do with this information? You know Nancy would never survive prison."

I scrutinized them, noting Cate's protective stance. This was a chance for Mrs. Long to start over. Get away from this town that held nothing but sadness for her. I glanced down at the envelope in my hand. If it was what I thought it was, it was a chance for a new beginning for all of us.

"I'm going to do nothing," I said, looking at them carefully to make sure they understood. "I came home after the restaurant reopening and the two of you were already gone. Waiting for me on the table was this envelope and nothing else because you hate goodbyes. By then, the two of you were long gone from Shady Palms and had left no trace of your whereabouts. Do you understand me?"

They looked at each other and nodded. "Understood. And, Lila, thank you."

"Don't thank me. I'm just doing what I think is right. Justice isn't always so clear-cut," I added.

I put the envelope on the table and gathered my things to join my aunt and grandmother at the restaurant. Mrs. Long gave me a big hug.

"Do great things. You hear me? Live the life Derek never could. The life I was always too afraid to live." And with one last squeeze of my hand, she and Cate were gone.

It worked out exactly as I'd predicted. Tita Rosie, Lola Flor, and I all came home to find the envelope on the table. Adeena and Elena were there, too, because I'd asked them to sleep over, saying we had a lot to discuss about the future.

Inside was the deed to Tita Rosie's Kitchen, which I had expected. What I hadn't expected was the addition of the deed to Java Jo's. She'd signed over full ownership to me and I knew exactly what I wanted to do.

I looked over at Adeena and Elena, who were screaming over this revelation. "Well, ladies, what do you think? With my baked goods, Adeena's drinks, and Elena's herbal remedies and beauty products, I think we'd have one magical shop."

Elena clapped her hands. "Yes! And I have the perfect name for us. The Brew-ha Cafe!"

Adeena looked confused, so I explained, "Bruha means 'witch' in Tagalog and Spanish. It's a pun."

Adeena groaned. "That's not how you say 'witch' in Urdu, and you know how I feel about puns, but I'll let it go. All I really want to know is, does this mean you're staying? Are you staying here with us in Shady Palms?"

I looked around the room. At my family, who'd been watching us silently, at my best friend and her new girlfriend, and I knew this was where I belonged. Forever? Maybe not. But for right now . . .

"Yes, Adeena. You're all here, which means Shady Palms is my home. And there's nowhere I'd rather be."

Acknowledgments

How do you even begin to thank the people who helped make a life-long dream come true?

I guess I should start with the women who made this all possible: my amazing agent, Jill Marsal, and my awesome editors, Angela Kim and Michelle Vega.

To the rest of the Berkley/PRH team: Brittanie Black, Natalie Sellars, Jessica Mangicaro, and Vi-An Nguyen (LOVE my cover!), Carla Benton, Megha Jain, Christine Legon, Hope Ellis, and Dasia Payne, thank you so, so much! Your support and hard work to make *Arsenic and Adobo* a success means the world to me.

Writing is often a solitary act, but I never would've gotten this far without all of my communities. Some of you fit into more than one group, but I'm listing you in the ones I associate you with most.

My Pitch Wars mentor, Kellye Garrett, has seen me through a million revisions, multiple books and agents, the hell that is the submission process (twice!), quite a few breakdowns, and so much more. I love you, my petty DM buddy. I don't know how I would've done this without you.

Speaking of Pitch Wars, I'd be remiss if I didn't do a shout-out to my fellow 2017 mentees. All these years later and I can still count on you for support and commiseration. I particularly want to thank Robin St. Clare and Marilyn Chin, who have been there through various iterations of both my novels and have provided invaluable support and feedback again and again. I love you both, and this book wouldn't be nearly as good without your input. Also, Robin, thank you for screaming at me about HIPAA violations because I'm pretty sure my nurse brother would've never let me live it down. Maz, thanks for geeking out with me about food since it is my favorite thing in the world. I also want to thank Anna Collins, Robin Lemke, Julie Christensen, Karen Hsu, and CJ Simone for their feedback on earlier versions of *Arsenic and Adobo*.

My Pitch Wars–adjacent Chicagoland writing crew: Layne Fargo, Reese Eschmann, Rena Barron, Rosaria Munda, and Lizzie Cooke. I miss our writing dates, haunted retreats, and the endless laughter, support, inspiration, and commiseration you all bring. And, Jeff, we miss you and all your young people references. Don't forget about us when you make it to the big time.

Since we're already on my local support groups, I've got to thank my MWA-MW critique group: Allison Baxter, Irene Reed, Shevon Porter, Bo Thunboe, and Adam Henkels for being there for me from the very beginning, as well as the Banyan: Asian American Writers Collective.

Being a part of Banyan, having other Asian diaspora Midwestern writers to surround myself with, has been transformational. The openness and vulnerability that you all cultivate within our group continues to astound me, and I wrap myself up in your warmth and understanding. Every Banyan member has made an impact on me, but I particularly want to thank M.G. Bertulfo, Jane Hseu, Karen Su, and Hiroki Keaveney for critiquing the opening chapters, and Isabel Garcia-Gonzales for her work in organizing and leading so many of the Banyan workshops and events along with M.G. and Jane. Mahal kita!

To all the CWOC members, but particularly Abby L. Vandiver and Kia Dennis, for helping me out with the legal aspects of my story (any and all mistakes are my own), Jessica Laine Mork and Raquel Reyes, for their feedback throughout my various revisions, and Gigi Pandian and Naomi Hirahara, for constantly going to bat for me and supporting me in so many different ways. You have no idea how much it all means to me, but I hope to pay you all back somehow.

To Sisters in Crime, especially the Eleanor Taylor Bland Award committee, who saw promise in the early chapters of what would become this book and selected me as the 2018 winner, thank you. Thank you so much for your tireless work in trying to support, uplift, and educate writers from underrepresented backgrounds in crime fiction. I particularly want to thank Lori Rader-Day, who's supported me from the beginning and is continuously awesome.

To everyone who provided blurbs, cultural feedback, endless support, and more, I'm eternally grateful. I especially want to thank book blogger/booktuber Your Tita Kate (yourtitakate.wordpress.com), Roselle Lim, Kellye Garrett, Gigi Pandian, Naomi Hirahara, Olivia Blacke, and Lynn Cahoon.

And to the people who aren't part of the writing side of my life, but who've supported me all the same: The Winners' Circle AKA my besties, Linna Loek, Jumi Kim, Kimsan Iep, Robert Otero, and Sam and Orouge Awan (yes, I totally stole your last names, love love!); Amber Hayes, who gives me all the dirt in the book world and points me toward job opportunities (our Shady Palms joke lives on for eternity! Or as long as this series is in print, whatevs); the EF Chicago (RIP) staff, who were the most amazing coworkers and never once rolled their eyes at me when I said I was writing a book.

To my family, who've always encouraged me to go after my not-Asian-approved career choice of writing. Especially you, Mommy—you introduced me to the world of mysteries and shared your love of culinary cozies with me. This whole series is for you. Daddy, I will never bring the care and attention to cooking that you always did, but I hope you tasted the love all the same. I miss you so much, but I hope I did you proud.

And finally, to James. Marrying you for insurance was the best decision I ever made, and not only because I could finally get those wisdom teeth taken care of. Thank you for believing in me when I lost faith in myself, providing for us so I could focus on my dream, and allowing me to have all the dogs. I love you so much, and you are my true soulmate (just don't tell Linna, it'll break her heart). There's no one I'd rather spout random Simpsons quotes with than you.

To anyone who's read this far: from the bottom of my heart, thank you. Whether you loved my book or hated it, you gave me your time and attention (and hopefully your money, as well) and I truly appreciate it. Maraming salamat!

Recipes

Lila's Ube Crinkles Recipe

Ube has a subtle, delicate flavor—think mild sweet potato
with vanilla overtones. This simple, chewy cookie
that Lila created allows that flavor
(and lovely color) to shine.

YIELD: 3½ DOZEN USING A MEDIUM-SIZE (2¾") COOKIE SCOOP

Ingredients

3 cups all-purpose flour
2 tsp baking powder
½ tsp salt
1 cup butter
1 cup brown sugar (white granulated sugar is fine, but
  the brown sugar adds a little something special)
2 eggs
1½ cups ube jam / halaya*

> 1 tbsp ube flavoring (I used the McCormick Ube Flavor)
> 2 cups powdered sugar

Preheat oven to 350 degrees F° and line cookie sheets.

Whisk all the dry ingredients in a bowl—flour, baking powder, and salt.

Cream together butter and sugar using a mixer until well combined, then add the eggs one at a time.

Add in ube jam and flavoring and mix at high speed until fully incorporated. Once the mixture is a lovely, uniform violet color, turn the speed down to low and gradually add in the dry ingredients mixture. Mix until just combined.

Cover the bowl with plastic wrap and chill for a few hours or overnight. Do not skip this step as the dough is very sticky and hard to work with while warm.

Using a medium-size cookie scoop, roll the cookie dough into balls (or scoop with a spoon and shape into roughly 2¾-inch balls) and coat with powdered sugar.

Bake on lined cookie sheets at 350 degrees F° for 10 minutes or until firm around the edges and slightly underdone in the center (but not doughy). Enjoy!

Want to make the ube halaya from scratch? Check out Mia's blog at miapmanansala.com and get the recipe for free!

Derek's Salabat-Spiced Banana Bread
(Filipino Ginger Tea Inspired)

When Lila first got into baking, she devised this recipe for Derek and it remained his favorite despite the change in their relationship. She couldn't blame him— as a fellow ginger fiend, she finds it absolutely delicious with a nice milky tea.

YIELD: ONE 9X5 INCH LOAF

Ingredients

Dry:

2 cups flour
¼ tsp cayenne
½ tsp salt
½ tsp cinnamon (heaping)
1 tsp ground ginger
1 tsp baking soda

Wet:

5 medium to large bananas (VERY ripe)
5 tbsp melted coconut oil (or melted butter)
½ to ¾ cup honey (depends on how sweet you like it)
2 eggs
1 tsp vanilla extract

A few swipes of calamansi or lemon zest
   (about ¼ to ½ lemon)

Optional:

½ to 1 cup chopped crystallized ginger
1 to 2 tbsp instant salabat mix*

Preheat oven to 350 degrees F° and prepare a 9x5 loaf pan (grease/spray/line).

Whisk dry ingredients in a medium-size bowl and set aside.

Mash the bananas in a large bowl, then add the coconut oil and honey. Mix well then whisk in the eggs and vanilla extract. Grate the lemon peel or calamansi directly into the bowl and add the crystallized ginger, if using. Mix thoroughly.

Add the dry ingredients to the wet ingredients and mix lightly with a rubber spatula until just combined. Don't overmix, it will still be slightly lumpy.

Put mixture in a prepared loaf pan and sprinkle top with instant salabat mix, if using. Bake for about an hour. Check the banana bread about halfway through the cook time, and if it's browning too fast, cover with aluminum foil.

It's done when a knife or chopstick inserted in the middle comes out clean. Let cool and enjoy with a nice cup of tea!

*Don't have access to instant salabat mix? Combine 2 tbsps sugar, 1 tsp ground ginger, ½ tsp cinnamon, and ¼ tsp cayenne.

Lola Flor's Minatamis na Bao
(Coconut Jam)

This rich coconut caramel spread is one of
Lola Flor's specialties. It's traditionally served with
pandesal (Filipino soft bread rolls) and kakanin (Filipino
sweet glutinous rice cakes) but it's delicious in many
other applications (Lila once used it to fill a layer cake!).
A great way to jazz up breakfast and tea time.

YIELD: ABOUT 1 CUP

Ingredients

1 can coconut milk (13.5 fl oz)
⅔ cup of dark brown sugar*
2 pandan leaves, tied in a bow, or 1 tsp pandan extract
(optional)

Put all the ingredients in a thick-bottomed medium saucepan and
bring to a boil.

Once boiling, lower to a simmer and stir the contents until the
sugar dissolves.

Using a rubber spatula, stir the jam until it thickens to a honey-
like consistency and is a lovely dark brown, about 45 minutes.** Make
sure to stir the contents, scraping the bottom and sides, often so that
the jam doesn't stick to the bottom. If you want to be sure it's done,

drop a small amount of the jam into very cold water and see if it forms a soft ball.

Remove from heat and pour into a clean glass jar. Allow to cool and thicken a bit more before using.

*If you don't have dark brown sugar, you can substitute the same amount of white sugar plus about 2 tbsps molasses. I actually prefer doing this because it gives a deeper flavor.

**You might want to remove the pandan leaves about 30 minutes into the cook time, when the mixture is still fairly liquid. If you wait till the end, the jam clings to the leaves and you'll lose quite a bit of it. It's too delicious to waste!

Tita Rosie's Chicken Adobo

Adobo is often considered the Philippines's
national dish, and is more a style of cooking than
specific food. The main ingredient and seasonings vary
according to region (it's an archipelago of over 7,000
islands, after all) and even according to family,
but this is how Tita Rosie makes it.

SERVES 4-6

NOTE: This dish tastes best when marinated for several hours, so start it early. Also, the ingredients are highly adjustable. Want it saltier? Add more soy sauce. Tangier? More vinegar. Is the flavor too strong? Add more water. Want to switch up the meats? Sub in a pound of pork belly for a pound of the chicken. Adobo is a personal experience.

Ingredients

3 to 4 lbs of skin-on, bone-in chicken legs, thighs, or drumsticks (avoid chicken breasts, which are too dry for this style of cooking)

¾ cup soy sauce (Datu Puti brand preferred)

1 cup vinegar*

1 cup water

1 tsbp sugar

10 cloves of garlic, minced

1 tsp black peppercorns

2 bay leaves

Put all ingredients in a large pot or sealable plastic bag, making sure the chicken is mostly submerged. Marinate in the fridge for four hours to overnight, turning the chicken or bag around several times so the marinade is distributed evenly. You can skip this step or cut the time down to only thirty minutes, but it won't be as tasty.

If you used a bag, empty the contents into a large pot and turn the heat to high. If it's already in a pot, you can skip straight to heating everything to boiling. Once the liquid boils, turn the heat down to medium-low and cook for 15-20 minutes until the chicken is cooked through, but not falling off the bone. Remove the chicken to a plate using tongs, but keep the marinade simmering in the pot.

Heat a separate pan on high and add a splash of oil. Brown the chicken on all sides, in batches, until the skin is crisp. Alternatively, crisp the skin under the broiler. Set aside.

Turn the heat back up to high under the marinade pot and boil the sauce for 20 minutes or more, until it's reduced by at least half. Some people like it a little drier, others saucier, so boil it until you have the desired amount. Return the chicken to the pot and stir to coat with sauce, then serve with white rice.

Filipino cane vinegar is preferred (Datu Puti is the most common brand), but apple cider vinegar is an OK substitute. White distilled vinegar is a bit harsh, so you might need an extra bit of sugar or water to balance it.

Keep reading for a special preview of

Homicide and Halo-Halo

Coming soon from Berkley Prime Crime!

Curls of smoke drifted around the Brew-ha Cafe, a pleasant floral aroma filling the space while hints of an unknown herb tickled my nose, making me sneeze.

"Salud," said Elena Torres, the pierced and tattooed woman holding the smoldering bouquet, and wafted a bit more smoke toward me. Adeena Awan, Elena's girlfriend and my best friend, stood next to her, breathing the mixture in, basking in the smoke.

I held back a cough. "Didn't we already sage the place?"

Elena nodded, circling me with the smudge stick in her hand. "Yes, but I did some research and saw that guava leaves were used in ancient Filipino practices the same way the indigenous people here use sage. Thought it would bring some good energy into the shop and be something nice for your ancestors. This smudge stick is a special blend of guava leaves, white sage, and lavender."

Ah, so that explained the floral scent my trusty nose detected. I wasn't as into the woo-woo stuff as Adeena and Elena, but I appreciated how thoughtful Elena was being. Besides, the place could use a good cleanse after what happened here back in March.

She continued, "I'm really liking the vibes this blend is bringing. I'll need to make more for the altar."

We all glanced toward the corner in the back of the shop Elena had set up with a cloth-covered table, candles, crystals, and photos of her deceased father and Adeena's deceased maternal grandparents. She'd been bugging me to add something to the altar, "something for the ancestors," as she put it, but I kept putting it off. I knew what she really wanted were photos of my dead parents, but I refused to put them on display. They weren't for public consumption, even in a way that was meant to honor them. Besides, I wouldn't even look at the photos of them inside my own home—what made her think I'd be comfortable seeing them in my place of business?

"It's getting way too hot in here. I'm gonna close the door now. Can you turn on the AC and make sure it's not acting wonky anymore?"

Adeena had propped open the door earlier to "let out the negative energy" and the sweltering summer heat rolled in, the temperature having already reached a stifling 86 degrees at seven in the morning. Any of the bad juju Elena had managed to cleanse would be replaced with my dark mood if it got any hotter.

The air conditioning kicked in, and I breathed a sigh of relief as the cool air washed over me. Summer had just started and the cafe had been closed since the . . . unpleasantness, but we were finally ready for our soft opening in a few days.

I looked around the room, once a monochrome minimalist space, now full of color and life. We'd outfitted the area with Adeena's artwork, Elena's plants, and my . . . well OK, so I hadn't added any personal touches to the cafe yet, but I was more of a back-of-the-house person. I handled anything administrative, such as ordering, sourcing suppliers, bookkeeping, etc. I was also the baker, so my contribution would be more evident once we opened.

If we opened.

I couldn't shake the feeling that we were missing something, that we were rushing into opening too soon. This was my dream, after all. It needed to be perfect. It needed to be a success. It needed to be *right*.

Before I could voice these doubts, Adeena said, "Stop it. We're not pushing back the opening."

I struggled to keep my facial expression neutral. Had I been thinking out loud or had Adeena finally progressed to full-on mind reader? "What are you talking about? I didn't even say anything."

She studied my face. "You didn't have to. I know you and I know the way you think. Plus you had that look on your face."

I crossed my arms. "What look?"

"The one where you don't know whether to run away or puke. You really need to start dealing with your anxiety and stop sticking your head in the sand over every little thing."

"What Adeena is trying to say," Elena cut in, giving her girlfriend a warning look, "is that we're worried about you. You've seemed really stressed out and—"

"Of course I'm stressed out! We're opening on Monday and we're so not ready. We haven't even—"

"Haven't what? We've done everything possible." Adeena ticked off the list on her fingers. "We've replaced all the furniture because neither of us could stand to look at it anymore. We hired industrial cleaners to go over the entire place," here her eyes flicked over to a particular spot near the door, "and the space is sparkling. It's even cleaner than your family's restaurant, which is really saying something. We've registered the business with the state, had my brother draw up all the legal papers, gotten every freakin' license possible. We could've opened even sooner if it hadn't taken the county so long to replace Mr. Nelson."

Mr. Nelson was the previous health inspector, currently in jail after I'd exposed his shady dealings with the help of Adeena, Elena, and some of the other Shady Palms restaurant owners.

She continued, "And it's not even our official opening on Monday, just the soft opening. Which you conveniently won't be present for since you decided to take that judging position without consulting us." She put her hands on her hips. "You know. Us? Your business partners? Who have just as much riding on this as you do?"

I sighed and toyed with my necklace, already tired of the conversation. I'd agreed to judge the Miss Teen Shady Palms pageant yesterday, after one of the judges had to drop out at the last minute. As a former winner, the pageant committee had wanted me to be part of the original lineup, but I'd turned them down. I'd already had my hands full preparing for the cafe opening and didn't need to be reminded of my pageant past, especially with Elena harping on about remembering those we'd lost.

However, with the pageant down a judge and the first event happening later tonight, the committee had decided to play dirty. They not only offered the Brew-ha Cafe the catering contract for all the pageant events plus a free booth and advertising at the Founder's Day Celebration, our town's biggest holiday, but they also brought in the big guns: The Calendar Crew, aka my godmothers—Ninang April, Ninang Mae, and Ninang June.

Nobody, but nobody, wielded guilt and tsismis the way these three women did. Once those aunties got involved, it was all over. How could I have possibly said no when Ninang June, my mother's best friend, said things like "Ay, Lila, it would mean so much to Cecilia, God rest her soul. You know how much she loved the pageant and believed in helping the community. Paying it forward, diba?"

Nothing like conjuring up the name of my dead beauty queen mother to convince me to do something that I absolutely did *not* want to do.

Which was what made Adeena's comment so unfair. If anyone knew my complicated feelings about the pageant and my mom, it would be her.

"You act as if me taking on the position is a huge inconvenience for you. May I remind you that I'm the one stuck dealing with this for the next three weeks? And that my sacrifice ensures a strong opening since we'd never have been able to afford a booth or the kind of advertising that they're providing? Not to mention the catering contract, and that I was able to convince them to hire Terrence to design everything!"

Terrence Howell was one of our closest friends, and he did freelance graphic design. He'd finally quit his construction job to do his design work full-time and I wanted to support him as much as possible. He'd already designed the Brew-ha Cafe logo, website, and social media banners, and did the same for my aunt's restaurant, but it wasn't enough. I knew he was hurting, both emotionally and financially, after the mess his fiancée, Janet, got him into a few months ago.

Elena, ever the peacemaker, stepped in. "She's right, Adeena. Besides, it was my idea to do the soft open, remember? We agreed it was the best way to work out the kinks in the system before officially opening since we could test what our customers are drawn to. Plus, I'm still trying to figure out the shop's energy. Without it, I won't know what other plants to bring in."

The three of us brought very different skills to the table. Adeena was our potion brew/barista and had come up with an impressive menu that offered the usual cafe staples as well as more creative drinks, drawing from our collective Pakistani, Filipino, and Mexican backgrounds. Elena was our green witch, providing not just the décor, but also ingredients from her family's greenhouse and garden. The herbal remedies, teas, and natural bath and beauty products that she and her mom made lined the shelves, scenting her corner of the shop with a lovely, subtle aroma. And I crafted the baked goods, putting a Filipino spin on coffee shop classics.

Or at least, that was what I was supposed to do. One of the biggest reasons I was hesitant to open was something I could never admit to Adeena, something that pained me to even think about. Something that proved the timing wasn't right. Because *I* wasn't right.

And as if on cue, Adeena asked about it. "OK fine, I'm sorry. I do appreciate all the publicity you're drumming up for us. But we still haven't seen your part of the menu. When do you plan on getting it to us?"

The tinkling of the door chimes interrupted us, announcing the arrival of an unexpected savior, my not-related-by-blood cousin, Bernadette. The sight of her got my adrenaline going, as if my body were gearing up for a fight, but I tamped it down. A year older than me, we'd been rivals almost our entire lives, but had formed a truce a few months ago when things were bad and I needed her help.

"Hey, Ate Bernie. What's up? Do you need me to let you into the restaurant?"

She shook her head. "This isn't a social visit. You're needed next door."

I'd barely succeeded in calming myself down and those words got my blood pumping again. "What happened? Are Tita Rosie and Lola Flor OK?"

A look I couldn't read crossed her face. "Detective Park is there and he wants to speak to you. He needs your help on a case."

Photo by Jamilla Yip Photography

Mia P. Manansala is a writer and book coach from Chicago who loves books, baking, and badass women. She uses humor (and murder) to explore aspects of the Filipino diaspora, queerness, and her millennial love for pop culture. A lover of all things geeky, Mia spends her days procrastibaking, playing JRPGs and dating sims, reading cozy mysteries, and cuddling her dogs Gumiho, Max Power, and Bayley Banks (bonus points if you get all the references).

CONNECT ONLINE

MiaPManansala.com

f 🐦 📷 MPMtheWriter

Ready to find
your next great read?

Let us help.

Visit prh.com/nextread

Penguin
Random
House